The Rose Guardian

BY LORINA STEPHENS

FIVE RIVERS PUBLISHING
WWW.FIVERIVERSPUBLISHING.COM

Five Rivers Publishing, 704 Queen Street, P.O. Box 293, Neustadt, ON N0G 2M0, Canada.

www.fiveriverspublishing.com

The Rose Guardian, Copyright © 2019 by Lorina Stephens.

Edited by Aerin Caley.

Cover Copyright © 2019 Jeff Minkevics.

Interior design and layout by Éric Desmarais.

Titles set in Vivaldi Font designed by Fritz Peters in 1970. Vivaldi font is a Script Old Style font. Vivaldi font attributes include 1970s, elegant, script.

Text set in Manuale designed by Pablo Cosgaya and Eduardo Tunni for editorial typography (books, newspapers and magazines) in print and online.

Published in Canada

Library and Archives Canada Cataloguing in Publication

Title: The rose guardian / by Lorina Stephens.

Names: Stephens, Lorina, 1955- author.

Identifiers: Canadiana (print) 20190059672 | Canadiana (ebook) 20190059680

ISBN 9781988274614 (softcover)

ISBN 9781988274621 (EPUB)

Classification: LCC PS8587.T4654 R67 2019 | DDC C813/.54—dc23

As always
For Gary

Contents

We are such stuff as dreams are made on
And our little life is rounded with a sleep

The Tempest Act 4, Scene 1
William Shakespeare

Endings

Irealize now innocence, once lost, can never be retrieved. We yearn. We search. But that search is vain; only the vestiges of what we once had remains.

It was of innocence I thought as the officiant droned on. He spoke of a woman he didn't know. He attempted to convince those of us gathered in that sombre and neutrally appointed room Una Cotter was someone to be remembered, a vital part of her community, loving mother, devoted wife. There was no denying she was all that.

Una Cotter, descended from Norman conquerors. Or so she liked to say.

I remembered a woman I both loved and feared. There was little of softness about Ma. Estranged, widowed, hardened by experience, she was as capricious as Canadian weather. The only thing on which you could depend was in her winter, it was bitter. In her summer, it was glorious.

White Cotter roses bookended the funereal urn of plain, penny-wise stoneware; a digital display on the wall above, sequencing through images of Ma from femme fatale to fatal crone. She died so very small, coiling into herself as though gathering all her effort for one final, full-colour explosion.

I had few illusions I would escape the repercussions of that explosion, like thunder in the heart, or the tsunami after the quake. For now, there was this calm. I should feel something, I told myself. Surely this marked some sort of personal shortcoming that I couldn't squeeze out even one tear. As a woman of age, had I become as impenetrable as Ma?

Finally, a pause in that fabrication from the lectern, and in that space a song about time to say goodbye, meant I was sure to elicit profound weeping from the host of mourners. Ma was like that. I didn't know whether to laugh or rage, to feel fondness or scorn. How was I supposed to feel after all these years, after all this history?

I could hear someone cough, the rustle of cloth as bums shifted on padded seats, the breathing of so many people who had come to mark the death of this enigmatic woman. I stared at my knees where black silk noile draped down to touch the tops of my black leather flats. I wanted to shift my own bum, rid myself of the casing of spandex designed to make the Rubenesque feel svelte. Or at the least acceptable. Dear god I was getting too old for this.

I wondered vaguely if they'd stuffed Ma into spandex underneath her funerary garb. Or had they simply taken her to the crematorium and incinerated her, gardening clothes, gloves, and all?

My brother, Bennet, who in true Irish form styled himself Benneit, sat to my right. His wife and their adult children were behind us.

Ben glanced at me. He was as always clean-shaven, beautiful in a hoary, stag-like way, and closed as he had been since he learned we were not fully siblings. How long ago was that? Fifty years? Somehow the taint of that was something he'd never accepted. Or forgiven. As if I was responsible for our parents' shortcomings.

I wished I could read him, gauge what lay beneath that polished exterior, wished somehow we could regain the laughter and lunacy of childhood. I managed a smile, not much more than a lift of the corner of my mouth, an attempt to say *I know, it's okay, death is just part of life.* But Ben didn't need that. Ben, like Ma, knew how to survive. They were both expert masons. Their walls were impenetrable.

Ah, there was the great, fully-orchestrated crescendo *I'll go with you upon ships across the seas, seas that exist no more....*

I glanced to my left where Uncle Ianto sat, and good the gods he bent over his knees, tongue between teeth, a quarter clamped in thumb and forefinger. What *was* he doing?

"Uncle Ianto!" I hissed. "For the love of god!"

That song went on about being together, forever, endlessly on.

He looked up at me, an idiot grin on his face and a mesh of lines around those recklessly blue eyes. He turned his attention back to the task of deconstructing the kneeling rail in front of him. I should upbraid him, I thought, tell him to show a little more respect for his sister's memory. The officiant shot a frowning glance in my uncle's direction. I had the strangest urge to giggle. *Jesus God, hold it together!* If I started now I'd never stop. And then would come those tears I thought myself incapable of shedding. Foolishness. Liar.

No. No tears. I swallowed, wishing for this service to

end, wishing for home and the sound of waves on the shore, of loons and their wild asylum cry.

I wanted to help Uncle Ianto take apart every last rail—Uncle Ianto who likely had more understanding than any of us about this funeral and what we marked.

Thank god, an end to that saccharine song.

The officiant—what was his name?—made one last futile attempt to urge either Ben or me to deliver a eulogy, and when met with a fidgeting, twitching silence, broken only by the scraping of Uncle Ianto's makeshift screwdriver, intoned his last words on the subject of Una Cotter and made his way to the door. That was a signal, I supposed, the service was at an end.

I elbowed Uncle Ianto to his feet, and managed to get him to leave off his deconstruction. We shuffled by the officiant, grasping hands, thanking him for his efforts. There was no invitation extended to him to join us at Ma's for the small refreshment we'd arranged. Mean spirited, I'm sure, but none of us needed this hired mourner to intrude upon the acrimony to come. That kind of vitriol is best savoured among the willing few.

We retired to the room set aside for family. Ben was already in discussion with the funeral director. I stepped forward to join in, thought better of it and retreated to where coffee had been provided. I swirled cream into a cup, watching it shift and billow, then finally settle into beige, heard my name and turned. Ben was there, introducing me to our host. What the woman said I hadn't a clue. It all seemed lost in a bubble. Nodding and smiling seemed in order, so I did that, shook her hand, mumbled thanks.

Ben took the velvet bag the woman handed him, hefting it to the cradle of his elbow. She withdrew. I looked over to Ben, tried to articulate my thoughts, but he said, "We're taking her ashes back home. I figured that was okay, given history."

He might have asked. I wanted to offer a bridge, found myself without the equipment to do so, and so only said: "Of course, Ben. Whatever you wish." But then, from somewhere, the courage to say: "I've missed you."

He seemed startled, his face softening for a moment. I saw the boy, my brother; then the man reasserted himself and Ben was lost to me. "We live in an age of communication."

I didn't think you'd want to hear from me—left unsaid, not knowing how. "I'm sorry," came out instead.

"So am I." He glanced down, then to the door. "We should go."

"Of course." Easier to fall back on duty. Easier to leave the demons chained.

Escape wasn't to be swift. There were the niceties of polite society, the acceptance of people's apologies— for what did they apologize?—the offer of comfort, of empathy, hands grasped and joggled meaningfully, faces full of well-intentioned emotion meant to convey solidarity in the face of the enemy of death. There were even hugs, unsolicited, unwelcomed, and my impotent hand patting a shoulder, a back, lips responding with platitudes and clichés, and the brain running ahead, anticipating bridges that might be blown or secure. Navigating. Always navigating.

"Should you need anything, Violet—"

Who was this? Don't remember. "Very kind of you to offer. We're all good. But thanks." The withdrawal of my hand from the clasp of two, a vague attempt to remember a name for that face. Glancing off to the doorway where Uncle Ianto fidgeted, laughing of all things.

"I need to get him in check," I said to Ben who stood next to me. "Rendezvous at Ma's." No response. None expected. I steered a course through the flow of bodies, keeping my attention anchored to my recalcitrant, unpredictable uncle.

At last I hooked my hand around his elbow, and head down, beat a retreat to the parking lot.

Relieved was how I felt when I buckled myself into the car, a moment's respite. I could feel Uncle Ianto about to explode into comment and criticism. What was it about the Cotters made us so willing to shake our fists, rattle sabres, beat shields? We should all just paint ourselves with woad and be done with it. Go charging off with the Wild Hunt.

I closed my eyes, feeling sunshine hot and penetrating on my face. A balm, a blessing. If there were any heroes in our family they'd long since vanished in the mists of Ireland, too insubstantial to make the journey to Canada. We were refugees, all of us, whether from famine or history made little difference.

"The hell with your brother," Uncle Ianto muttered. "Unmitigated shit!" I laughed, opened my eyes and turned to him. He looked like a radish. Blood pressure, I thought. Time to calm him down. "I never liked that little turd." That last salvo apparently just for good measure.

"Hush, Uncle Ianto," I said. "Let's just get through this." I raised a warning finger to him. "No shenanigans, okay? Behave yourself."

"Damn right, my girl. Damn right. Get through this and get back home."

I really am getting too old for all this melodrama, I thought.

It was about a twenty-minute drive from the funeral home to Ma's. On the way, Uncle Ianto and I spoke mostly about our plans for the remainder of the day and his departure tomorrow. It was agreed we'd try to quickly wrap the après deuil, have a quiet evening together, and stay in touch throughout the following week. I'd keep the car, drive Uncle Ianto and David— my ex—to the Waterloo airport where we'd arranged a hitch on a small charter. David would drive Ianto home at the other end, stay with him while I was away. David, another dangling thread in the fabric of my life.

But for now, we'd be a team, my uncle and I, with David conscripted in; we three dispossessed in uncertain territory.

I headed west out of Paris into the triangle of rural country between Highways 401 and 403; mostly flat, arable land now given over to the growing of ginseng and cereal crops, a few upstart vineyards creating nouveau vintage by marketing the ashtray flavour of tobacco to youthful trendsetters. Orchards joined those vineyards along with agritainment farms for the urban family seeking reconnection with the land.

When we turned north and rattled along the washboard gravel sideroad that led to Ma's farm, I felt my heart stutter. The last time I'd travelled this road I'd been in tears, David dispensing advice and indignation in equal measure at the wheel of the car.

Twenty-five years ago. And too many years of

silence before we found a way through the fog of that particular war. It's always too late for regrets.

I slowed when I approached the maple-lined laneway, observed for a moment the old stone house, a Loyalist, utilitarian box, twenty-six windows, and one thousand acres of land given over to woodlot, a pond that was more a lake, and gardens that would have put any public horticultural centre to shame. The service entrance for the business side of Ma's property came in from the north, and it was there the trial beds of Ma's roses were situated, along with the greenhouses, labs, and office facilities. At least that's what I remembered.

Crown land deeded to the immigrant Loyalist Cotters.

"Still a sight to behold," Uncle Ianto said. "She always had style, did your Ma."

She did.

I eased the car up the shaded lane and drove into the courtyard created by virtue of a converted carriage house to one side of the house, and a renovated stable to the other. All, apparently, a reconstruction of the farm the Cotter's had left behind in Burt, Donegal. When I stepped out onto the gravel drive I paused, listening, remembering it was quieter when I grew up here. You had to go a long way north now before you could achieve that kind of quiet, where the reverberation of traffic didn't underscore everything. I had that at home, at my refuge at Meldrum Bay.

Then the mood was broken by a goldfinch's trilling, a sound to penetrate the heart and fear, a song of such joy as to make a mockery of the sombreness of a funeral. Here was life.

Are you there? Are you there? I still thought of goldfinches as throwing queries into the air.

I looked to the copse of trees in the distance, trying to find the brazen yellowness of the bird. But no. Only that glorious sound, and despite myself I smiled, allowing such simple pleasure to touch my apprehension.

I scanned the lawns, the gardens, watching a little girl dart amid the rose parterre, her red capris and white shirt as defiant as the goldfinch's song.

"Who's that?" I said, nudging Uncle Ianto.

He looked up at me, frowning. "Who?"

"That girl."

"Where?"

"There." I nodded to the parterre where this imp of a child now stood, waggling an admonishment at a white rose.

"Yer daft," Ianto said. "There's no girl there. Just Una's roses."

I opened my mouth to protest, snapped it shut. She'd gone. No matter. I steered Uncle Ianto past other vehicles in the drive, guests who plainly arrived ahead of us, along to the front door that was thrown open to the beauty of this May day. Ma would have fetched a fit. Letting in mosquitoes and blackflies and who knew what vermin. Nature was perfectly fine kept ordered and in its place, all ugliness eradicated.

My nephew, Colm, greeted us in the foyer, all hugs and exuberance, tall and no longer the boy I remembered. He laughed with Uncle Ianto, found someone to guide our fey relation into the parlour and get him settled and seated. Alone with Colm, I asked, "Would it be silly of me to say you've grown?"

He grinned and looked down at me. "A bit, Aunt Vi. But

I'll forgive you." He gestured to a diminutive woman beside him. "This is Aislinn." I shook her hand, raised an eyebrow to Colm, who said, "We've been together a few years now."

"I'm the last to know anything." I nodded into the house. "I gather your father doesn't approve?"

"Living in sin and all that."

"We just didn't see the point in contractual love," Aislinn said. "And weren't sure how you'd feel, so we just kept things quiet."

I smiled. "Manitoulin's a long way away, but you're always welcome. You and Colm both. Might as well find out how the rest of the non-conformist Cotters live."

"It's a date then," Colm said. "Give me your keys and I'll fetch in your bags." Colm gestured to the parlour off the foyer. "Dad's in there with Mum and Erin. I know for sure at least the females will be glad to see you."

"Thanks for the warning."

I stepped through the wide archway into the parlour, dodging ghosts and memories, listening to the susurration of voices both present and past. Not much had changed since last I was here. Light still flooded the room from a long bank of deep-set windows. There the fireplace with its ornate fire-screen and potted plants, the Regency-style sofas like bookends, the butternut bookcases and leaded glass, leather volumes carefully arranged alphabetically by author. The Heppleworth knock-off secretary, the Persian carpets, occasional chairs in conversation groups for conversations that never took place.

"Can I offer you refreshment?" my sister-in-law was asking, I realized. I turned toward her.

"It's good to see you, Evelyn." I declined the offer of

a drink. "The only time we Cotters seem to gather is at weddings and funerals, and not so much the former as the latter." *You're being unfair,* I thought.

"It was a lovely service, don't you think?" she said.

"Mmm, yes. Ma had it all arranged, I'm sure."

"Down to the obituary notices for the papers," Ben said, drawing abreast. He watched me over the rim of his glass, garnet wine catching the light. Why was it I always felt there was subtext?

You're too paranoid. Just fergawdsakes stop being so damned anti-social.

I gestured to a settee and eased to the jacquard cushions, fitting myself into a corner. A shrink would rub her hands with glee over that, I'm sure. Uncle Ianto, radar zeroing in on potential family conflict, thumped down in the opposite corner of the settee, looking like a cornered hound.

There was an uncomfortable pause, and then my niece arrived, all effervescence like her brother, and asked about life on the island. I responded, asked about her doctoral studies.

"Bio-ethics isn't it?" I said.

She confirmed, talked about the Third World crisis in medical care, of human experimentation by the giant pharmaceutical companies, and while I watched her face illuminate with passion, I thought I couldn't be too harsh on Ben and Evelyn if they could create a woman with this kind of commitment and intelligence.

It wasn't long before her brother joined in the debate, and that kept us all occupied for the next twenty minutes. By now other guests arrived. The room filled, people spilling out onto the back terrace where spring breathed. Where I needed to breathe, so I rose from the sofa, made my excuses, and wove my way through mourners to the freedom outside.

A surprise, yes. Ma's death was quite sudden.

In good health? Yes, she had been in good health. Or so we thought.

Stroke. Yes. A surprise. Yes, a surprise.

I wondered what it had been like for her, ass to the heavens in the garden, endlessly eradicating weeds. Had there been pain, a dizzying moment of disorientation? Had she pitched into her beloved roses and wondered if now, these many years and sins later, she was to meet her Maker. Had there been fear? Had there been regret? Had she been lonely, dying alone, the perfume of flowers her last absolution and sacrament?

I found myself sitting on one of the stone benches in the rose parterre, remembering when first Ma had taken spade and shovel to the ground, digging out the shapes to make a Maltese cross and medallion. I had been no more than five or six. She had been frenetic, I remembered, furious, tears cascading with sweat down her face, her dark hair a jumble of curls escaped from the bun in which she customarily contained it.

I had wanted to comfort her. But even that young I knew Ma's view of comfort was grim, a sign of weakness.

"You're not to come home from school with your father," she'd announced suddenly. "I've made other arrangements."

I didn't ask the obvious, the genesis of a lifetime of avoiding crisis. Dad hadn't been at dinner that night. Nor at breakfast the following morning. Nor any meal thereafter. Our neighbour became my after-school ferry and safe house while Ma earned our keep. Uncle Ianto came to live with us about a year later, after Ma had been in hospital.

"They talk to you if you listen."

Startled, I looked to my side, unaware I'd been joined by the little girl I'd seen earlier. She shifted her bum on the cool stone of the bench. I smiled.

"Who talks to you?" I asked.

"The roses."

Such a serious little face. There wasn't any artifice there, not even a suggestion of mischief.

"The roses talk to you?"

"Sure. Don't they talk to you?"

They used to, I remembered, after Ma planted them, encouraging slips she'd nurtured in the greenhouse, a feather forever in her pocket with which she'd dust and broadcast pollen like a human bee.

"Not for a long time," I answered.

She considered that for a moment, then: "Well, maybe they're just waiting for you to say something."

"Vi!"

Startled, I looked up, bringing into focus a face I knew well. I swallowed regret. "David. You came. I was just talking to—" I looked to where my young guest had been to find only the cold bench.

"Yourself?" David asked.

"No. To...where did she go?"

"Who, Vi?"

"The little girl I was talking to."

"There's no one here. Just you and me."

"But...I...." I winced, looked back up at him. "I'm glad

you came," I said instead, confused, suddenly unsure of everything and this entire day.

"I promised you."

"That was gracious of you. You certainly didn't owe Ma anything."

He shrugged. "I owed her at least for the gift of knowing you."

I looked down and away. "I suppose the whole bloody island knows."

I heard him laugh, looked up at that familiar face. "It's a big island." And together we said, "Largest fresh water island in the world," and giggled like kids caught telling a dirty joke. He joined me on the bench.

"You sure you're okay taking care of Uncle Ianto?" I asked.

He nodded. "It's all set. We'll get back to Gore Bay tomorrow afternoon, late. Just came down for the service and to help with Ianto. I'm staying at Featherstone's B&B tonight if you need me. You figured about two weeks you'd be here?"

"About that. There are apparently details of the will that need to be addressed fairly soon for the smooth continuation of the greenhouses and guesthouse. Not sure how long that will take. I'm hoping we can get the majority of it addressed in the next two weeks while you holiday with Uncle Ianto, and then I'll take care of any further details via email and the like."

"Good thing the ferry's open. It'll make getting back easier for you." He nodded toward the open doors of the terrace. "You and Ben talked?"

"Not really. Hasn't been time yet."

"You going to be okay?"

I laughed and ran my fingers through the cropped curls on my head. "Oh sure. You know me."

"Tough old bird. Like your mom." I stiffened, looked at him. "Vi, relax. All I meant was you're a survivor, whether you realize it or not. All of you Cotters are. It's just that in you, survival doesn't come at someone else's expense." I closed my eyes on tears, sudden and hot, felt the rough tips of his fingers along my jaw. "If it weren't for her...."

"I know," I said, looking at him, at that face I'd known and would always love. "It was an unfair war in which I placed you." I kissed the tips of his fingers, pushed his hand to his chest where I let mine linger a moment. "I should go mingle." Stood and left.

The room and Ma's mourners enclosed me. In the end I sank back into the corner of the settee where I'd started, sipping water. Conversation flowed and ebbed around me. I answered questions, offered comments and gratitude, pulled a smile from my pocket of theatrics and pasted it on my face. I wished there was booze in the cup, was grateful there wasn't. After awhile the afternoon became a blur and then past tense as the door closed on the last guest, and Ben brought us back to the funeral, and the miracle of medicine that had allowed Ma such longevity.

"Ninety-four," he said.

"Ninety-eight," I said, and once again realized how much she'd risked, even then. She'd always said it hadn't been convenient for her to have children. Convenient. Children. Yes, that was Ma.

There was an uncomfortable pause, and then I said, "I suppose we should talk about the logistics of the estate. I can spend a few weeks down here to help. It's not like my boss is going to fire me."

"That's true," Ben said. "Unlike you, some of us do have responsibilities to employers."

I closed my eyes, chewing on the bait, rejecting it. It was just Ben's way of stirring things up. "I have a show coming up, but I'm well ahead," I said.

"Where are you showing?" Evelyn asked, arriving with a new tray of refreshments and fixings. There was a moment's interruption as people moved to clear space on the coffee table.

It was Uncle Ianto, ever my defender, who answered, "She's showing at the Manitoulin Festival of Art."

"Ah, art for the indigenous," Ben said.

"It's a fundraiser," I finished, throwing Uncle Ianto a warning glance. What I didn't want was an all-out fracas. Bad enough we fired ranging shots each other.

"I can do this on my own," Ben said. "There's really no need. But thanks."

"Really, it's okay," I answered. "I figured I could go over the will with you tomorrow, start organizing. I thought it might take some pressure from you." And now he knew where I stood. I wasn't going to be sidelined, and while it wasn't like I was hoping for some buried treasure to be unearthed in this sorting of the deceased's effects, I did want a chance to be alone with Ma's memory, with the possessions she'd gathered around her like a shield. Nope, Ben didn't like that one bit. What I wasn't prepared for was his next statement.

"The will's been changed, you know."

Ah, there it was, the quake. "Oh?"

He smiled. "You and Uncle Ianto are welcome to read it."

"You've got that right, my boy," Uncle Ianto said. "Isn't that so, Violet, my flower?"

"Perhaps we can do this tomorrow morning?" I asked. And suddenly I felt as though my navigation had foundered my ship. Why couldn't anything to do with Ma ever just follow a simple course?

Ben swirled the wine in his never-empty glass. "Actually, there's a meeting over at the greenhouses with the CEO of Cotter Greenhouses tomorrow morning to discuss the smooth transition of the greenhouses and business. But of course, if you'd rather not attend...."

I hesitated a moment, never good in the line of fire.

"I can go with you," Uncle Ianto said.

Not a great idea. "You're travelling home with David."

"But—"

"I saw him here. David." Ben said. "I thought that was all washed up?"

"People are capable of civil separations, you know."

Ben snorted. "Ah, my sister the diplomat. You'll talk yourself into anonymity."

"And have a clear conscience."

He shrugged in that judgemental way he had. How was it he could raise violence in my sensibilities where no one else could? All I wanted to do was break my fist on his face.

It was Colm who said, "Whoa, Dad. Ease up, eh?"

I threw Uncle Ianto a look I hoped would convince him of my need to be here alone for the meeting.

"You sure?" he said.

"Absolutely." I turned back to Ben. "It would appear it's settled."

"Suit yourself," Ben said. "Nine. Ma's office. You remember?" He didn't wait for an answer. "I've retained some of the hired staff for the next few days."

"I don't know why," Evelyn said. "It's not like there's going to be an army of guests."

"My wife isn't serving my employees."

My employees. Ah. Then the will made Ben the new major shareholder of Cotter Greenhouses. As much as that information stung, I wasn't surprised, which was in itself a surprise. First the quake, now the tsunami, the stutter in the heart. I couldn't even bring myself to wonder why, once again, Ma chose to overlook me. Was I incompetent? Was that it? Was the fact I'd run away from her and a marriage and confrontation enough to tattoo failure on my forehead? How was it I could be a senior citizen and still feel like six even in the memory of her presence?

"Right then." I set my cup on the coffee table and rose, turned to Evelyn who looked bewildered by the duel that had just taken place. I managed a smile. "It was lovely, as always, to see you, Evelyn." To the kids: "If you're going to be around, would love a chance to chat over the next few days, catch up a bit." I levered Uncle Ianto to his feet. "C'mon, you. Enough excitement for one day." And made my way to the stairs, Uncle Ianto ready to sputter. The moment I had him in his room he broke into an uproar. And through it all he muttered, "The little shit."

I let him rant. Sometimes it's good for the soul to scream at the gods. Just be careful they're not listening. There was enough momentum in his anger it carried him through my administration of his meds, which usually was enough of a chore, and overseeing his trip to the loo.

"You can manage your pyjamas?" I asked.

"Of course."

I wagged my finger at him. "Don't you *of course* me. I know you. If I don't do a bed check you'll be sleeping starkers in the chair or flashing at the window."

"Oh, now, Violet, that's hardly fair."

I retreated to the door, continued to wag my finger at him. "Behave yourself. Pyjamas and right into bed. Your book's on the nightstand."

He thumped down on the edge of the bed and glared at me. "You're no fun when you're serious."

"And you're a pain in the ass when your balls are in an uproar."

"Such language."

"Go to bed, Uncle. And behave yourself."

He clucked a disgusted sound and waved me away. I closed the door on him and made my way to the adjacent bedroom where memories would ooze from familiar furnishings.

Despite my assurances to Uncle Ianto, I was under no illusion the settling of Ma's property would be smooth.

I ducked into the bathroom while the rest of the family were downstairs, removed cosmetics I detested, brushed and flossed, and padded my way back down and across the hall to the room that had been mine in another life. When I closed the door, I felt I might drown. There wasn't enough air. It was too congested with memory in here, and all of it bittersweet, both joy and sorrow, laughter and anger. I eased to the edge of the bed, remembering a satin-edged blanket where there was now a down duvet, flounces of floral bed skirts where now a neutral box-pleated skirt hung stiff with starch. But the bedframe was the same, cherry posts and headboard, a blanket rack in the footboard where one of Ma's amazing quilts hung. She had a way of painting with fabric, of employing colour and texture.

I slathered moisturizer onto my face, feeling the push and shove of my skin, no longer supple, ever thirsty, let my fingers linger over my closed eyelids, paused, swept in and up, paused again, and this time knew there were tears and that despite all my denial, all my own carefully built mechanisms, grief eroded it all.

Unable to face myself in the light, I snapped off the switch on the lamp, leaned over and curled myself onto the bed. I watched the last vestiges of the day darken from crimson to indigo behind the maples.

Why was it I always seemed to be crying myself to sleep in this bed?

I woke with a start in the night, heart skittering, disoriented, a face from childhood like a ghost in my mind. This wasn't home. This wasn't my bed. I could hear voices, and for a moment I thought perhaps there were trespassers on my property. With a jolt I sat up and realized I was in Ma's home, that she was dead, and we presumed upon her hospitality in her absence.

I eased off the bed, crossed to the armchair by the window and sank into it, after a moment opening the sash to the cool night air. It touched my face as I sat there, a relief, scented with wisteria and grass, the verdure of the garden. Far off there was the tenor whirr of an eastern screech owl, mysterious and lonely, and beneath that the spring treble of peepers and toads.

My heart stilled. It had been thumping, silent to all but me, the way an owl's wings beat unheard by both prey and predator. In that suspended moment, I wondered if I fell, like an owl from her perch, would I be able to effortlessly push away the air once, twice, rise in disdain of gravity and glide across the meadow to that far line of maples and spruce, find the gnarled ancient that spread limbs over the spring that fed the lake, and rest. And watch the water that flowed ceaselessly, deceptively warm to invited skin even in the bitterest of winters. Would I see that face again? Would those fingers rise as liquid cascades like skin shedding? Would I be able to conquer my fear? This time? Would I?

I let out a breath, gathered another, slowing my frantic thoughts, gathering reality and order out of the shreds of dreams and old fears. It had been decades since I'd thought of that face, a child's ripe imagining in the blue-green waters of a sulphur spring.

I looked up and out the window, feeling the night air bathe my febrile cheeks.

There was a full moon caught in the arms of the willow I called Grandmother as a kid. It always reminded me of her, of Grandma's long hair that she'd let down and allow me to brush in those rare, still evenings. When she was gone, and all that was left was her book of Shakespeare's sonnets and a lingering impression of the dowager empress, I began to sojourn with the willow, seeking out Grandma's spirit beneath its graceful cascade, reciting poetry she'd encouraged me to memorize. Ma did not approve. I was never sure if it was because of her impatience with my romantic adolescence, or the fact I broke curfew by escaping into the willow's variegated moonlight.

It seemed to me I was always part of her disdain quotient. Certainly, it was her disdain that finally shattered my fear of her and led to me not only hanging up on a telephone conversation with her, but smashing the phone into plastic gravel.

It was an outburst of violence that had shocked David, I remembered. He'd enfolded my rage into the harbour of his arms, while I gasped out my wish for her death. Careful what you wish for.

We were married two days later. Only Uncle Ianto and David's sister attended the civil ceremony. And from there we'd migrated north to Manitoulin and the hope of a life free from Ma's influence.

But sometimes we allow a person to linger in our minds, permanent residents that shadow all our brightest moments. Chiaroscuro. That was Ma.

And since then not a word. Either of us could have easily picked up the pieces of that conversation, glued together some semblance of a working relationship, mended pride. Yet I found myself incapable of forgiving her for her condemnation of David and our marriage. What were her reasons for silence I would now never know.

All that was left was regret.

I leaned back in the chair and apparently allowed the moonlight and cool night air to lull me finally into sleep. I kept hearing that wee girl's voice: *They talk to you if you listen.*

If you listen.

It was my niece, Erin, who woke me with coffee and a smile.

I sat up in the chair, full of imperative.

"It's okay, Aunt Vi," she said. "You have an hour."

"Uncle Ianto—"

"Is up, dressed and downstairs breakfasting thanks to Colm. We thought we'd give you a break. It's going to be hard enough for you getting through this meeting with Dad and the team at Cotter Enterprises."

"Thanks," I muttered, and took the cup into my hands, sipping this forbidden, rich brew. "You two staging a mutiny?"

"Oh, Colm and I have pretty much always teamed up with Mum to keep Dad in check. You Cotters, you know."

Erin squeezed my shoulder and retreated. I took a few moments to let the coffee work its magic, and then set about making myself presentable. A meeting with the executive of Cotter Enterprises was something for which I'd been unprepared, and rummaging through my suitcase after showering I realized I'd have to cobble together an outfit from the jacket and shirt I'd worn yesterday with the only pair of dress pants I'd brought with me. Jeans and t-shirts wouldn't cut it, and there was no way in hell I was going to struggle into spandex and pantyhose, let alone bother with cosmetics.

With a despairing glance at my wet and unruly head of curls, now mostly grey, I headed downstairs. I could hear David as I descended the stairs, the rise and fall of his husky voice. Down the hall I could see Uncle Ianto's suitcase by the front door. I turned right into the dining room where I found David, sitting back in one of the chairs, his legs stretched out and crossed in front of him, completely at ease as was his wont. Colm looked up from across the table, grinned. I murmured a general greeting, waved off offers of breakfast from the small buffet on the sideboard.

"Car's picking us up in half an hour," Ben said.

"We couldn't walk?"

"You can. You'd better get started. It's a hike."

"Take the car," Evelyn said. "Leave the walk for when you're not on a schedule."

"Good point," said Colm.

"The indignities of getting older," I said, which generated a few chuckles and a stony silence from Ben. I wanted to confront him, ask exactly what it was I'd done wrong, why he continued this antagonism. After all this time I just wanted a little peace. But the truth of it was I was afraid to open the subject, afraid of what might result. Learned responses have a way of creating negative instincts.

The moment passed when David sat forward and nudged Uncle Ianto.

"We'd best make tracks," he said.

"You're carting me off, then, is it?"

"Afraid so. We've a flight and then a bit of a drive."

As a unit we all rose and followed David and my uncle to the front foyer, embraced, and said our farewells. Colm and Aislinn stood with them, a ferry to the charter.

Uncle Ianto patted my hand. "It will be fine. Never you mind."

I looked at the gnarled knobs of his knuckles, hands that had known hard work. "You think so, do you?" I said.

He leaned close and hugged me, whispered in my ear, "Shall I come with you, take apart the chairs just in case?"

I laughed, pecked his cheek, and turned him toward the door. Watching him drive away I smiled again thinking of him bent to the task of deconstructing rails. The memory seemed almost inappropriate given what was to come, and even more so when Ben announced what we all could see, that the car from the office had pulled into the courtyard. He descended the steps without another word to either his children, his wife, or me. I supposed that could be considered adversarial.

It was later I understood there was nothing adversarial in Ben's actions. His was the surety of the victor.

Una: March 15, 2000

I've been to Hoffman's today. Got myself tarted up in silk and perfume to prove to that insignificant toad of a man the old gal still has her wits about her. Didn't matter much. Old people are never taken seriously. We're lumped in with the idiots and cripples. Why do these younger folk (Hoffman young? That shit's easily forty-eight and not yet convinced middle-age is upon him.) think we're all deaf? I'm right here, you moron. No need to shout.

Anyway, I've been to see my lawyer. Figured it was time to update the will, make sure all's in order. I've left the whole thing to Ben. He figures it's his anyway, so why make things harder for Vi? She won't see it that way, sullen child, won't understand I've done her a favour, and in return she will do one for me. But I'm done with mothering. She'll get the patent to the Cotter roses. Ben gets everything else. I'd give anything to see him go into a tizzy over that, the greedy little shit.

At least with the patent in Vi's hands I can be assured it won't get sold off to one of those soulless agribusinesses, running around inspecting fields to make sure no one's growing anything without a royalty coming to them.

Still, I wish there was a way I could reach her, make

her understand that despite everything—the sundered homes, my lack of talent as a mother—that I love her. I had to be tough with her. The world isn't kind to women. Best she gain a thick hide, and maybe it's not too late for that.

Ianto, of course, disagrees. He thinks I should have been kinder, given the girl the grace of no expectations. The hell with that. What does he know about being a woman in a man's world? Find a successful woman and you'll find a lonely one. Where a man shows leadership and decisiveness, in a woman it's called arrogance and bitchiness. We're supposed to be walking dolls. Boobs and batting eyelashes. Smart, but not too smart. And smile. Yes, fucking smile through all of it. Don't you dare show temper or petulance. Don't you dare have an off day. Do that and you'll immediately be branded hormonal, as if our entire lives are governed by our ovaries.

So, I've decided this evening, to bequeath one last thing to my daughter who doesn't understand, who doesn't speak to me, and that's the gift of understanding. I'm instructing Hoffman to give Violet my diaries.

Lettie: Over There

The sky is purple now, the colour of her bedroom. Out here it's cold. She glances at the orange windows of her house, sees Ma walk by one, dishes in her hands. She should go in. Ma will want help. She looks back to the sky. Her breath puffs like smoke through her scarf. She blows again, watches the white burst of air, watches it thin as it rises up and up, and disappear into the cold. Does this air from her body have part of her in it? Does it go out into the cold to become another one of her? Are there ghosts of her walking around she doesn't know about?

It's creepy to think about.

She wiggles her bum on the snow where she's sitting—a throne she carved into the bank—smoothing the surface. She wishes it was ice not snow, wanting the throne to look like crystal. Diamonds. That would be a better throne for a fairy queen. No princess for her. She is a queen.

She glances back at the windows of her house where steam paints grey smears. She really should go in. That would be smart. It's just she doesn't get to stay out late, watch the sun set, especially not in winter, and Ma seems busy as she walks by the windows. Maybe it would be okay to steal a few more minutes. She polishes the arms of her throne with her red mittens, looks back up to the darkening sky.

There, see what the clouds are doing now, that magic thing. They've broken from where land meets sky, showing a lake of gold and there, what seems a lifetime away, are the red and purple hills rising to mountains. Sharp against the sky, towers of white unfold into cities and castles, pink forests huddled near the walls. She wonders if there are birds Over There. Does a cat like Timmy Cat prowl for mice and tease a yellow dog like Bella? She stretches out her red-mittened hand as if she really can touch that place, that land where there is no fear. She knows there's no fear there. These people hug and laugh. These people eat ice cream and strawberries all day, the red strawberries, not the hard, green ones Leslie leaves for her in the patch they raided in June.

Maybe if she wishes really hard she can go there, Over There.

She slides off the ice throne—which is really diamonds—and bows to the ships she sees coming across the Golden Sea. She must do something special to greet the ambassadors coming to her. They will be dressed in robes of purple that go swish, swish. They will have pale faces and speak quietly like the rumble of thunder in the distance.

What can she offer these ambassadors? What does she have? She has only her throne of diamonds, her magical red mittens that grow diamonds from the balls of snow crusted in the wool. What do they need with diamonds? They have everything Over There. Everything.

But maybe they don't have dance. That's right. She can

dance. She can spin and spin like one of those funny dancers all dressed in white she's seen on television.

And so, she sticks out her arms like blades, like wings, and sets her feet in motion, a turn, and turn, and spinning, the snow hardening to diamonds under her feet. The mountains and hills of purple Over There spinning, round and round and round, the lane, the buildings, all stretched out into blurred bands of colour. She's like water draining from the sink—what do they call it? A vortex. She's a vortex, yes, and if she keeps spinning she'll spin all the way to the ambassadors, those beautiful ships of gold that sail a golden sea from Over There.

Bequeathal

So it was I lost my last vestiges of innocence that morning I sat in the board-room of Cotter Enterprises Inc. with my brother, the CEO Cam Daniels, their head of research Susan Wong, and the head of legal Izzy Hoffman. It seemed the final irony I should be bequeathed roses and their patent; not just any roses, but Una Cotter's award-winning creation. Ben, at first apologetically smug, offered to help gather my winnings. It wasn't until Hoffman pointed out it was the patent, not the roses themselves I owned, that Ben and I completely understood what it was Ma had done. While Ben had title to the business and Ma's private holdings, the engine in Ma's machine was mine. The patent was everything.

"You'll, of course, sell it to me," Ben said.

I declined. I caught Susan ducking her head, and wondered for a moment if that was a smile I'd seen flit across the cool reserve of her face.

The CEO, Cam Daniels, pushed a box across the table to me. "Your mother also asked that we deliver these to you, Violet."

I raised an eyebrow.

"Her journals," he said. "Everything from her personal memoirs to her botanical notes. She asked if

Izzy and I would read them before entrusting them to you. We have. They're now yours. I digitized them, as she requested, in case something should ever happen to them. They are in an encrypted file to which only you, Izzy, and I have access."

"So, she's essentially ham-strung me," Ben said.

"From selling everything off, yes. It was Una's greatest concern that her life's work remain part of a whole, cohesive unit. And she felt, as do we, that ownership of the patents to her roses is key to the entire enterprise."

"So, the house, the—"

"Everything is tied to the corporation, and the corporation tied to the patents. While you, Ben, retain rights to all tangible properties, your sister, Violet, retains the rights to all intellectual properties, of which the exact genetic signature of the Cotter roses is part. So even if another grower wanted to license the Cotter roses for cross-pollination, you could negotiate the deal, but the decision whether to license would remain with your sister.

"Equally, you have controlling interest in the corporation, which means the greater share of dividends goes to you, whereas your sister earns no revenue whatever from any of your mother's estate."

"So ,what am I supposed to do with a house no one wants and a business about which I know nothing?"

The CEO looked over his glasses at Ben a moment, and then, "You might trust in the people she assembled to run this business. As to the house, it could easily remain a B&B, or be transformed and used as housing for interning university students, visiting business associates. With a little imagination it could easily be upgraded to an inn or a retreat, which was another of the projects your mother had always wanted to pursue, but never found the time. There are a thousand acres here of prime, arable land that are used not only for the roses of this enterprise, but leased to a vineyard that has often approached us about leasing the house for an inn attached to their culture of wine. Unlike many of the other vineyards in the area, that have had to favourably market the flavour of tobacco in their wine, the vineyard that leases part of the Cotter lands has the benefit of floral influences from our roses. They're keen to see our enterprise flourish."

"A perfect symbiotic business relationship built on cooperative and sustainable earth practices," Susan said. "Something that's actually been lauded in scientific and agricultural journals."

"What you're saying is Ben should take the long view," I offered, which was met with a grateful smile from the CEO and a scowl from Ben.

"Precisely," said Cam. "She may not have been an easy woman to either work for or live with, but she was shrewd and had an uncanny understanding of complimentary business and agricultural relationships."

I almost laughed aloud at that statement, wondered if Cam knew just how well he had assessed Ma's abilities.

"I can, of course, contest this," Ben said.

"You can. I wouldn't," said Izzy, without looking up from his tablet. "Una Cotter knew all about acquiring the best, and I think you'll find yourself tied up in a legal snafu from which you may never recover."

"Which is precisely what you're supposed to answer."

Susan tapped Cam on the hand with her pen, raised

an eyebrow in query, to which Cam nodded. She said, "I realize you're disappointed, Ben. But you might want to trust to her judgement. None of us here could say we were ever close to your mother. Hell, she scared most of us silly. I think the most endearing name anyone had for her was Dragonlady. But that's not to say she didn't carry a great deal of respect among the people she employed and the business associates with whom she dealt. If you're to follow in her footsteps as the major shareholder, you might want to remember that."

Which did not sit at all well with Ben. I watched his face close with anger, the way he folded his hands together on the table before him. "And that's that. Nothing left to do but sign the paperwork, hail Caesar, and carry on."

"Pretty much," said Izzy, finally looking up from his note-taking. "You can stop by the offices tomorrow when our legal staff will have the papers ready for your signature. The house, of course, is at your disposal until you and the Board decide what should be done with it, if anything."

"Then we're done?"

Cam nodded.

Ben rose, didn't offer to shake hands, and beat a retreat. I took a look at the box and wondered about getting it back to the house, feeling more than a little bewildered.

"I can have someone drop it off for you, Violet," Cam said. "And I can arrange a separate car for you, if you'd like. I gather you and your brother aren't getting on too well."

I smiled. "Families. You know how it is." I patted the box. "It's likely all in there, I expect."

Cam pursed his lips in a tacit agreement, shrugged.

"I'd appreciate it, and will accept the offer of having this dropped at the house, thanks," I said. "As for a lift for me, I think I'm going to take the walk I didn't coming here."

"There's one more thing," Susan said. "We were reluctant to bring it up with Ben here. Your mother also wanted you to have a pot of the award winner."

"The white rose."

She nodded.

"The ones that were at her funeral, no thorns, heavy Damascus scent."

She smiled. "You know your roses."

I inhaled sharply. "Ma and I may not have spoken for decades, but it would seem I am very much her daughter." I looked back up at the three of them, these professional people who could speak so freely and candidly about a woman I spent most of my life fearing. "I'm grateful. Is it possible to have the pot brought to the house with the journals? I'm assuming the rose is as hardy as its creator and can take a week or two bound in a pot?"

"Just water it."

I smiled. "I think I can manage that."

I shook their hands and made my way out into the afternoon sun, a little shell-shocked, a lot unsure.

The walk I took back to the house was dogged by memory. It had been so very long since I'd strolled this footpath beside the laneway that connected the house to the business. I remembered graders coming in when I was a brooding teenager, remembered the screaming argument between Ma and my step-father, Daniel Mcafferty, while the construction crew paid attention to their work. He'd stormed out of her life that day, leaving Ben in an angry grief, his crew under threat of unemployment, and me in relief.

I crossed through the maples and across fields now under viniculture, until I came to the red barn that still stood, built by Cotter pioneers. After Daniel left we'd found truckloads of empty beer and rye whiskey bottles.

"Good riddance to bad rubbish," Ma had said. Ben had cried. I knew enough to say nothing and kept loading bottles into the farm's pickup.

I wondered now if our Irish forebears had staged a gathering after raising the barn, wondered if there'd been good Irish whiskey swilled amid the sorrow of Irish wives. We'd been flax-growers in County Donegal back in the 18th century. Good aristocratic officers who had raided with Cromwell, been rewarded with land, and lost the land when weather, failing crops and cheap imports had sucked the life from industry and tradition. And so, the New World and a new world, again rewarded by the British Government, but this time not so easy. One hundred acres yours if, after the first year you were able to clear ten, raise a house and barn, and this with no hard cash to hire in help, nothing but your pig-headed determination not to fail this time.

And somehow, they hadn't, those early Cotters. And when settlers around them had been unable to meet the commitment, we Cotters had swooped in like the raiders of old and succeeded in gaining yet more land from the Crown to add to fortune. Land was wealth. Wealth was in land. So, it had always been with we

Cotters. So, Una Cotter believed and taught Ben and me.

Now Ben had the land. I had the idea of it.

By the time I made it back to the house it was late afternoon. I'd taken my time. Idling by fences, wandering up rows of roses or grapevines, hearing laughter and tears, wading through memory. I found myself shunning thought of my early childhood, from the days before Daniel Mcafferty and the birth of my brother, Ben.

I entered the house through the old summer kitchen, now a mudroom. Out of habit I kicked off my shoes and barefoot went into the kitchen, the old slate floors cool on the soles of my feet. Some of the staff Ben retained were occupied with the business of *mise en place* for the evening meal. I eased to one of the press-back chairs at the old harvest table, not wanting to be in the way, and asked if it would be possible to have a glass of water or lemonade.

"Violet Cotter, yes?" one of the young women asked, pouring a glass of real lemonade for me. She set the sweating glass on the table before me.

I nodded, thanked her for the drink and gulped down half. I grinned up at her. "Haven't had anything so good since I was a kid."

Some of them chuckled. Another brought me a plate of munchables. I ate cucumber spears and radishes, coins of chèvre and pear wedges, relaxed in their chatter and forgot the ghosts walking among them in this house of history.

It wasn't to last long. It was prep for dinner and I asked when was service.

"We were told seven," said the woman who seemed to be in charge of catering.

I murmured some sort of acknowledgement, which the chef seemed to intuit when she said, "If that doesn't suit, we can easily bring something to your room. I understand it's been a stressful few days for you."

I felt embarrassment flush my face, looked down and away. "Very kind of you," I muttered. "I would be grateful." I looked back up at her. "What is for dinner, by the way?"

"Pork tenderloin medallions in a port reduction. But if you'd prefer something lighter that's no trouble at all."

"Did a psychology course come with that chef's hat?" I asked. She grinned. "Lighter would be great. In fact, something noshable like what you just gave me. And tea. I'd kill for a pot of tea."

"Consider it done."

I thanked her and the staff, scooted up the back stairs to the second floor and retreated to my room before anyone could find me. The box of Ma's journals was already in my room when I entered. I wondered where they'd put the pot of roses, figured it would be somewhere safe, and rolled down to the bed.

I was apparently worn out by the day's activities as the next thing I knew one of the staff had knocked and entered with a tray, which she set on the side-table by the window and the armchair. I sat up on the bed, cross-legged, scrubbing sleep from my eyes. In a moment I scooted over to the other side of the bed, dragging the duvet as I did so, and poured myself a cup of tea. God that was good!

I set down the mug, lifted away the lid of the box and

pulled out the first journal that came to hand, which, in typical fashion for Ma, was the first she had ever written.

Back in the chair, comfortable with tea, nosh, and journal, I read.

Went skating today on the Grand. Some of the men from town have cleared a long stretch where the ice is deep and the bank easy to climb, just off Homestead Road. It was really cold and so I togged up in my woollen stockings and the overalls I usually wear when I go out to help old man Bailey on his farm. Even wore Ianto's sheepskin cap with the flaps cause I didn't want my ears to freeze, and with him still somewhere on the continent fighting in this never-ending war, it felt kind of good to have my brother's hat on my head, stopping me from becoming an icicle-keester. Mostly I just wanted to get out of the house and have some fun, cause it was such a long week. I swear if that creepy boss of mine asked me to work any more overtime I would have quit. Well, not really quit, cause Ma depends on the money, especially now Granny's living with us and Da's dead.

Anyway, went skating. And boy was it fun! Hardly anyone was there on account of it being so cold, so that meant I had most of the ice to myself and I could fly along just as slick as you please. I think even Barbara Ann Scott would have approved; course I don't have her tiny figure or her wardrobe. Down on the smoothest part of the ice some boys were playing hockey. They always nab the choicest ice, leaving the rest of us to deal with lumps and bumps and the sculpting of the Grand. Have to be careful in some places where the ice thins. Just three weeks back the Harding twins sailed right onto rotten ice and down into a deep pool, never came up. Never seen. We all went to the funeral. The parents all grey and red-eyed. Mrs. Harding had to be helped to walk she was so stricken with grief. Ma said it was a tragedy, but certainly those twins never displayed the common sense God gives cabbages. I thought that was a bit hard. But had to agree, really. Why would they take a chance like that? Especially when everyone knows how tricky the Grand can be? Anyway, today was good, like I said, cause of there being so few people, so there was no worry about skating off into areas one aught not.

My ankles were getting sore and so I skated back to where I'd left my boots and flask, plunked myself down on the bank and had a nice cup of tea, letting the steam warm my nose, which then of course started to run like a spring freshet. I thought I'd die of embarrassment. I'd just fetched out my hankie from the depths of my coat when this man, bold as brass if you please, thumped down on the bank beside me and said he'd been watching me skate, and wasn't I just a graceful gazelle. Did I know what a gazelle was, he asked, as if I was some kind of rube, thank you.

I told him I didn't talk to strangers, especially strange men, and gave him my back. And he, brazen as that, says, "I'm no stranger. I see you all the time in Frasers' Hardware."

And what was I supposed to answer to that? If I continued to ignore him word could get back to Mr.

Fraser and I'd catch it for sure, be called rude and shiftless and doing his business harm, and that could cost me my job, and that paycheque Ma needs to make ends meet. It's been hard on the farm, with everyone broke, and so many out of work. Even we can't pay for help, because we had to sell our crop for less than it cost us to bring in. And while I miss school, I'd miss the farm more, so I offered to go to work in town. It was a long walk until I got the bike, but now it's back to walking on account of the snow.

Anyway, this man kept chatting me up, so there was nothing for it but to turn to him, to play polite and apologize, but what I was really doing was making sure there would be butter with our bread, cause I couldn't afford for him to run tales to old man Fraser.

Anyway, we got to talking and I think maybe he's okay. Seemed nice enough anyway after that rude start. Even offered to drive me home, but I said no thanks.

After I finished my tea I went back skating and he said goodbye and that maybe he'd see me at the hardware store or skating some time. I smiled and waved at him, and wondered why I'd want to meet him again, him being so much older than me and all. Have to admit, though, he certainly was fine looking.

Lettie: Dungeon of the Darkies

From winter to spring and now early summer she waits for the ships to arrive. But every evening when the magic of sunset reveals Over There, the ships are still sailing. She can see them there, out in the middle of the Golden Sea. It must be a long way to come, she thinks. It must be a very important journey the ambassadors make.

She thinks this while she's in bed. It's very late, she knows. Her room is black. She closes her eyes and sees black. She opens them and sees black. She thinks this blackness would be a perfect place for bad things to hide. It's the Big Black Dark. All she can hear is her own breathing. It's too loud. She wishes she didn't have to suck in air so hard, that her lungs would work the way other kids' lungs work. In the Big Black Dark her breathing will give her away for sure.

She has to pee. Ma said if she peed the bed one more time she'd catch it for sure, that Panda the Bear, Trixie the Dog and Greenie the Teddy would be thrown in the trash. They stank, Ma said. Hanging from the laundry line, her friends looked miserable. For their sake, if not her own, she would try to get up, cross the Big Black Dark to the stairs and down, across the hall to the basement door. The toilet beside her room is forbidden—too many times with too much toilet paper—and so she has to face worse than the Big Black Dark. There is the basement and the Dungeon of the Darkies, and there, in the middle of the dungeon, on a raised platform like a stinky throne, the other toilet. And above that is a long string to the only light, like an evil moon shining on her where she'd sit and pee, exposed and sure to invite every slinking, slimy, evil thing in the Dungeon of the Darkies.

Maybe she can hold on until morning. Maybe. She squeezes her eyes shut, holds her breath. Sweat beads her upper lip. She lets go of her breath in a big whoosh. No use. She is sure her eyes are yellow she has to pee so badly.

"Will you come with me?" she whispers to Panda, touching his glass eyes, his rubber nose.

Of course I will.

Good ol' Panda. She hugs him, kisses him, and gathers him into her arms. Carefully, holding one leg, she lets Panda gently over the mattress so he can check under the bed.

No Furries, he says.

That's a relief. You never know when the Furries will scuttle out from under the bed and wrap up your ankles. The floor is cool against her feet when she slides off the bed.

So far so good.

She turns the knob on the door, kissing Panda's head for luck, and peers out into the darkness of the hall. Clear. There's pale light at the end of the hall. It's the moon that glows and floats on the hardwood. What if the hall were to become a river? Not enough magic tonight, she decides. It will be safe. She pads to the stairs, grips the banister with one hand, clutching Panda with the other, and slides her heel off the tread and touches the cool wood of the next. And again. And once more until she reaches the lower hall and from there to the basement door, kisses Panda again, opens the way to both relief and fear, and carefully, placing her feet just so, she steps down and down into blackness as deep as dreams.

For a moment she hovers there on the grit of the concrete floor. It feels like ice. This isn't ice she can control. She hasn't made it. It's not like the ice of her throne. It's not ice that can be diamonds.

"I'm afraid, Panda," she whispers and clutches her friend closely, wanting very much to cry. It's so far across to the toilet and the light and who knows what is out there in the darkness?

There's nothing in the darkness that isn't there in the light, Panda says in her ear. His rubber nose is cool against her skin.

She squeezes her eyes shut for a moment, gasps and then tears out into the darkness, hurtling toward the place she thinks is the toilet, one hand stretched out ahead of her to guard against falling or colliding with something unwanted, or the toilet. There it is all of a sudden, the damp coolness of the toilet and she climbs up the step, reaches up with her free hand into the darkness, finds the thin cord for the light and yanks.

Light floods the darkness. She whirls on the dais, peering out to the edges where she knows the Darkies lurk.

"Please don't hurt me," she whispers. "I just have to pee."

With a clatter and a gulp she flings back the toilet

lid, peers into the bowl to make sure the Uglies aren't there—clear—and thumps down just before her bladder bursts. She watches steam rise between her legs. Then, keeping track of the shadows, she leans this way and that, peeing in different directions to drown any hiding Uglies in the toilet. By now she's shivering, trying very hard not to cry, not to whimper like the baby Leslie says she is.

She rips toilet paper from the roll and scrubs her bottom and leaps up, flushes, bangs down the lid, yanks on the light and bolts for the stairs, the hall, the next stairs, down the hall to her room.

She figures it's okay to cry when she catapults back into bed, clutching the sheets around her head, safely surrounded once more by Panda, Greenie, and Trixie.

Meldrum Bay

The following morning, foaming at the mouth with toothpaste, I realized I wasn't needed at Ma's, that despite everything I'd assumed, she'd in fact taken care of all the details, and what was really required of me now was to sign off on the paperwork, and head home with Ma's journals and the potted rose. There was no point mooning around here chasing memories I didn't want.

Settled on a course of action, I showered and dressed before the rest of the household was up, and walked the lane to the offices. The doors had only just been opened when I entered, told reception I was here to see Izzy Hoffman. I signed, he signed. I was told copies would be sent once Ben had signed, had my physical and email addresses confirmed, and walked back down the lane to the house.

The pot of roses I found sitting outside the summer kitchen, nestled into the herb garden. I found a watering can stowed where Ma had always kept one, in what used to be the spring house against the stone garden wall, gave the roses a drink, and then watched the antics of birds in the small fountain that was fed from the odiferous artesian well that burbled summer and winter, despite all extremes of temperature.

From there, despite my earlier determination to be out with dispatch, I wandered aimlessly, through gardens and gazebos, along pathways Ma had constructed to look like crumbled ruins. Everywhere was fragrance and texture, colour and contrast. In summer she painted with flora; in winter with textiles. It was almost as though her inability to nurture relationships burst into brilliance in soil and needle.

In the years I'd been away she'd polished and perfected the bones of what she'd laid down when I lived here. Everywhere there was her distinctive signature. And in witnessing all of it I wished I had understood the frenetic, creative energy that had driven her and kept her from being able to connect with me in any positive fashion. How was it she could create such harmony here, and such discord between us?

I spent the next few hours deciding whether to have a full-scale, self-indulgent nervous breakdown, or just get on with things. I chose the latter. It took too much effort to do a proper breakdown. I mean, if you're going to do that sort of thing, do it with panache: voices, Joan of Arc delusions, stigmata—the whole thing. But, no. I'd cling to this hard-won sanity, this island of calm in the hurricane that had been life with Ma.

I dined that evening with Ben and his family, delaying, hoping I supposed for some miracle reconciliation, and knowing full well it would be the last I would see of them for some time. Evelyn I could have counted as a friend, but Ben's animosity would prevent that. And despite good intentions, I was enough of a realist to recognize that both Colm and his wife Aislinn, and Erin his sister, would have every good intention of visiting their reclusive aunt on Manitoulin, but would likely never get around to it. Life was like that.

I retreated into the safety of silence, watching the evening slide by like celluloid. Most particularly I watched Ben, an ache where there had been childhood laughter.

A little boy, a brother, a voice husky in whisper: *Where are we going?*

It's a secret.

And his scrubbed, moon of a face grinning up at me. An afternoon spent slinking through woods, adventure bright on our skin. Hijinks. Antics. I wondered how I'd managed to make it all go wrong.

I looked down to my plate. The lamb was perfectly pink, the jus rich. Greens from the estate's gardens. Pinot noir in my glass. Untouched. I watched Ben swirl his, nose it, tilt, and taste. I pushed my food on my plate the way I pushed words in my mouth, tasting none of it. There were words enough around me, carrying conversation to places from which I demurred.

We lingered past coffee. I said my good-evenings early, with notification I would be gone before sunrise as I had a long journey ahead. Ben gave me a nod. I turned away.

When I was about to hike up my feet and into bed, there was a knock on my bedroom door, and when I acknowledged, Evelyn stepped into the room, in her hands an old ivory carving I knew very well. Every line, every graceful curve of the old woman bent over a hoe I had admired from the moment Ma and I had found it buried in a junk shop outside of Paris.

Evelyn now extended the carving to me. "I know how

you like this piece," she said. "I thought you should have it. Ben doesn't know. Best that way. I doubt he'll miss one more item he'd regard solely for its monetary value."

I received the carving into my hands, looked up at her. "That was very kind, Evelyn. I honestly don't know why you put up with him."

"He's good to me, believe it or not. I think he looks at me as the only person he can trust. But then I've never had anything he thought should be his." She turned away. "I'd like to say we could correspond, but I've never been very good at keeping secrets. This one will be hard enough. But it's only one moment, one thing, not many."

I watched her face, the lines of worry that had set in, the soft brown of her eyes, almost like burnt butterscotch. I realized how little I knew of her, and how much she must have shouldered coming into this contentious family. Brave soul. Gentle soul. I marvelled, finally, at her ability to retain such halcyon in the face of us all.

"I understand," I answered, and gave her a smile, a small token of acknowledgment and understanding. It was, perhaps, the most profound discussion we'd ever have. "And thanks again."

When the door closed I looked down at the carving, remembering that afternoon from so long ago. I could almost smell the naptha from mothballs in that old junk shop, again see the chiaroscuro of light where it spilled through dusty windows. There had been an oak Arts and Crafts sideboard and hutch against the wall, crammed with tin toys and boxes, and there hidden at the back, this ivory relic, this old Chinese woman hoeing a non-existent garden. She stood maybe twelve inches tall, a beautifully rendered moment, even then yellowing with age, a crack from lack of care running up the back. But I didn't care. I'd crept away from where Ma had been ogling some Fenton milk glass and had the cashier ring through the purchase. I hadn't even asked how much. Just handed her my credit card and stowed the surprise in my handbag which in those days resembled more of an Edwardian valise than anything fashionably small and petite. I remembered thinking how that carving would be my ma decades later, how she was never so happy as when her hands were dark with dirt. I had given it to her when we got back into the car before heading home. It had been just before David and I married. A happy afternoon. Tea and scones in a wee shop afterward. Ma's face glowing with pleasure, me basking in that warmth.

And now here I sat with the old ivory in my hands, overcome by memory, weighted with regret. I lifted the carving to my nose and inhaled. It even smelled like her.

I reopened my suitcase and nestled the ivory in among my clothes, giving it a cushion and protection. I called Uncle Ianto, to be sure he was fine; he threatened to contest the will, to face down that little turd of a nephew, and generally spiralled into a tizzy I was sure escalated his blood pressure. I assured him I would be fine—to how many people had I given that assurance?—and guided him into safer conversation. The house was fine, he said. Meldrum Bay waited for me. The loons were back. David had been by to make sure he was settled. Once again Uncle Ianto offered not so subtle opinions that I'd been insane for ending that relationship. Irene from the village had driven up our long lane to deliver soup and pie.

"Apparently, I can't cook," he'd said. "Light the barbeque, fire the burgers, slap them between bread and there you go. If nothing else, Weetabix works in a pinch."

"You need more fibre than Weetabix," I'd said.

And that had set him off about vegetarian nonsense and another attempt on my part to settle him down.

And finally, at long last, we rang off, my travelling itinerary delivered to him. I texted the same to David just in case, turned out the light and slept. It was not restful. There was a parade of dreams which woke and haunted me. I struggled to sleep again only to find myself strangling the pillow, or soaked in sweat. When the alarm on my phone trilled, I struggled up through exhaustion, showered and dressed, and crept out in darkness like a thief escaping. The pot of roses was in the back of the car, roped off against any possibility of tipping, my suitcase nearby. The box that held Ma's memoirs sat on the passenger seat, the sack of my purse atop.

So, packed and prepared, the drive north should have been typical, a start in darkness before the land suffuses with colour, later dawn like hope on the horizon. Coffee to hand. Silence in the car. Alone this time. Uncle Ianto ahead of me tending the home-fires, as it were, while I drove to catch a ferry and from there to a retreat that had been my home ever since I made my escape from the sprawl and the confusion of southern Ontario.

An island. A solitude. A refuge from the world and myself. A refuge from the past with all its remembered wounds and terrors and losses. Loneliness as large as this morning sky, something that should have brought comfort but instead only rendered me insignificant in the face of the universe.

That damned phone vibrated in its cradle on the dashboard, like some frenzied Mexican jumping bean. Now the ringtone kicked in: *A caller, Madam. Shall I tell them to fuck-off?* and I thought perhaps I'd been a bit insane to think that an appropriate ringtone for unknown callers. And then the thought: How did I get to this point? Always at someone's command. Land line. Cell phone. Internet social networks. E-mail, snail mail, mail rising in my In-basket like a nervous breakdown. Ma. Always at Ma's command.

Now beyond her command. And there was the problem. Every form of freedom has a cost.

"Oh shut-up!" I barked at the phone, and listened again to the rush of the wind over the sun-roof, the whine of tires on asphalt, every sense stretched and yearning for the landmarks of my progress: Guelph, Fergus, Mount Forest; Markdale, Chatsworth, Owen Sound; now Cruickshank, Clavering, Wiarton at last. Six-thirty of the blessed A.M. now, and hope of another coffee to keep the crust and sting from my eyes. Tim Horton's, icon of Canadian travel. Clean and country chic, a washroom with the welcome smell of recent disinfectant, small-town staff with encompassing smiles that touched their eyes. I felt inadequate against their quiet energy.

Coffee, double-double, please, to go.

They kindly fulfilled my request. I paid one forward. On my way out the door, I swigged down a gulp, hot and dark, like crack to an addict.

I listened to the car engine tick as it cooled while I took another slug of coffee, cradling the cup under my chin, chewing on tears that threatened now that reality was setting in, and I stubbornly refused to shed. This was no place for an emotional scene, the parking lot of Timmy's. I couldn't let go. Not now. Not ever. I'd fought too hard to find sanity in the insanity that had been life with and without Ma. Now gone. She's now gone. Beyond all contact. Beyond all hope of understanding.

How did it come to this? How is it that anger and hurt now became regret beyond all redemption?

God, I'm going to lose it right here in the parking lot, right here amid coffee and Timbits, contractors rushing to a morning fix and a day of customers and work, farmers gathering for gossip and a connection with the living.

Hang on. Sweet freaking Jesus just hang on.

I thumbed the button to unlock the car, heard locks click, opened the door and slid into the driver's seat, hauled the door closed.

A big breath, held, let go in a long, shuddering sigh. *Okay. I'm okay.* I glanced at the phone, a pang of guilt. I set the cup in the holder and picked up the smooth silver apparatus that was really a mini-computer of miracles. A few taps at the screen and I revealed a text message from Uncle Ianto.

For godsakes, Vi, let me know you're okay!

The tears welled and I couldn't help it; let them slide down my face. The hell with what anyone could see. They shouldn't be looking anyway.

I jabbed at the keypad.

I'm sorry. I'm OK. I'll let you know when I reach the ferry.

Everything's okay. And added, like a kid, *Don't be mad.* As if my every action might bring down retribution.

Uncle Ianto's response was swift: *You sure you're okay?*

Yes. It was so easy to give him that deceit, assure him all's well with his quickly dissolving niece. Don't drag him into your misery.

I'm still pissed, he texted.

I'm sure you are.

His response was slower this time. I knew he struggled to find the right words. There was no questioning his concern. It was as true as the sun rising, the cycles of the moon. Uncle Ianto was just like that.

I saved him the effort of trying to stumble through a suitable response.

I'll let you know when I'm on the ferry. Don't worry. And set the phone back in its cradle.

I swallowed another gulp of coffee, gathered a breath, another sip, placed the cup back in the holder, hauled the seat belt around me, heard the snick of the buckle, and turned the key in the ignition of the car. Checked the mirrors, my blind spots—I should have checked the metaphorical ones years ago—backed out, shifted into drive, and out again to Highway 6 and north to Tobermory, the ferry to Manitoulin and a two hour respite in which to collect my senses before I headed north and west once more.

Running. That's what I was doing. I should have told Uncle Ianto I was running.

Always running away from something or toward something. Right now, I ran back to the security and safety of Meldrum Bay and the home I'd forged there. Away from Ma's funeral and all the memory that resurrected.

Just leave it for now. Just get to the ferry. It will be okay.

And so, I drove through the almost non-existent towns of Mar, Edenhurst and Ferndale, checked the time, watched the sun rise higher, through Miller Lake and past the signs that proclaimed the Bruce National Park and hunting grounds for First Nations. This was true escarpment country, rugged limestone grinning like teeth, endless forests of hardwoods, ancient cedars, and white pines. Finally, into the tourist and diving mecca that Tobermory had become.

The highway bypassed the town core stacked with scuba shops, galleries, inns, and purveyors of collectibles. I headed out to the Chi-Cheemaun's terminal, made the requisite check-in for reservations, and then crossed to the restaurant attached to the building.

There was an hour to sacrifice. I decided another pee break, libations of orange juice and chamomile tea were in order. I'd been drinking far too much coffee and regular tea, and with the respite of the crossing I could relax a little, begin the slow purge of my system. Migraines would no doubt plague me once I got home. The last time I had to withdraw, I'd been a right bitch for two weeks, shakes, temper, and all.

I settled into a window seat where sunlight bathed the green laminate and butter-yellow oak table. There was heat under my rump from sunlight on the chair. Despite myself, I let out a sigh and sucked back the orange juice as though I hadn't had anything fresh in my mouth in months.

On the wall in front of me hung a painting, and I shook my head when I realized it was one of my own. How many of these bits of me were out there? Not high art, no. But accessible, yes. The quintessential Canadian landscape. And mine looked lonely, I had to admit. It was like looking at a photograph of yourself from years ago and realizing your heart's right there for anyone to see.

I drained the bottle of juice, looked away to the harbour and the bulk of the docking ferry. It occurred to me if I didn't have something to worry about I wouldn't be happy. Anything to distract me from the rising storm of sorrow and regret. Relief flooded my sensibilities when I saw cars disembarking from the Chi-Cheemaun. On cue, I returned to the capsule of the car and drove into the queue that would take me home.

Home to Meldrum Bay and haven.

Una: February 1945

It turns out his name is Conner Bannon, and he's thirty-two and for some reason I can't figure out he's a bachelor. I think he must go to the skating pond every Saturday, cause every time I show up he's there. He's taken to bringing hot chocolate in his flask, which he shares with me. He must make good money at Penman's if he can afford cocoa. He's a mechanic at Penmans, maintaining and repairing the knitting machines that make the cotton jersey for underwear and hosiery. I have to wonder, though, about his character, as I suspect he has seen no military service whatsoever, unlike so many men who signed up in town, some who will never come home. I'm wishing Ianto would come home. We all miss him, want him back safe and sound. But I'm wandering off again.

Today Mr. Bannon showed up at Fraser's when I was working, and had me fetching and pricing and working up an order he wanted delivered. I asked him what he was going to do with all this pipe and stuff, and he said he was putting in an indoor toilet. I asked him what for, when an outhouse was good enough for most people. Course I spoke too soon, cause I quickly realized most people in town were connected to the mains, unlike those of us out of town. And he smiled and leaned in closely (he wears some sort of spicy cologne or something) and asked which was better, a frozen arse or a warm one?

I nearly died of embarrassment!

Besides, he said, and he was laughing at me I swear, he figured if he were going to bring a wife into his house he had better make sure the house was all modern and attractive, couldn't have her coming into a rundown nest, now could he? I asked him when he was getting married. He said he didn't know. I asked him who was his intended? He said he couldn't say. Why ever not, I asked, and he leaned in close again and I felt my face get all hot, and he said, 'cause she doesn't know yet, now does she?

I didn't like that. I didn't like the way he made me feel, and the way he seemed to think he was pulling a mickey on me, and when I moved away to write up his order he pulled me back by the arm and asked when I got off work. I told him. He said he'd be by to pick me up and take me for a coffee. I said I couldn't and had to go straight home. Then he'd drive me home, he said, but when Mr. Fraser walked by, he went all quiet and shifty-like and I hurried away to the counter and finished off his order. It was relief, for a change, to have Mr. Fraser hover over me to make sure I got all the details right.

When finally Mr. Bannon left, Mr. Fraser turned to me, and not unkindly, said, "You be careful around yon Conner Bannon, Miss Cotter. It's an ill wind that blows nobody good."

Well, that's set the fear of God into me, I swear. Mr. Fraser isn't known for friendly advice; why, I've rarely known more than a reprimand and sharp orders from him. But he seemed truly concerned, and that got me thinking. I wanted to ask Ma about Mr. Conner and what Mr. Fraser meant, but I admit I was afraid to. I feel almost as though I've been involved in something bad, and with Ma always going on about how careful a girl has to be about her reputation, I'm afraid somehow I've done something wrong, and that was why Mr. Fraser gave me a warning. I can't imagine he meant me any kindness. Mr. Fraser's never been kind. I even had to work right up till six on Christmas Eve, even though there wasn't anyone at all in the shop, let alone on the street. And besides, who goes shopping for anything in a hardware store the afternoon of Christmas Eve?

Anyway, I've decided not to go skating for awhile. I think maybe I should pay Mr. Fraser's warning some heed.

We had a letter from Ianto this week. He'd written before Christmas, saying they were on the move in Holland, but he couldn't say where, exactly, for reasons of security. He writes of the terrible hardships of the Dutch people, how they're facing starvation and cold, but says we're making headway. He says when they're marching, those long hours of fear and drudgery, seeing all the farmland stretching out before him reminds him of our own good earth and he hopes to again walk upon it, not under it. He sends his love. We, of course, send him ours. Ianto, I miss you. I wish you home safe.

Lettie: Mary Hamilton

For the most part, it's better during the day, in the safety of sunlight where everything is seen and known and her world can be identified. Only the Uglies slither around during the day, but at least they live in the toilet bowl. They don't lurk under the bed, or the basement. And as long as she pees on them they can't ooze up and over the toilet rim.

Today, however, is cleaning day. She can't stay home while Ma and Granny clean. It makes her sick. Her chest gets all heavy and wheezy. It's hard to breathe, harder than usual. So, she goes to the Harris' house just across the road and down the hill a bit. The Harris house is different from hers. It has red bricks. Hers has stone blocks. Inside, the Harris house is like hers, but the wrong way round. Sometimes she wonders why it was made that way. She wonders if having the rooms face one way or the other makes a difference in the magic of a house. She thinks it must, because it's always so warm-feeling in the Harris house. Except for when Leslie is there. He's like one of the Uglies.

Still, she likes cleaning days, when Mrs. Harris will give her green pea soup and tea biscuits for lunch. She likes these things. She likes the colour of the soup. She slurps it noisily until Mrs. Harris tells her to eat with her mouth closed. Mrs. Harris looks annoyed.

Oh. She didn't know she had to do that—eat with her mouth closed. She doesn't want to make Mrs. Harris angry. She likes Mrs. Harris as much as she likes the green pea soup, so she carefully puts the whole spoon in her mouth—it's hard to fit the big spoon in her small mouth—wraps her lips around the stem, and pulls the spoon back out, empty. The metal hurts the corners of her mouth a little. She swallows. Yum. Looks up at Mrs. Harris for approval, who shakes her head and laughs, giving her a hug.

"There's a good girl."

She smiles. It's nice to be hugged by Mrs. Harris. Her bosom is all squishy and big, and she smells of flowers and laundry hung on the line. She likes Mrs. Harris' apron. It's yellow with little white roses and green leaves and fits over her shoulders and ties in the back. It's almost like a smock.

She finishes the soup and the biscuit that drips butter down her chin. This time she remembers to chew with her lips clamped firmly shut. Why didn't she know how to do this before? There's so much less noise now and she can hear Mrs. Harris singing something sad in her husky voice.

Arise, arise, Mary Hamilton. Arise and tell to me,
What thou hast done with thy wee babe I heard weep
and lie by thee?

She uses the linen serviette Mrs. Harris has placed for her. This is something else Mrs. Harris taught her. There are so many rules about eating politely. Is it any wonder she doesn't know all these things?

I put him in a tiny boat, and cast him out to sea,
That he might sink or he might swim, but never come
back to me.

"Is Mary Hamilton bad?" she asks.

Mrs. Harris turns away from the kitchen sink where she's been washing dishes. "Mary Hamilton? Whatever are you...oh, yes, Mary Hamilton." She smiled. "Goodness, girl, no. Whatever would make you say such a thing?"

"She sends her baby away."

"Oh, aye, she does. But no, my wee bairn, she is no bad, least not so I figure. In her way she tried to protect him."

"Why does she put her baby in a boat?"

"Oh, now, that's a sad story." She wipes her hands on her apron. "But I'm not sure it's one for telling a wee lass as you."

"Doesn't she love her baby?"

"Oh, very much. But the Queen doesna."

"So, she sends the baby away so the Queen can't hurt him?"

"Something like that, aye."

"She sends the baby Over There?"

"Over there?"

"Beyond the Golden Sea, where there are white castles and people who love children."

"You mean Heaven, lass?

She thinks about that. Is Over There really Heaven? She's not sure. The Ambassadors who were going to come for her didn't have wings. But maybe they were saints? The pictures of saints she's seen on the church walls didn't always show saints with wings. Some were without. She wondered how they managed to get from Heaven to here, but maybe that's what the boats were for?

She nods in answer to Mrs. Harris' question. "If I were Mary's Queen I wouldn't do that. I wouldn't make Mary send her baby away."

Mrs. Harris laughs and takes the dishes to the sink. "I don't expect you would at that. Now off with 'ee. Go see what that boy Leslie is up to."

She slides off her chair and goes out to the lounge—it's really a living room, but Mrs. Harris calls it the lounge—where Leslie hunches over books. He's on his stomach on the hardwood floor. She asks what he's doing. He tells her to go away.

"But I'm supposed to be here," she whispers, afraid of making him mad. Leslie always gets mad at her, and then he teases her and tells her stories that make her clutch Panda at night. It's Leslie who told her about the Uglies. And Leslie who showed her where the Darkies live.

So, she sits on the floor near the honey-coloured bookcase that has two rows of Encyclopaedia Britannica on its shelves. She can read a little bit, and sometimes if she's lucky there are pictures that help to explain the big words on the page. She makes herself sit very still so Leslie will forget about her, and when he starts writing stuff on the paper, and flips back and forth through the books around him, she inches one of the encyclopaedia from the shelf and lays it on the floor beside her. It's a G book. A picture of a tall animal is on the page to which she opens. It has a really silly, long neck, and what looks like horns on its head that have knobs on the end. The animal is covered in brown spots. She looks at the letters of its name, sounds them out in her head, tries to string them together and whispers, "Guh-ear-af."

"Shut-up!" Leslie says.

She winces and keeps her gaze away from him, sitting absolutely still, hardly daring to breathe. After a moment, she continues to look at the words on the page, but they are too big, too strange, but the picture is pretty and she studies everything in it, the grass, the tree that spreads out flat on top. Giraffe. Such a funny word for such a funny animal.

She makes up a song in her head about giraffes. Before she knows it she's singing it out loud, a happy sort of song because the giraffes look like happy sorts of animals. She puts her whole body into the song, rocking side to side.

Leslie slams her book closed, his pimply face close to hers. "You like giraffes?" he asks. She nods, afraid she's answered wrong. "Well let me tell you about giraffes. They're ugly, mean things that hide in tall things. Yeah, tall things like trees. And at night, when there is no light, the giraffes wake up and wait for something to eat. And you know what they eat?"

She is afraid to ask, but shakes her head no, watching Leslie's red lips, the way his eyes narrow to icy blue mirrors.

"They eat people. But their most favourite people are little girls. They really like girls with brown hair."

She throws a glance to the lounge window where she can see the big trees along the drive. She knows her own lane has trees just like this.

Leslie laughs and slumps down to his books again.

"Just wait till you go home tonight. You'll have to run fast before the tree-giraffes wake up."

She slides the book back to the shelf, afraid to look at the giraffes any longer, and levers herself up, pulling the hems of her red peddle-pushers down to her calves. She goes out to the front of the house to escape Leslie and his mean stories, plops down to the grass near the red flowers that have long, trumpet-like blooms. There's sweet juice in those flowers, and she carefully pulls one off and sucks, feeling a small burst of syrup on her tongue.

She'll wait here until it's time to go home, she decides, that way she can be on the road and run for home faster, before the tree-giraffes wake up and eat her. To pass the time she sucks on another flower. It looks like a little soldier, and, lying down on her belly, she carefully threads the base of the flower onto a blade of grass. She does this with the other bloom she'd discarded.

By the time she hears the phone ring and then Mrs. Harris' announcement it's time for her to go home, she's created a protective ring of flower soldiers around her. The sun is low on the horizon now. She can see the Golden Sea, but she can't wait for the ships this evening. She must go, and go quickly, step out of the protection of the circle and onto the road.

"Please keep me safe," she whispers to the little red soldier flowers, and casting a fearful glance at the lane of trees, races for her house, past the Harris' gate, up the hill to her lane and the courtyard with the out-buildings and their own laneway of trees. She pauses with her hand on the handle of the door, panting and her lungs filling with cobwebs. She looks out to the courtyard. The sun sinks. With a jolt of fear, hot and liquid, she fumbles with the doorknob. She can see the glowing eyes of a tree-giraffe. The long neck of it is mottled in the sunset, just like the giraffe in the book. She hears it hiss.

Finally, she's able to make the knob turn and she flings into the house, gulping air, her heart a wounded bird in her chest.

Art Classes

It's amazing what familiar and friendly territory can do for your sanity: the sweet, fragrant fullness of orange tea in my mouth; the deep warmth of sunlight on my face; the doumbek drumming of water under my dock where I sat, legs dangling, watching terns bomb the water. Mist still dabbled up the shore, iridescent where those low shafts of sunlight touched it.

Meldrum Bay, where the road ends. Home.

A week since I returned. A children's summer course was to start today. I should shift. I should enter the world. But it was hard to leave this place between sleep and industry, hard to abandon the smell of the bay and the woods. Hard to focus my mind on the now, and not the past.

All those things Ma and I should have said and didn't. The things we did say and shouldn't. Regret. Is that what experience and wisdom teach us?

Stiff, I levered myself up and walked back up the dock, fingering the wall of the boathouse where David kept his sailboat, from there to the thin grass, and tossed the dregs of my tea. Gone were the spring blooms of forsythia and daffodils. Peonies and iris now unfurled in preparation for summer. Uncle

Ianto had worked his magic here, tucking touches of his Ireland into the ancient Ojibwe landscape. Me, I cultivated indigenous flora. Manitoulin isn't kind to tender imports.

There, beside the pergola David and I built when we first made Meldrum Bay home, was the pot of Ma's roses. The famed Cotter roses. My heritage. My legacy. My bitter memory.

I'd plant them today, dig a bed and enrich this meagre soil with compost and bone meal, make a good start for another tender import. Roses on Manitoulin. Rugosas were one thing. But this Cotter rose? The thought was absurd. But for now I returned to the house to prepare for the day, make myself presentable, and ready myself for the adventure I would begin with the children who would unsuspectingly come to me for discovery and tutelage.

The chairs on the porch were studded in dew. Seeing that I realized my feet were cold and wet. I looked down at red sneakers that were soaked through. I wriggled my toes, felt the squish and gelid mess, aware of the ache that had penetrated with stealth. Foolishness, I thought, to be so preoccupied not to notice such a thing.

The smell of herbs lingered in the house when I stepped into the mudroom, toeing off my shoes and replacing them with the comfort and warmth of worn sheepskin slippers. I set my cup in the sink, listening to the sounds of this old house, of logs settling in the woodstove, of the carriage clock in the living-room chiming the quarter hour.

Ma never knew this home, I realized. Too much silence, too much to do. Too much between us and not enough. How had we let things spiral into such distance? There is always time for regret. Never enough for the things we should say.

I ascended the stairs to the second floor, turned left at the landing and closed the door after myself when I entered my room and let the warmth of the shower infuse me with some equanimity. By the time I presented myself, shiny-clean and fragrant in the kitchen again, Uncle Ianto was up and boiling eggs.

He stood there wedged between the counter and the range, sunlight spilling over his shock of silver hair where it tumbled across his forehead, forever errant, like his own nature. He looked up, the corners of his eyes crinkling, his cheeks like apples.

"Sit you down, my flower," he said. "I see you've already been out."

"Gorgeous morning," I answered. "Great day to start classes. You didn't have to do breakfast."

He waved away the latter. "How many registered this session?"

"Six." I swallowed orange juice. "Two girls, four boys, all middle-school."

"You're going to have your hands full."

"I am that."

"Do you ever wish you'd had your own?" he asked, setting breakfast before us and easing to his chair.

I felt a small ignition in my chest. I looked away, out the window where I rested my elbow. "No."

"David never wanted a family?"

I looked back at Uncle Ianto. "Why the sudden interest in my failed marriage? That's a bit old now, don't you think?"

"Don't be techy. You know very well you're a good runner."

"And what? You're saying I ran from David?"

He shrugged.

"It wasn't me who called an end to nuptial bliss," I said.

"All I'm saying is people work at these things."

"So, what, we're discussing my failures this morning?" I decapitated both of the eggs on my plate. "A few decades late for that, don't you think?"

"I'm just worried you're going to go into a depression again."

"Why? Because Ma's gone?"

He nodded. Yolk spilled over the edge of his egg where he'd crammed a soldier of toast.

"I did all my grieving a long time ago, Uncle."

"And you're not harbouring any grief about the will?" He mopped up the viscous yellow goo.

"What is this about entitlement? Who says progeny are entitled to the estates of their parents?"

"That sounds like an attempt at rationalization."

I tore the serviette off my lap and dumped it on the table. "Look. I have a class to teach this morning. Four boys in that six. All of whom are likely to be typically busy boys. If I'm going to do any deep thinking today it's going to be about strategy and cleverness, and failing that, all out subterfuge in order to get them to sponge up what I've been paid to teach them."

"I can see the sand kicking up under your heels."

I shrugged. What was there to say? That he was right? That it was typical? That Ma always had a way of reaching out of time and distance to wreck havoc on my life? To this day I didn't know if it was jealousy, or malice, or some other convoluted rationale that made her take innocence and twist it into something grotesque. *How could you marry an Indian? What's wrong with your own kind?* Even now from beyond the grave.

The only time you ever call is when you need something.

And you never do, Ma.

"It was never her money I wanted," I said and buried my face in my hands, pressing back tears, closing off anger.

"She was a fool."

I heard Uncle Ianto leave, the soft pad-pad of his slippers on the hardwood. In my chest there were other rhythms, irregular, stuttering. I looked out the window to honey light on the lawn, to shadows under trees, to the single white bloom on the Cotter rose waiting for me to give it a home and nurture.

There didn't seem to be enough air. I sucked at the atmosphere like a fish out of water, gulping, blinking.

No, don't do this. Not now.

And as I always did, I gritted my teeth and turned to work, putting on the mask that would become my own face in a little while. I'd learned at one of the annual Wiki pow-wows the Iroquois have an ancient belief if you put on a mask not your own, the spirit of the mask possesses you. In this case it might be a good thing.

After cleaning up our aborted breakfast, I crossed the property to the implement shed that was now my studio. No matter how many times I walked into that space of creation, I was struck by the aromas of my trade: the fungus smell of watercolour papers, the citrus-sharp pungency of oils and turps and glazing mediums. It wasn't a designer's dream, this space, but it was mine, put together with invention and reclaimed materials. And the light was fabulous after I'd scrounged enough to put in skylights and a bank of windows on the north wall. David and I had built this. Full of hope and dreams then, a fortress against the world. But sappers can breach walls. Every fortress falls.

I heard a shuffle at the doorway. My first unsuspecting subject hovered there, his face wary, his dark eyes animal-bright. He took in the room, sized me up, and moved forward at a nudge from a woman behind him, his Ma, I assumed. I let the mask of my face become a smile, extended a hand first to the boy, then to the woman.

"Vi Cotter," I said. "Welcome." To the boy then. "And you are?"

"Jason."

"Well hi, Jason. Do you like to draw?" And guided him into my world, giving him sketchbook and pencils, eraser and pens, easing his apprehension with chatter and involvement. As the others arrived, I gathered them into our expanding conversation, until at length they all forgot they were in a strange place, with a strange person, doing something likely against their will. Parents hovered, and when it became apparent they weren't going to be included in the developing dynamics, waved themselves out. It worked every time.

Thirty minutes later, there were tongues in teeth, frowns of concentration and a palpable energy as my class discovered the principles of basic shapes, light and shadow, and the secrets of creating the illusion of three dimensions where there were only two.

All did well, pretty much what I expected. Their silence and concentration weighted the air. Sunlight poured like syrup across their faces. I turned to the windows, to that starkly white bloom in the shadows. I remembered my own first attempts at this exercise my students undertook, remembered the portfolio I later acquired, sliding those early sketches like sacred texts into protective pockets.

I felt a tug at my sleeve, brought my attention down to old-fashioned ringlets framing an oval face, dark eyes like the recesses of shuttered rooms. Did I know this child? Hadn't I seen her recently?

The girl extended her sketchbook to me, on the open page a cone, a cylinder, cube and sphere, shaded with panache. She'd even printed her name in minute letters in the lower right corner. *Lettie.*

Now that was an old-fashioned name to match her ringlets, one that could very well have been from my own past.

"This is very good," I said. She smiled and turned away, took a seat apart from the other two girls, the four boys. No one else paid her any mind. So, she would be the shunned one of the class. There was always one. I never understood why people thought children so sweet. Certainly there was example enough of the cruelty of children, the politics of the playground, the devastation of peer groups. Growing up could be a war zone with hidden bombs.

I looked back out to the roses.

Una: June 1945

I haven't written in such a long time, and so much has happened I hardly know where to begin. The best news is after all the VE celebrations in May we had a letter from Ianto who says he'll be home around mid-summer, at the latest end of August. Can hardly wait to see him again, have him home, unharmed, safe. It's been such a long time, and now news of the concentration camps is coming out it is horrifying to think he faced such an enemy.

But while all that was going on, out of sight, mostly out of mind, it seems I've waged and lost a war of my own. The heart is such a treacherous thing. The short of it is I've gotten myself married, and a baby due around Christmas. Ma cried. It wasn't with joy. She told me I'd live a life of misery with Conner Bannon. She may be right, but with a baby in my belly there's not much I can do. Is there.

I wore blue, believing: *married in blue, always be true.* True to what, I wonder now. True to yourself? True to your nature? True to some ideal of the perfect woman, wife, mother? Are we, all of us, Mary incarnate, virgin brides, virgin wives, virgin mothers? Is that concept of unexplored territory, even of innocence, or perhaps ignorance, such an aphrodisiac to the men who govern the world, and we—the women who love them, marry them, serve them without question or expectation—the prize? The kewpie doll awarded to he who can smash down walls.

The blue dress—silk and a gift from Ianto before he left—is now rags for polishing, beyond repair, a bitter reminder of the caprice of promises.

It's odd how bruises and cuts heal, but the invisible wounds bleed silently and in the darkness of our thoughts.

Princesses become prisoners, whether of their princes or themselves matters little when the key to freedom is beyond reach.

I think Ianto and I will find much in common when he returns.

Lettie: The Secret World of Loons

She's watched and waited for the Ambassadors from Over There, but every evening she looks and still the ships sail. She's watched through rain and snow. She wonders if there is some sort of evil magic that keeps them on the sea? Maybe they are caught in some sort of time thingie? You know, like one of those awful dreams where you run and run and can't get anywhere, where you bend over and push yourself along the ground to help gain speed, and still you're in the same place. Maybe it's like that for the ships.

She's thinking about that now, sitting under the big pine near the cottage. Mummy sent her to spend two weeks with the Harrises, up here where there's no dirt but lots of black and pink rock, and huge pines whose branches spread out like green clouds to the sky. Mummy said she had some things to sort out, that it would be good for her special girl to spend some time up north.

Panda sits between her legs, and together they're trying to make the sound of that bird—what did Mrs. Harris call it? A loon? *Oooo-oo. Oooo-oo.* Yes, a loon. She figures the bird is called a loon because it's as crazy as it sounds. What bird would spend so long holding its breath under water? She tracks them when they bob up like a cork, tries to find where they go down and then come up again, counting off the seconds—one Mississippi, two Mississippi, three—and whispers to Panda about how crazy they are, and he agrees.

Still, though, they're pretty, like a black and white ink drawing. She figures their craziness shows up in their red eyes.

"You don't think they're bad, do you?" she asks Panda.

Of course not, he answers. *They're natural creatures.*

There's something important about what Panda's said, and she tries to figure that out. Maybe animals don't know how to be bad. They just do what they're made to do. Like Timmy-cat chasing and eating mice. Or Bella chasing Timmy-cat. Or the lions on the TV in Africa chasing those pretty deer-like animals and eating them, their cheeks all bloody as they stare without blinking over the dead and steaming body. It's scary what those animals do, the way they eat other animals that are still alive. But she thinks it's maybe more scary the way humans do things. She thinks maybe humans just like to do things, sometimes, that hurt other people, just because they can.

Like the way Leslie teases her. That's the only thing she doesn't like about being here with the Harrises.

Her waiting is rewarded when a loon she's been tracking pops up.

"That was a long time," she says to Panda, who agrees. She hugs him. "Why does Leslie tell me awful things?" she asks after awhile.

Because he's a teenage boy, Panda says. *You must be careful around Leslie.*

She agrees with that. He's been hanging around her a lot lately, not even bothering to scare her, and that makes him even more scary because she's wondering what he's up to.

She calls again to the loons, "Oooo-oo. Oooo-oo." And watches the water. There's a little family of loons that have come into the cove. The chicks are almost as big as their mummy and pestering her for food. She knows perfectly well the chicks can feed themselves by now. It said so on that nature show she likes to watch.

Her tummy growls and she laughs. Panda laughs with her, tells her she's like one of the chicks. She gets up from the ground—it was getting hard anyway—and walks around under the tree, wiggling her bum like a water bird and flaps her bent arms. "Oooo-oo. Oooo-oo," she calls. Panda answers, *"Oooo-oo. Oooo-oo. Let's go see if lunch is ready."* She tucks Panda under one arm—that's really a wing—and swims her way back to the cottage, through the trail among the pines, swimming up over pink and black boulders, tree roots like huge, frozen snakes. She can hear chickadees peppering the air overhead, and now she becomes one of them, singing in their stuttering, piping speech.

By the time the screen door slams behind her, she's back to being a girl. She wipes her sneakers on the mat and crosses into the big room that's all kitchen, dining, and living room. She likes this room, likes the way it makes her feel as if she's living inside a tree. Sunlight slants through the windows, making the log walls yellow. She smells grilled cheese and sure enough there's Mrs. Harris at the funny old stove, with a cast iron pan and a metal lifter. Her face is shiny and pink, ribbons of hair escaping the bun on her head.

"Go wash up, lass," Mrs Harris says.

She takes Panda with her into the bathroom and scrubs her grubby hands, swipes the backs and fronts on the towel and then hurries back out to the table. Leslie's already there, dipping grilled cheese in ketchup, chewing, watching her with cold, blue eyes. She settles to her place, hands on the red and white plastic table cloth that feels cool on the tips of her fingers. She avoids looking at Leslie, and is relieved when Mrs. Harris sits down beside her, placing plates of the gooey, golden sandwiches before each of them.

Mrs. Harris asks her what she had been doing that morning, and she tells her all about the loons and the chicks. To Leslie Mrs. Harris says, "Did you finish with the garbage?"

"Yeah."

"And you made sure the rocks are back on the lids?"

"Yeah."

"Then you can have the afternoon for yourself."

After lunch Mrs. Harris sends her to her room for a nap and says she'll be just outside reading. Lying on the quilt with Panda, she looks out the window at the shards of sunlight through the pines, listens to the sound of wind in their branches. She's drifting into dreams when Leslie comes in and lies down beside her, whispering her to silence. She can feel him trembling as though he's scared, and now she's scared too. He presses his lips to hers and she's afraid of suffocating and pushes him away, but he tells her to shush, that it's okay, that this is what people do when they love each other, and she does believe he loves her, doesn't she? And this will be their secret, won't it? And she's too afraid to say anything and just closes her eyes. When he pushes Panda to the floor she whimpers and sends her thoughts down to him where he stays until Leslie is gone, and now she knows there are things to fear in the day as well as the night, and that Panda, after all, had been wrong.

Fairy Roses

Uncle Ianto and I sat round the expanse of the kitchen table that evening, long after the dinner I made, sharing a moment, recounting the day, planning for the next. There was fresh bread from this afternoon, one of the miracles of the bread machine, and tender gnocchi and asparagus. I enjoyed the last crusts of bread while Uncle Ianto indulged in a strawberry torte.

"Great class today," I said.

"I was about to ask," he said, fork before his mouth.

"They're keen."

He scraped the last bits from the plate. "Ah, the exuberance of youth."

I leaned to the window, resting my elbow on the wide sill. Certainly, the children in my class were exuberant. But exuberance wasn't the word I'd have used for Lettie. Determined. Focused. A steely resolve that was quite adult. Yes, she was all those things.

"Look, Uncle Ianto," I said. "I'm sorry about this morning."

"There's nothing to be sorry about, my flower."

I shrugged, looked back at him, at the pouches under those ultramarine eyes, the rosacea that tinted the apples of his cheeks. He always had this manic look to him, partly because of his unruly mop of silver-white hair. I remembered playing scatter-the-ants with him as a child, of the dog-chain spinning and his fey laughter. "Still. I shouldn't take my bad temper out on you."

He lifted a shoulder in a shrug, nodded out the window after a moment. I knew what was coming. "And so, when are you going to plant those legacy roses? You wouldn't want your inheritance to up and die on you."

"They're too hardy to die," I said.

He barked a laugh. "If I know one thing about my sister, she couldn't stand weakness or things out of order."

"You shouldn't speak ill of the dead." But Uncle Ianto's statement was true. There was no room for the faint of heart or the imperfect in Ma's world. I knew that first hand, remembered being set outside the door of our home in white organza and patent shoes, ribbons in my sausage curls, told to play but not get dirty. There'd been cool, squishy mud in the virgin territory of our new back garden, dangerous allure to a young explorer. A dog kennel. A new father. And Ma singing with happiness. "In all fairness Ma isn't here to defend herself," remembering that day, how her joy became anger as quickly as a storm descending. Confusion on my part. Remorse on hers once the storm was spent. Tears and hugs. Promises.

"So, you'll do it for her? You?"

It had been Uncle Ianto who intervened that time. God! Why remember these things now?

I braced my elbows on the table and held my forehead. "Please."

"You know I'm right," he said. Great, so now he was going to have at me, deliver the broken child. "I'm the first one to say respect your elders, but I think there are extenuating circumstances here."

I looked up at him, watched that weathered face. "Et tu, Brute?" I saw the barb sink deeply, the wound bloom. Your Ma's daughter.

"This isn't an assassination. You know that." Such rebuke in that voice. I felt like a shit, but he had no idea, none, of the hell he courted.

I felt his hand on mine, felt those sausage fingers dig in and caress. "I'm just concerned for you."

I glared at him, not wanting his concern, his pity, his hovering anxiety. Don't be an ass, I told myself, and promptly ignored that bit of sanity. The hell with him. The hell with the whole thing.

I stood, hearing my chair scrape on the old plank floor, and flung out the door. His astonishment was as audible as a shout. He didn't follow, for which I was grateful. I just wanted some space. To think. To sort it all out. So many words left unsaid between Ma and me. So many scenes rehearsed and left unperformed. The role of aggrieved heroine cancelled due to an empty house.

Caught between rage, sorrow, and regret, I threw open the door of the garden shed, tossed spade and shovel, bone meal, and pruners into the wagon of the garden tractor, climbed into the seat and turned the key in the ignition. When only a stuttering groan issued from the blasted thing, I christened the machine with profanity and turned the key again. This time the ignition caught. Bloody right. Slammed the gear into go and let her rip out into the evening light. I almost two-wheeled it when I rounded the bend to the compost.

You're being a fool, I told myself. Tantrums get you nowhere. Ah, but it felt so damned good throwing a tantrum. For how long had I been told to be a good girl, to do as I was told, to be nothing less than perfect.

But you're a grown woman. A senior citizen fergawdsakes.

Oh, fuck all that.

I threw compost into the wagon as though digging for answers, heaved in the shovel when I was done, and roared off to where those famous Cotter roses lurked beside the garden that bordered the stone terrace. Early on, I'd planted roses there, all of them scented, one break with indigenous plants. The plan had been to let fragrance spill out onto the sitting area, create yet another still pool where I could perch, contemplate, and connect. It hadn't occurred to me until now what I'd really done was create a bridge to Ma, to memories of playing amid blooms, of watching her prune and hum and fuss her way through the roses she so loved and cosseted.

For a moment, I remained on the tractor after I'd switched off the engine, let the stillness of the evening settle around me, smooth my pulse, evaporate my tears. An oriole warbled in the trees that edged the property. I looked up to the branches, searching for the flash of orange that would reveal the songbird. There, like sunshine in leaves, a male notifying the world of his territory.

This place is mine. This place is mine. Isn't that what we all did, no matter the species, claim and mark territory and let the world know here is where we make our lives; take it at your peril.

Do you hear that, Ma? This place is mine. I plant your damned roses, and now they're mine, part of my world, my domain.

And yet I wanted her to be there, wanted to hear her hum and coo and chatter to the plants on which she bestowed such care. I wanted to swim in the eddies of the wonder she could create. So much we could have shared if only I'd found a way to cross that bridge, to meet her half way, to try to understand. Instead I'd chosen the Cotter pas d'armes. In the end she'd chosen not to fight, and I had her token, which I knew was not a mark of humiliation but rather one of reconciliation and peace, a treaty written in a rose.

There was little room in the existing bed, and so I set to lifting away turves and sifting out gravel, expanding into a ring that hung like a bubble off the arc of the existing bed, a giant comma to separate the clauses of my life. The soil here was poor, but with care and time it would amend. I inhaled its fragrance, worked in compost and forked the soil over until I had a loose loam for these roses. They were hybrid rugosas, virtually thornless, completely white, dense blooms, and a fragrance that harkened back to the old Damascus roses. The years it had taken her to create this prize, this amazing strain of flora.

And a sobering reality when I acknowledged she had created it for me. A fall into the fragrant rugosas as a child. Limbs threaded with thorns and blood, her tears and trembling hands when she'd plucked out thorns, anointed my wounds, swearing she would create a rose for a child. For her child. For her daughter.

Before Ben came along, when she and I were an island.

By the time I finished it was dark. I strolled back across the dew-damp grass and sank down in front of the new addition to my garden. I should have been pleased with my work. Truth to tell I was too tired to care, and too numb to recognize the warning signs.

She left me roses and their patent, something that had taken her a lifetime to create and perfect. I supposed I should have been touched by that. I wasn't. I felt over-burdened, yet again, marginalized by my brother and his status as not only the male child Ma always wanted, but the most recent, the current, the vogue. There were no others after Ben. No one to take Ma's attention and affection. We could, after all, only love the most current creation.

Not that Ma didn't love me, I knew. She did, in her own warped, singular fashion. But it was a shadow of me, a dream and fabrication she loved, an image into which she tried for so many years to make me, and in the end, frustrated with my increasing lack of pliancy, tolerated.

For me the patent, the responsibility and a memoir. For Ben all else. Poor Ben. Dear Ben. Bennet the Blessed.

Petulant, pitiful thoughts. I detested that. And so, I opened the dark door through which I periodically peered, allowing all my transgressions to parade and drown my thoughts, so that I could wish only for a quiet oblivion, an escape from all the anguish and hurt and lack of perfection in so much of what I called my life.

They came then, those tears, hot and silent. I lay

myself on the grass, yearning for the earth to open and swallow me whole, cover me with a mortal blanket.

Why couldn't she have seen me? Loved me? Why? Why was it always obligation and duty, responsibility and appearance? Why was there never room for spontaneity, impetuosity?

And no answers to the many whys. Only tears and regret and loss greater than death.

At some point I heard the unmistakable lilt of a tin whistle—Uncle Ianto reaching for his own memories through music. I sat up and took in the growing dusk, the violet scarves of mist in the trees. Lights danced there, fireflies, hundreds of them, like faeries in the tree-line, a fog of them across the lawn. And laughter. Very definitely there was laughter, a child, a girl, playing with the faeries, her marble-white feet dancing brightly against the dew-damp dark lawn. I watched her curls bounce, watched her turn and sway, cupping handfuls of fireflies as they flickered and then flowed into a ring around the old apple tree.

I pulled myself up, my heart a staccato beat. What *was* this child doing playing on my property? When she danced up to me, her face alight with wonder, I said, "You need to be home, Lettie. Your Ma will be worried."

"Ma won't know." She turned the white oval of her face to the apple tree. "Will she?" She laughed. "He's pretty, isn't he?"

I threw a glance at the apple tree, raised my eyebrows, looked down to her, the red pedal pushers, the white blouse. "Who's pretty?"

"Ghillie Dhu." A fairy? One of the Sidhe? Here among my roses? This was a child's imagination, an elaborate *let's pretend.* "He says you're not going to be able to see him. Is that right?"

I waved to the tree. "Lettie, there's nothing there. It's just a game."

She shook her head. "Nunh-unh. Ghillie and Zeegwun always talk to me. They're going to help me find a way to get to Over There."

Irish and Ojibwe legends? But instead I asked: "Over there?"

She raised an arm and pointed to the horizon where clouds flamed in the last light of the sun. "You remember Over There, don't you?" She cocked her head as if listening. "Oh. I didn't know that." Looked back at me. "Zeegwun says you've forgotten how to dream. You really can't see them, can you?"

"Lettie, where is your ma? Where do you live? I can walk you home. You shouldn't be out so late."

"Ma's dead." All I could do was nod, feel the painful bang of my heart. I had memory of that hammer-stroke, a signal for fight or flight although it was usually flight. "They want me to let you know they'll watch over the roses until the roses can take care of themselves. You want that, don't you? You want the roses to live?"

Well of course I bloody wanted the roses to live. It's all I had of my Ma. All she left me. But instead of saying this, all I could do was nod. I should have ushered Lettie home. I should have tried harder to figure out her fantasy play. But I felt as if my limbs were not my own and I was pinned to that place under the old apple tree, caught between dreams and fear.

"Good!" She laughed. And Lettie, wee Lettie, skipped off across the grass, the whiteness of her calves and feet visible long after she had, in fact, melded into the night. I stood, turned heel and made a brisk exit from the garden to find the sign-up sheet for my art classes, and a solution to the puzzle of this seventh child.

Una: August 1945

Conner's made me quit my job at Fraser's. He says it isn't decent for a woman to be seen in public in my condition. I never thought being pregnant was something a woman should conceal, but then he is my husband, and I suppose I should pay attention. I can't ask Ma about this, as I've been forbidden to see her. He says she's an interfering harpy. And while I know Ma doesn't approve of him, I long for someone to talk to about all this wife stuff.

I would talk to Ianto, because I can talk to him about anything, but I'm not allowed to see him either. Even when he came home from overseas, discharged and safe, Conner found every reason why I couldn't welcome my brother home.

So I am alone. And without my income I'm not sure how we'll manage with a new baby and all, on what he makes from Penman's. And he keeps starting new projects in this old house, but they never seem to get finished, and that indoor privy he was going to put in hasn't transpired, so I guess it's a cold arse after all. He'd smack my mouth if he heard me repeat that.

Lettie: The Darkies

She lies sweating in her bed, the thin, cotton sheet clutched to her neck while purple dusk gathers at her window. Around her is an army of friends: Panda the Bear, Trixie the Dog, Greenie the Teddy. A stir of air rustles the plastic drapes, false promise of relief. She longs to lay back the sheet, neatly, without disturbing dust that will have her wheezing inside of moments, but that means lying exposed in her room and she had learned the better of that decision. Safer to lie sweating with the sheet as armour and the peaceful purple of this long, long moment of twilight to rock her.

The purple at her window is like the purple of her walls, clean, dreamy. She sings a song about that, silently, because it wouldn't do to make noise and draw attention. Besides, there are some things too special to say out loud.

> *The purple grows outside my window.*
> *The purple grows inside my room.*
> *Darkness coming in the garden.*
> *Darkness coming in my room.*
> *The Darkies, the Darkies, soon they will come.*

She'd made peace with the Darkies. They'd heard the plea she'd flung into the Dungeon and instead of pouncing on her fear they championed her nights. Two nights ago, she discovered them in the four corners of her room. Two nights before that there was only one, and that a shadow of a boy-not-quite-man here to watch over her, here to care for her.

Leslie, small and dark, like a monkey she thought, with that scary look to his eyes like the monkeys in the zoo who watched you and knew, they *knew*. He had the name of chieftains, so Mummy told her. She wondered if all chieftains dealt so sneakily, so cruelly. He had been just a shadow in the corner of her room long after the purple faded from her window and the world dissolved to darkness and shadow, blacks and blacks with only the silver and grey of moonlight when it shone through the glass.

She had been singing—well, humming—quietly so as not to bring down Leslie's anger. Leslie didn't like noise or bother or disturbance when he babysat. The song was one she made up for the beauty of the night. When the shadow in the corner of the room separated from the walls and took on the form of Leslie, she stopped singing, that last note silenced in a moment of fear.

The monkey was loose. And he knew; he *knew* things that would make her silent. To her bed he crept, like the bogie-man himself, dark and silent. In her head she sang:

> *The purple grows outside my window.*
> *The purple grows inside my room.*
> *Darkness coming in the garden.*
> *Darkness coming in my room.*

Then he was there beside her bed, his hand on her mouth, in her face the smell of pee and sour toilets.

She doesn't want to remember that and feels sweat trickle down her face and slide round the curve of her neck. She pulls the sheet closer still, making sure the edges wrap tightly under her arms.

> *The purple grows outside my window.*
> *The purple grows inside my room.*
> *Darkness coming in the garden.*
> *Darkness coming in my room.*
> *The Darkies, the Darkies, soon they will come.*

In her head she hears them, long, slender people-shapes that are neither man nor woman, all blackness and shadow. Darkness drips from their long fingers, flows from their long hair and grows like grapevines across her walls.

We are here, they sing, all whispers like breathy angels.

> *We are here. Sing, sing, sing, for we are here and*
> *darkness grows,*
> *Outside the window, in your room, darkness coming*
> *in the garden,*
> *Darkness coming in your room.*
> *We are here.*

Relief floods through her and for a moment she dares to let go her grip of the sheet, sit up and bow to each of them, elegant creatures. They bow in return, like dark water rippling. She sinks back down to the bed, the foam pillow, and holds the sheet to her throat. For a while, she will be safe. They will watch. They will sing with her. And tonight, tonight, maybe when Leslie comes she will find the courage to sing out loud and end her torment.

For a time they sing the Song of Darkness, silently, all of it weaving like heavenly music through her head. They sing low, like a slow-moving river, like the wind in autumn. She can almost smell these things rich and healthy unlike her and her sickly lungs. For her part they let her take the high notes, and this she does gladly, in her mind letting her voice slide like a wheeling bird high and higher, rising and rising to the moon.

She is almost there when another shadow joins them. Her singing stops. The Darkies' does not. She still hears them like the earth itself, rocking, comforting.

None shall harm thee,
Child of the night, and child of the morning.
None shall harm thee but that thou sing
Sing, sing and be free!

Her throat tightens and she tries to breathe, feels her chest freeze and her lungs betray her. It is as though Leslie puts his knee on her chest from where he stands in the doorway, suffocating her. He moves, gracelessly, through the doorway and quietly closes the door, turns and continues to the side of her bed.

As always, he says nothing, hobbling like a beast. His hand closes over her mouth. She can see nothing of his face, turned as it is away from the window. He is all shadow and beast-strength, smelling of sweat and food. She knows what will happen next, shrinks at the thought of it. She tries to be small, so small she will disappear under his hand, that her mouth will not be large enough to do what he wishes.

In her head, the Darkies sing:

None shall harm thee
Child of the night, and child of the morning.
None shall harm thee but that thou sing
Sing, sing and be free!

Free, oh, Ma Mary, yes, she thinks, let them be free, please Ma, let them be free; and all at once she feels her song in her head, feels the notes travel there in their sweet, sad, purple sound, rising and rising. She opens her mouth. She hears Leslie sigh with pleasure. Song spills out of her, thready and hoarse, but song nonetheless.

The purple grows outside my window
The purple grows inside my room.
Darkness coming in the garden.
Darkness coming in my room.
The Darkies, the Darkies, soon they will come.

Leslie retreats a step, she thinks surprised at her song. She sings the song again, trying to find enough breath to finish. Out of the corners, she can see darkness flowing, detaching from the walls. It moves like cloth through the air, fluid and comforting, and then tears apart like scarves to wrap Leslie softly, all the while their music like madness in her head:

We are here!
Sing, sing!
For we are here and darkness grows
Outside the window in your room
Darkness coming in the garden
Darkness coming in your room.
We are here!

She hears Leslie gasp. By now the Darkies lose all form and are no more than flowing scarves around his body, his thrashing limbs. He does not cry out, and she is glad of that because she is afraid to make any noise but for her singing which is soft. She dares to sing higher, higher yet, her lungs cooperating and giving her breath, while the Darkies' song lowers and slows like the wind in autumn, like the chittering of dry leaves. Soon Leslie is all but invisible inside that swirl of darkness. She sings her last, trembling notes as the scarves fade and melt away.

And Leslie is gone. The screams are gone. And finally, she cries into warm and familiar arms.

An Old Bridge

I'd been yelling in my sleep again, sobs exploding, and there in the darkness just my own voice—*it's okay, it's okay, just a dream.*

I listened to the percussion of my heart, gathered a deep breath, let it go, groaned and ran the back of my hand over my eyes. There, my pulse slowing, the impact of it behind my ears diminishing. Now only the creak of the house around me. This old house that had been abandoned until I rescued it after the dissolution of my life with David. A project to numb the nerves. Industry to escape failure. An uncle who followed me because of a tearful phone call one night, and ended up staying.

"Why?" I whispered into the night, inhaling the smell of woods and water. Dreams and darkness like molasses in my mind, my tongue thick with it, my eyes heavy. All of the *why* revolving around Ma, the scope of one word too vast to be contained in three letters. No answers of course, at least none that were definitive. I wanted black or white, and knew there could only ever be grey, shadings, tones on tones on tones until absolutes were muddied under the nuances of life and perspectives and mitigating events. Life as a painting, transparent glazes like coloured films over an event.

I turned onto my side, pulled the duvet to my chin. Out the window I could see moonlight like broken mirrors on the bay. I wondered if I'd ever be free, if I'd ever be given that chance, or, were I honest, if I'd ever allow myself that chance. It occurred to me happiness was something we chose. It wasn't a gift or a right. It was a state of mind we chose, and even at that only fleeting moments. Much better to strive for contentment, something that would endure and buoy the spirit.

And so, unconsciously, I'd practiced the slow tai chi of finding contentment, looking for it in the zen of a sunrise, the endless horizon of the water, the whisper of the woods cocooning my home. So, my life so far hadn't gone exactly according to plan. But, then, what had been the plan? Someone with whom to share my life. Someone who would see me. Well, we all knew how that worked out. And while David and I remained friends, it was clear my life was better a solo than an intense tango in stiletto heels.

Why? A breath. *And still why?*

It would seem even my determination was no match for the exhaustion of the past days; at some point I finally closed my eyes to those shards of light on the bay. I woke to the balm of sunshine and the wail of the kettle. The orioles were in full song, a gorgeous cascade of notes, periodically a crackling chatter that warned off intruders before the birds fed. They must have a nest in the trees, I thought, for such activity to be so constant.

I stretched and rolled to my side, facing the bedstand where steam spiralled lazily from a majolica mug of chamomile. Uncle Ianto's doing. I lifted the mug into my hand, inhaled the fragrance, sipped, smiled, sipped again. There was honey in the tea.

Why should I long for Ma when I had all this?

Because she was my Ma, I thought, the most sacred of trusts, the foundation of all else.

And with that tears rose. I fought them, sipped, listened to the orioles, the starlings piping, to goldfinches cascading arias. I heard that blasted pipe bang, Uncle Ianto yelling at the caprice of water nymphs, footsteps on the stairs. There was the smell of sweet bread toasting, cinnamon and fruit.

Life. And time for me to enter that hurry and hustle. The familiar routine of the morning's shower and tooth scrubbing went a long way to restoring a semblance of normality to my thoughts, so that by the time I stepped into the kitchen to yet again offer my apologies to Uncle Ianto, I felt capable of meeting the demands of the day.

He just looked at me with humour, and squeezed my shoulders in his hands. He smelled of spices. There were other memories suddenly, not of this place, not of this time.

"It's okay," he said.

I looked down and away, grateful for his grace, could find no response, and, balancing toast plate on my mug, simply made my way out to find that sign-up sheet and make inquiries about the unexpected third girl in my children's art class.

As I stepped off the porch, I saw there was absolutely no sign of wilt on the roses, the one, pale bloom quivering with dew. I remembered Lettie speaking to her imaginary Ghillie Dhu and Zeegwun, strange mix of cultures and legends. I remembered Lettie dancing with the fireflies, her white feet like silver slippers on the moonlit grass. I remembered other roses in Ma's garden when I was a girl. There were thorns. It was as a girl I learned beauty could make you bleed.

I flinched when a child said, "It's pretty," looked down and to my right where Lettie stood. "Ma liked roses."

"Did she?" I answered, wondering from where this child had come. "Did your Ma plant roses?"

She nodded and leaned toward one of the new bushes, reached out a finger and touched the stem. "No thorns." She snatched her hand back. "I don't think it likes that."

"The rose?"

"Roses need something to protect them. It isn't natural for roses not to have thorns."

"My Ma didn't like thorns."

"No. She didn't." Lettie looked up at me. This was a child it could be so easy to love, a face that expressed the shift of her thoughts and emotions, a direct way of looking at you that melted all the barriers we learn to build as adults. "Are you going to teach us today?"

"Yes, I am," I answered. She slid her hand into mine. Together we crossed to my studio and once there I abandoned the toast to Lettie, and gulped tea, realizing how late I was. The other children now gathered, and so the morning submerged into the mysteries of light and shadow.

An hour later, my children arrayed themselves on the grass outside, studying trees, reducing those forms to simple, basic shapes, and then creating composition from those shapes, using the density of detail and shading to make dimension. For the most part the children were biddable, the boys, as always, chaffing to be set loose. My two girls huddled together in a tight knot, Lettie, as yesterday, apart from them all.

Her isolation was a palpable hurt. I remembered bearing the brunt of that as a child, but also knew that to afford her special attention would be to isolate her even further, so I let her be, left her to sketch, her tongue caught firmly between her teeth. There was a frown on her brow, her dark curls spilling over her shoulders.

I walked among the children, offering guidance, praise, sometimes kneeling down beside them to show how I would handle a tricky part by sketching on my own pad. It was a rule of mine to never put my hand to their work. Give them ownership and they could soar. I'd seen it happen. How was it that so many of the rules of the road I learned came about through reversal?

"You see?" I'd say, and they'd nod with conviction, attacking their own work with renewed zeal.

One fellow decided his composition of trees required a race car in the foreground. There was no point mentioning to him the car wasn't part of the exercise, because he'd rendered the car in very carefully placed basic shapes, the source of light in keeping with the remainder of the composition. I also chose not to draw attention to his embellishment. Give him too much latitude and I'd find myself hung.

I looked up then, counting heads, found Lettie wasn't anywhere near, turned around and found her far across the grounds, cross-legged in her red capris beside the Cotter rose. She seemed to be talking to herself, and as I came closer, I realized she sang, swaying to the rhythm.

Her sketchbook lay in the hollow of her legs, pencils

lined up like soldiers in front of her, rank and file. The image on the paper, as yesterday, was beautifully done. I'd have thought the child familiar with art classes and when I queried her about that she said, "No. This is my first time."

"Then you must draw a lot at home."

She shrugged. "I guess."

"I see you made it home safely yesterday."

A nod.

"You must live nearby."

"Yeah."

"I guess your da's picking you up, eh?"

She shook her head. "Can I draw the rose?"

"If you follow today's rules, sure. If your da's not picking you up, then who—" And then a shriek across the lawn, the boys rolling with laughter, the two girls huddled together like cornered hens. "Okay, what's the commotion?" I yelled, striding back to them.

"A snake!" the girls wailed, pointing and tracking movement like hunters.

"It's just a garter snake!" one of the boys said. "It's no big deal."

Indeed it was, a beautiful green ribbon sliding through the grass. "All right. Leave the poor creature be. Back to your drawings."

The girls sidled away and tentatively settled back to the ground, the boys chuckling and tumbling to their work. Lettie, however, stood nearby, her eyes owl-like. There was utter horror on her face, her mouth opening and closing as though trying to push out words.

"What is it?" I said, squatting beside her.

She looked at me then and it was as if the weight of some terrible knowledge crushed me. I wanted to hug her, to weep, to tell her everything was okay, everything was fine. Hush, Lettie, hush, be still.

But she turned from me and walked back to the roses.

When I glanced at the other children they were oblivious to the drama that just unfolded. Just as well. No point giving them cause to ridicule her. I continued my audit. And so the morning evaporated.

I kept my attention on Lettie when the children were being collected. One of the mums snagged me. By the time I was done reassuring her of her boy's progress, everyone had gone. I watched the last car turn around in the lane and drive away. And of course Lettie was nowhere to be found. Foiled again.

In the stillness that followed I found Lettie's drawing of the rose abandoned on the grass near the new Cotter rose. The way she used negative space, light and shadow and texture demonstrated an intimate, instinctive understanding. But beyond technique, there was that immeasurable thing we call talent, that artist's eye that made a person's work unique and startling. And she was so young.

I took the drawing into my studio, tucked it into my portfolio for safe-keeping, closed the door and wandered to the shore with my empty cup and cold toast neither Lettie nor I had eaten. I settled on my favourite perching rock. The toast I tore into small chunks and tossed up to the ever-present gulls. Their wings beat the air. Some landed on the cobble shingle, scurrying close and veering away, squabbling with each other over the morsels I threw them. Uncle Ianto said I shouldn't feed them, that I was making a cross to bear. He was likely right. They seemed to know when I came to the shore, sometimes bombarding, but always present. My thoughts, however, were on Lettie. Not only had I failed to find out where she lived, but who were her parents, and for that matter even her last name. If I had that I could at least do a bit of sleuthing. Of course, if I could have just been a bit more organized I would have remembered to look up her student registration, which I realized once again I'd forgotten to do. I'd been too absorbed in studying her work.

And of course the greatest shock of all was that I found myself adrift, and my difficulty tracking one student was only a symptom of a greater illness. In all of my perfect planning I hadn't anticipated having much of a reaction to Ma's death. I honestly thought I'd drive down for the funeral, settle things with the legals and Ben, come home, and carry on. It wasn't as if we'd talked to each other. It had been years. The last time I'd hung up the phone in anger. Pulverized the damned phone, in fact. I remembered how David tried to reconcile the two of us and ended up a casualty of war. I'd collapsed into a pool of anguish after that. Somehow, I always thought she'd make contact, that David would forgive us both, that the rainbow after our storm would result in treasure.

Instead I bought this old house where the road ends. And now Ma was dead. And I had a legacy of roses and journals, and a student I knew nothing about.

I threw the last of the toast at the gulls, returned to the house with acid in my empty stomach.

I was about to discuss that very subject with Uncle Ianto when he handed me a list and pointed toward the door. "Ah, yes," I said. Groceries. "Do you want to come?"

"And waste this afternoon in a car?"

"But it's okay if I do."

"Aye, well, you're younger." He thrust my pack at me. "I've taken the liberty of being sure your phone and wallet are in there."

Resigned, I slung the pack over my shoulder. "Just make sure you're around when it comes time to put things away. We're both seniors, you know." He snorted derisively. And with that I turned and retraced my steps back outside, along the walk to the garage and flung myself into the car. I could have sailed to Gore Bay, but, like Uncle Ianto, I didn't want to waste more of the day than necessary doing something as mundane as filling our larder. Besides, the boat was David's, dry-docked in the boathouse and likely not even sea-worthy. Neither of us had sailed since we'd separated, and by mutual agreement he kept her secured here rather than seek out marina arrangements in Gore Bay, and he hadn't the heart to sell her. I didn't mind. It was the least I could do after all the hurt we'd shared.

Once I headed south out of the long lane of our drive, I felt my spirits lift, and thoughts of Ma, and Lettie, and my smug brother blew out the window. There was rarely much traffic on County 540 into Gore Bay. Today was no exception but for the few farm vehicles. There was the ripe pong of eau de farm in the air, and despite my attempts to breathe shallowly it wasn't long before I felt as though I'd eaten a paddie sandwich.

The hour it took to get to Gore Bay slipped by quickly enough, and the temperate morning turned to bright heat when I pulled into the Valu-Mart parking lot. I went through the usual routine of parking and snagging a shopping cart, lobbing my canvas bags into the shallow compartment designed for children or fragile fruit. Head left to the produce department —romaine, green onions, vine tomatoes—the smell always drove me nuts—some lovely leeks and bok choy—Uncle Ianto would fetch a fit—nice Ontario crispin apples, bananas for his cholesterol watch, grapes for me. I called them boops as a kid. Then straight through produce to the deli and from there down to the bakery, meat, dairy and then the looping course through the aisles to stow cans and bags and boxes into the cart. I realized I hadn't done a proper shop in some time when I found little room for the economy sized plush toilet paper, the last item on my list.

I hoped there was enough in my account when I headed for the check out, and was too proud to make the circuit again to put items away I likely should not have claimed. So, I white-knuckled it while I waited for the last items to be scanned through, and then just to add to the grocery store drama, David walked up and grabbed my bags, all grins and hellos as if there had never been any sorrow between us, as if our tentative start at a marriage hadn't ended in an enduring but sterile friendship. There were thrashing wings in my chest. I couldn't deny it was good to see him again after the funeral, to watch that quick-fire smile, the folds of his cheeks around his mouth, not quite dimples. He'd grown a beard since last I saw him at Ma's funeral. It looked good, I decided.

"Forget to shave?" I said.

He scrubbed his chin. "Got tired of it. The result of a lazy man."

"No one could accuse you of that."

We reached for the same bag of pasta and laughed,

when the clerk said, "Two, twenty-four, thirty. Will that be cash or debit?"

I withdrew my hand and un-zippered my pack, fumbled to retrieve my bank card and swipe it through the terminal. She keyed in numbers, messages appeared on the screen in front of me. I made the appropriate responses and another small miracle saved me from embarrassment. The till spewed out the remainder of my receipt.

"Let me help you out with this," David said.

"Sure." And we headed out to my car.

"You have time for lunch?" he asked as we loaded my bags. I looked up at that face I knew so well, wondered how he managed to keep us friends. "I thought you could use a bit of a break."

I heaved down the hatch on the car. "Lunch would be good. You have time?"

He laughed. "I'm the boss. I can make time."

"Oh, the meat and dairy," I said, realizing it was warm enough to cause spoilage.

"Right." He gestured to the car. "I don't mind storing them in the store's cooler if you're willing to shuffle things around."

"Oh, I dunno, David. Seems like such a lot of bother. Maybe—"

"Oh, c'mon, Vi. We haven't really talked in weeks, and you look like you could blow off some steam."

I was an idiot for botching this relationship. With a nod, I consented. We repacked bags, stowed them in the store's cooler and then walked out to Meredith Street and the ritual of breaking bread. In the end we took fish and chips down to the shore. There was a brisk on-shore breeze, enough to keep off the black-flies.

"You okay?" he asked after awhile.

I nodded. Mostly what I felt was numb, until I was alone and the boo-rattlies jacked my heart into a staccato. "I try not to think about it."

"She hadn't been ill?"

"Apparently not. Truth be told I think Ma just made an appointment with fate."

"Sounds like something she'd do."

"She left me the patent to the Cotter roses." Now why'd I tell him that? What possible significance did that have?

"And Ben got everything else?"

"Except for her journals, yeah."

"She kept journals?"

"Apparently so."

"How do you feel about that?"

I looked over at him. "You practicing analysis now?" He raised a brow and gave me one of his looks. "Yeah, okay, don't be a bitch, Vi, right?" He nodded. "Sorry. How do I feel? Sweet the saints like I'm supposed to know? Doesn't matter how much I prepared for Ma, she always surprised me. As capricious and unpredictable as the damned weather."

"I think we have better luck with the weather than the element that was Una Cotter."

And David should know. I looked back out to the north channel, watched a sailboat tacking up-wind. She was having a hard go of it. "You never forgave her, did you?"

"No, I suppose not. You can't say she didn't come between us."

"I think it was more me than Ma."

"Water and bridges, Vi. Water and bridges. How's Ianto?"

"Good. Pissed as always. But that's also a Cotter trait."

David laughed and the sound of it was infectious. "You've got that straight. Lord, don't be near ground zero when one of the Cotters goes off."

"Boom!" I looked back at him, watched the wind toss his hair around that lean and pockmarked face. I still loved that face. Loved the ruggedness of it, the honesty that was there, the life. "You should have seen Uncle Ianto at the funeral. He tried to deconstruct the chairs with a quarter."

"No kidding?" He laughed again. "I'd have given anything to have seen that. But I was stuck in the back with the cheap seats."

"Just one more element of the surreal world that's the Cotters."

"Truth that." He stuffed a few fries into his mouth, swigged back the iced tea he'd bought. "And you have a show coming up."

"I do."

"I'm proud of you, Vi."

How did he do that? How did he always manage to unhinge me, reach through all the bullshit and touch my heart? I shrugged. "I'm teaching right now, painting most afternoons and evenings, but I look forward to classes ending so I can really concentrate on finishing up these last pieces." Although I'd miss Lettie were I honest.

"Do I get an invite?"

"Always, David." I looked over at him. "You know that."

He nodded, watching me closely. "Yeah. I think I do."

"And you? Anything new in your world?"

He shook his head, watching the sailboat as she made a starboard tack. I wondered if he remembered all the time we'd spent on the water. "Life is pretty much the store and keeping the employees happy. I have the garden in the summer, the workshop in winter."

"Quite the socialite."

He crumpled up the box from lunch. "Gotta head back. Set an example and all that."

We rose, chucked paper and glass into the appropriate bins and made the walk back up Meredith to the grocery store, retrieved my perishables and from there to the parking lot. As always we hugged. I still loved the smell of him and for a moment I wished I'd never told him that I wouldn't have his children, that I wouldn't be responsible for bringing another life into misery. But we live with the decisions we make.

When I looked into the rear-view mirror he still stood there, watching.

Una: October 1945

As it turns out, he smacks more than my mouth,
and for less than using the word arse.

Lettie: The Pussywillow Family

She's been bad. That's why Ma took away Cathy and Cindy, stored them back in their boxes on the shelf of her closet. It seemed that when Ma told her to go and play, after dressing her in a white dress and shoes—the pretty dress with the holes all over and fancy stitching—that what Ma really meant was sit somewhere clean and stay that way.

But she hadn't known that's what Ma really meant. Why didn't Ma just say that? So, she'd wandered into the back garden and found a cool puddle of mud made by the rain last night. That gave her an idea, and she snuck back into the house and dressed Cathy and Cindy in the pretty dresses Ma had made—that way they'd all be pretty together—and took them out to the mud puddle to make pies for their tea.

When Ma found her, Ma said she was a filthy little pig and hit her hard across her head. She saw little bursts of light when Ma did that.

Ma put her in the tub and told her to get clean. She knew better than to cry. Ma would just get angrier. So, she now sits in the tub and washes herself, watching the water turn a milky brown, and when Ma doesn't come back she sloshes the washcloth up and down, up and down, and then plasters it like wallpaper across her chest. It's interesting the way the washcloth rolls down into a sausage if she wiggles her tummy in and out.

The white bar of soap floats between her legs and she wraps her hands around it. The soap slips around, like a wheel. She does it again and watches trails of white swirl out into the water. It's like the water wheel she's seen on an old mill Ma and Da had taken her to visit. Look at that—a soap water wheel right there in her tub.

By now the water is cold and she is getting cold too. Ma still hasn't come back. Maybe she is supposed to dry herself as well? She chews her lower lip, thinking, and decides she must have misunderstood Ma, and that getting clean must also mean getting dry, so she pushes herself up out of the water—whoosh—and steps onto the bath mat—she must not drip on the floor—and scrubs herself with the pink flowered towel. There aren't any clothes in the bathroom for her, so she just leans back to the tub, yanks out the plug, feels a shiver of fear flash down her arms for fear she'll get caught in that draining water, and races for her bedroom before the water sucks her down the hole. Her feet make squeaking noises on the hardwood floor as she runs.

Breathless, and afraid that might mean an asthma attack, she flings herself on the bed and pants, trying to gulp air. She pulls Trixie and Panda and Greenie to her to cover her nakedness, whispers secrets to them, and lets a few tears leak out the corners of her eyes. In a little while she can feel her heart settling down. It's easier to breathe now.

"I'm okay," she whispers to Panda.

Get dressed, he says.

She kisses him and sets him aside with her other

friends, slides off the bed and pulls open the drawer with her panties—steps into those and yanks them up to her belly button—closes that drawer and opens the next one down for her blue pants and that striped top Granny made her, the one with the pointy front. Reluctantly she tugs socks and slippers onto her feet, only because Ma fetches such a fit if there are footprints on the floors. As an afterthought she pulls out a sweater, because she's always being told to guard against dampness.

The house is quiet. She doesn't know where Ma is, and as she tiptoes out to the hall, she sees Ma flung out on the bed, taking a nap. She should ask Ma if it's okay to go outside to play, but waking her up can sometimes mean anger, so she tries to be quiet as she makes her way down the hall, down the stairs to the back door. Her sneakers are there and she ties them on. Doing the bow is hard, but she manages after awhile. When she steps outside her tummy grumbles and she tells it to stop. It doesn't listen.

There will be bread in the bread box, she's sure. The bread man will have been. She walks along the side of the house to the box that's built into the wall of the house, lifts the latch and opens the door, and sure enough there's a lovely loaf of bread there, the knob sticking out of the brown paper bag like an invitation. She feels water in her mouth. Her tummy growls loudly. Unable to resist she reaches up and breaks off the knob—Mummy doesn't like knobs anyway—and crunches into the crust and the tender bread inside.

It's so yummy! She reaches up to the bread and pulls out a long ribbon of the tender white middle, remembers to chew with her mouth closed, takes another chunk, and another, and before she knows it the middle of the bread is gone.

What to do? She'll catch it again for sure! But then she remembers that when Ma cuts the bread she never takes it out of the bag, only moves a little out so she can saw through it. If she turns the bread around, Ma will never know! And convinced of the cleverness of her plan she takes out the shell of what was once a loaf of bread, turns it around, and leaves the remaining knob hanging out of the bag. Crime disguised!

She pushes the door closed on the bread box, fixes the latch, and brushes crumbs from her top and sweater.

Happily, her tummy no longer growls.

She leaves the shade of the house and walks out into the garden, talking to the flowers, making sure everyone is happy. There are pussy willows on the tree. She touches their silky fur and marvels at these creatures. Pussy willows had to be alive, like Timmy Cat. Why else would they have fur? But she feels sorry for them, glued like that to the branch. They never get to move around, waiting all day for visitors like she did in the hopital. She wonders if this is a kind of plant hopital, and if so are the birds and insects that peck and look and prod doctors and nurses? Are the pussy willows sick? Or are they waiting to go home?

"Would you like to play?" she asks them. She's sure they do, and carefully she pulls the fattest of them away. She pets it in the palm of her hand. In the sunlight she's sure she can almost hear it purr. But it will be lonely if it doesn't have another to play with, so she pulls one that's not quite as big, one that will be the Ma Pussy willow to this Da, and another that will be Baby. She kisses them each and takes them to the rose garden where she plunks herself down on her sweater so her bum won't get damp from the grass.

The roses aren't in bloom yet. That's okay. She likes playing near them anyway. She figures if they can protect themselves with their thorns, they can protect her too, and so through the long afternoon she adventures with the Pussy Willow Family, long into the slow yellow light when the Golden Sea unfolds again from the sky, and there in the distance rise the towers of Over There.

Eulogy

I hesitated for a moment, hand poised on mouse, cursor hovering on the *Publish* icon on my blog. Maybe it wasn't such a good idea to broadcast this eulogy to the world. Maybe I was being as self-indulgent and idiotic as those thousands of people who publicly proclaim the gruesome minutia of their lives. It seemed like extravagant exhibitionism to me.

Was this any different?

I looked out the window of my studio, watching evening settle under the trees, how the water of the bay glowed. There were clouds on the horizon, the air beneath them shimmering like another golden sea.

I nearly fell off my seat when Uncle Ianto put his hand on my shoulder. He laughed, tightened his grip, and let go.

"Sorry," he said. "It's getting on and I wondered if you were going to stay here and work, or come in?"

I relaxed and sank back. "You scared the shit out of me."

"You were plainly somewhere else." He thumped down in the chair near the small desk I'd made for my tablet.

I looked at his round face, the apples of his cheeks where tiny veins splayed like red webs. The thing about Uncle Ianto that was always so compelling were his blue eyes. I wondered why he was never snagged. In his younger days he cut quite the figure.

"I was sort of thinking of posting a eulogy on my blog," I said.

He shook his head, a long shock of white hair falling over his forehead to the bridge of his nose. "Why all of you are so interested in this internet thing baffles me. Baffles me, I tell you."

"Oh, don't start."

"Don't start? What's out there in this unknown place you can't find in a library or by talking to people?"

"Nothing. You're just able to find that information faster, and make contacts with people you wouldn't otherwise."

"Stuff and piffle."

"You're a stubborn old coot, you know."

"Oh, aye. And you're exempt from that Cotter gene?"

No. Not exempt. I looked back to the tablet where the eulogy waited for me to touch the publish icon. All of us stubborn to a fault, unwilling to admit or acknowledge our armour might be just a wee bit slight.

"That it?" he asked, nodding to the screen where the cursor still hovered. "That the eulogy?"

I nodded. "Would you mind taking a look?"

"Go up so I can start from the beginning."

I slid my finger up the screen, scrolling the page to the top. He dragged his chair closer, reading over my shoulder. I knew better than to watch his face; it always annoyed him, so I kept my attention on the screen, advancing when he indicated, listening to his measured breathing. He leaned back when he finished, one hand still on my shoulder.

"I think you should publish it," he said. Just like that. No qualifiers. No hesitation.

"You're sure?"

"I wouldn't say so if I weren't sure."

"You don't think it's too personal."

"This isn't gushing with emotion."

"Then it's too impersonal?"

"God grant me patience! No, it's neither. What I'm trying to say, Violet, my flower, is that I think you've hit just the right tone. If anyone chooses to take offense, they're an idiot."

"Well, it's the idiots I'm afraid of."

He squeezed my shoulder. "You think Ben will object?"

I nodded. Who knew what Ben was capable of? He had that ruthlessness of the Cotters, and when crossed could be brutal. I didn't want to risk that and feared if he saw this it would be the final brick in the wall that had come between us.

"What can he do?" he said. "Send you a message? Make a call? You really even think Ben takes the time to read that thing of yours?" I made a face. "Oh, now, don't go and look like that. Don't choose to take offense. You know very well I meant that we aren't important to Ben. Our orbit isn't his sun. Publish it."

One click. In this age of instant communication, everything can change in a moment. A breath. A blink. A click. One minute your life is this. The next it's that.

"You coming in now?"

"I think I'll paint for awhile. I need to get on."

Uncle Ianto let out a burst of noise which might have been a laugh. He patted my shoulder and rose to leave.

At the door of the studio he paused. Out on the bay a loon called.

"You still need to cry, you know," he said.

"I haven't seen an abundance of tears from you."

"Ah, well, we're not speaking of your uncle."

"But we are speaking of grieving. And you've no idea what I do in the privacy of my own room."

I watched him consider then, push back the hair on his brow. He looked over to the paintings shelved in one corner, the one in progress on the glass. The loon cried again. Uncle Ianto looked back at me, his gaze very clear and sharp in the gloom.

"I did my grieving for Una a long time ago. It just took a long time for her body to follow her spirit."

"What do you mean by that?"

"Read the journals that are your legacy, if you haven't been already. If she's been honest, you'll begin to understand. If not, well, we each of us carry our own version of truth."

He turned then and shuffled away, his back stooped. I watched him cross the grass to the house, the way his feet left dark stains in the dew already descending. By now the sun had slipped down behind the woods backing the house.

I closed the screen door of my studio, flicked on the light and picked a brush. Time to lay down a transparent glaze with gum Arabic, a coloured lens through which to view the world.

You can do that with watercolours so long as you use transparent pigments and are careful about which pigments are staining and which are not in case you wish to lift a section. Use a staining pigment in a glaze over dry paint and paper and you pierce all those layers, shifting the hue. Use an opaque pigment, and you obfuscate and sometimes obliterate what lies beneath. So, in order to create an image with depth, you choose transparent, non-staining pigments and lay them down in a thin wash over dry work, feathering the edges with water to allow the pigment to bleed and soften. Illusion. Trickery. Manipulation of light waves to fool the eye. It's amazing what you can do with manipulation.

Una: November 1945

Ma always said life dishes out in equal measure. So it does.

Conner's love put me in hospital last week, with purple bruises and a broken rib to show for it. And a lovely, healthy daughter to boot, despite being here early and in dire circumstances. I've named her Violet, with the hope of spring and new beginnings.

Ianto and Mr. Fraser set the police on Conner, so Ma says. Officially he's been charged with disturbing the peace. Apparently, that's about all can be done about a husband who punctuates his arguments with his fists. Unofficially, they've told him to sell up and get out of town; the next time they have to put him in lock-up he might find the drunk he bunks with not so forgiving as they.

And all of that's fine and well, good riddance to bad rubbish, but where does that leave me now? Here am I, a baby to suckle, no job, no option but to throw myself upon Ma's mercy and have her take this fallen woman home. And make no mistake I am a fallen woman. What else will people think when it's common knowledge I was unable to prevent Mr. Bloody Conner Bannon from using me as a punching bag? Won't matter he was old enough to be my father; all they'll see is he had a steady job at Penman's, owned his own house. We're all raised to assume it is the woman's place to hold the peace, to be the pacifier, the glue that holds together family and propriety and decent living.

Well what happens when the husband decides to undermine the peace? Just how much is a woman supposed to endure in order to keep that peace? And what does peace mean anyway? Is it peace at any cost? Is it peace at the price of slavery? Because I'll tell you right now that's exactly how I feel, a slave to his will. If he says the moon is purple I should agree, proclaim it as truth, despite what the reality of my own eyes tells me.

And then what happens when the husband refuses to acknowledge the right of the helpless child he's fathered? How is that child—a mewling, helpless lump—to defend against want, whether of love, or shelter, or sustenance? Who to defend her? And in the face of that, how does a woman choose? Does she accept the authority of his violence in order to protect the child? Or does she fight back in equal measure with the hope of breaking the bars of her cage?

Well, we know now I chose the latter course.

And then for me another realization: somehow, I felt closer to Ianto when I lay connected to tubes in the hospital bed; I began to understand some of the fears he must have felt during the war.

He fought one battle. I fight another. And the hell with the world.

Lettie: The Rose Guardian

The problem with adopting a family is you have to give them a home. She thinks about this. Thinks about where the Pussywillows might want to live. She wants them to be comfortable. She wants them to feel safe. And she needs to know she can watch over them as well, so their house has to be something not only small to fit them, but easy to carry and easy to disguise.

She sneezes again. There's a lot of that invisible stuff in the air—what did the doctor call it? Pollen. Yes. There's a lot of pollen in the air, she's sure, because it's hard to breathe and the sneezes are getting worse. Not just ordinary sneezing. Great big right from your toes sneezing, one right after the other. And then gobs and gobs of goo. Which means lots and lots of tissues.

She blows hard into one now, groans, drops the soggy tissue onto the bed with a pile of others.

And then the best idea of all comes to her. The pussy willows can live in the tissue box. She's always carrying a box around with her. How perfect is that?

"I'll be right back," she says, touching each of the tiny grey people on her bed.

I'll watch them, says Panda.

Assured all will be well, she scrambles off the bed

and checks the hall for activity. Clear. Carefully, she makes her way to the little desk in the living-room. She hears a pan go smack on the stove, Mummy singing —*Byelu baby bye, bye, byelu baby bye, bye*—and as she reaches the small desk hears a sizzle followed by that wonderful smell of onions and garlic. She wants to go see what Mummy's cooking, share the singing, but she has this important thing to do.

Carefully she slides open the drawer of the desk, finds the scissors and tape, pushes the drawer closed and returns to her room. She bends over the bed, touching Ma, Pa and Baby Pussywillow with the tip of her finger.

Panda says, *I took good care of them.*

She kisses him, and then in turn each of the Pussywillows.

It takes time, but she removes all the tissues from the box, keeping them in a tidy stack, and cuts the empty box to fit walls and floors. She tapes the new walls and ceiling into place, bending the thin cardboard where she's not been clever enough with the scissors. It all looks so bare. So, she pulls out her crayons and colours in rugs and paint on the walls, tapes up tissue drapes, and then decides The Pussywillows need to have clothes and uses more tape and tissue to create a skirt for Ma, a teeny-tiny tie for Pa, and a diaper for Baby. This latter, she realizes, she'll have to change often. But then thinks it might be better for Ma Pussywillow to do this, and instead carefully cuts tiny diapers and stacks them in the nursery of the new Pussywillow House.

"Do you like it?" she asks the family. She's sure they do, and places them inside, sets the ceiling into place, the tissues back on top. She's so excited about this she takes her new portable house outside to show the roses.

When she sits down in front of the large white rose bush it amazes her, as it always does, how quiet it is here. Mr. Harris' lawn-mower, Leslie and his friends screaming about a goal in the hockey game they play on the dirt country road—all of it is distant and hushed. Like one of the magi, she sets her gift at the foot of the white rose, rocks back onto her knees.

"Will you be their guardian?" she asks the rose. "Will you protect them with your thorns?"

She waits in the green stillness, hoping the white rose has heard her plea. The Pussywillow people are so small and soft. People like that need help.

Above her a chickadee pipes and bobs along the rail fence. It looks at her, its head cocking one way, then the other. It flutters and lands on a stem of the rose, picking off aphids. She realizes even the rose needs a guardian.

When the chickadee flits away she gets up and goes back to the house, leaving the Pussywillow Family in the shelter of the roses.

Ma tells her to come to dinner. Remembering Mrs. Harris' rules about table manners, she goes to the bathroom and waggles her fingers under the water, using soap as an afterthought, waggles again and then dries off, making sure to fold the towel just so the way Ma likes.

It's liver and onions, cabbage and potatoes for supper. She scrambles up onto her chair. Smiles at Pa. Smiles at Ma. They're not smiling back. She knows what that means, ducks her head and tries to eat quietly, the way

Mrs. Harris taught her. Be small. Be quiet. Be a mouse. No, not a mouse. Mice get killed. Be air. Air is always there. Invisible. Even when a glass looks empty it's full of air.

She doesn't understand why the other kids don't like liver. It's yummy. She places it carefully into her mouth, watching Ma and Pa out the corner of her eye. They're busy with their own food. She chews more. It's so quiet all she can hear is the scrape and scratch of utensils on the plates, of Pa gulping water from a tumbler, of Ma breathing heavily. Ma's angry, she knows.

She manages a forkful of cabbage without slopping all over. Something white whizzes by her face. She's hears it go smack on Pa. Shocked, she looks at him, sees mashed potatoes sliding off the side of his cheek. He's still eating. You'd think nothing had happened.

She looks over at Ma who lifts her fork to her mouth, chews, does it again.

And then there are mashed potatoes stuck on the side of Ma's face, clinging to her dark hair. Still, Ma continues to spear and cut, lift and chew.

She looks back at Pa. He's still working on supper. Back to Ma. She's still working on supper.

But they have mashed potatoes all over them!

This is going to be terrible, she knows. Their anger is like the air before a storm, heavy and sticky, so thick it's hard to pull in a breath. It's hard to eat now. Her throat is tight. But she manages in small bites, making little noise, being air. If she's quiet enough, if she's still enough, she can make it outside with Panda before the thunder.

But too late. Ma is at the sink, scraping dishes,

running water. Pa's chair bangs against the wall when he gets up. In two strides he's beside Ma.

"You're not going to class tonight."

"Don't be ridiculous. Of course, I'm going."

"I said you're not."

Ma turns toward Pa. She's smiling. It doesn't look friendly. "Give me one good reason why I shouldn't go?"

"He'll be there."

"Who?"

"That master gardener."

Ma reaches over and turns off the taps. There are soap bubbles mounded over the top of the sink. "Well of course he'll be there. He teaches the class."

"And what else is he teaching you?"

"Don't be ridiculous." Pa yanks her around. Ma laughs. "You going to hit me now? Like a man?" Her face is close to Pa's. "Go ahead and hit me like a man."

Pa growls like an animal, his big hands around Ma's throat. He bends Ma to the sink.

She doesn't know what to do. She should try to save them. She should try to stop this. She wants to yell, but her throat has closed, and breath is sharp and painful. She backs out of the kitchen, hugging Panda, step by step, turns when she reaches the hall and makes a dash for the door.

It's dark outside now. The air is cool and damp. She sucks in air, wishing she were air. Wishing herself invisible. She flees to the roses to check on the Pussywillow Family, to be sure they're not fighting as well. She kisses Panda over and over, wetting his head with her tears.

The Pussywillows are fine when she checks.

"They're fine," she whispers to Panda. He looks up at her with his glass eyes.

Of course, they are. They're with the roses.

"The giraffe trees won't get me here?"

She just about splits her skin in fear when the white rose touches her arm. There's a face among the blooms, all petals and yellow stamens. Its fingers are like briars, bristling with thin red thorns. It scratches but it doesn't hurt.

You're safe here, it says. She looks for the mouth, sees a gap among the dense leaves.

She hugs Panda tighter. *This is the Rose Guardian,* Panda says. *He watches over all of us.*

"But then why does he let the Uglies and the Furries be here?"

They can't hurt you. They just like to scare.

"And the Darkies?"

They're your friends. They protect you inside where the Rose Guardian can't go.

All this time. All this fear.

I have servants everywhere, the Rose Guardian says.

The tears come then, hot and urgent, and she hates herself for crying like a sissy baby.

Calm Waters

I decided today was the day I would discover who were Lettie's parents. The summer course was coming to an end by the close of the month, and not once had I seen either father or mother drop her off or collect her. Lettie just appeared. Lettie just disappeared.

As if that weren't troublesome enough, the other children remained oblivious to her. I decided that, also, would change today.

At the moment we worked out near the bay, under the shade of the pines where it was cool and fragrant, a breeze off the water keeping the flies to a minimum.

"Break into pairs," I told them. I was about to push Lettie into a trio when she gripped my hand and brought my attention down to her. She shook her head, such a look of pleading there. How could I refuse that? Despite my better judgement I acquiesced.

"You remember how we did faces yesterday?" I asked the kids, watching for signs of recognition, received seven nods. "Today you're going to sketch each other, using all the things you learned yesterday." The other two girls turned to each other conspiratorially, the boys thumping each other amid jests. They settled down fairly quickly. I strolled among them for a few moments, and when it seemed they were well on their way, I sank to the soft needles under the pines, my own sketch book in hand, and let Lettie sketch me, as I sketched her.

So much for integrating her with the others. She might have been air for all they noticed. Still, it was an opportunity to spend some relatively uninterrupted time with her. I was about to ask her about her parents when she said, "You have a boat."

I looked over to the boathouse. "Not mine anymore. But I let my friend keep it here."

"Do you still sail?"

"Sometimes."

"Can you sail for days and days?"

I nodded. "Do your mum and dad sail?"

She looked back at me. "No." And looked back down to her work.

"What do your mum and dad do?"

"Ma's a gardener. Pa doesn't live with us."

"Your parents divorced?"

She shrugged. "I dunno. Pa doesn't live with us."

"I've never seen you in the village."

She shrugged again, her focus entirely on her drawing which was in fact quite good.

"Does your mother drive you in?"

"I walk."

"Is it far?"

She shrugged.

"Do you have any brothers or sisters?"

Once again that shrug. She turned her drawing around for me to see. "Is this okay?"

It was more than okay. The basic shapes and forms I'd taught the others were plainly rudimentary for this strange child. She must have had lessons before, despite her earlier denial. I asked her about that.

"I guess so. A long time ago," she said.

What an odd thing for her to say. But then I remembered how it was a month could seem an eternity to a child. She looked up at me then and I felt my heart skip again. Why did this one little girl affect me so? It was like looking at a dream take shape before me. Or a memory.

"Do you go sailing a lot?" she asked.

Not like I used to, I realized. Not since David and I separated, despite the fact he kept the boat here. I'd let all the simple pleasures slip by. Guilt, I supposed, my own form of penance for failing as a daughter, failing as a wife. Better to employ that good old fashioned Puritan work ethic, nose to the grindstone and all that. Pleasure was the incubator of sin. Feel miserable and make everyone proud. How was it I'd bought into all that?

I looked over at the boathouse. "No," I said.

"You should. It would be good for you."

Say what? Where did this child come up with these things? And while I wanted to press upon her my curiosity, parents started to arrive to collect their children. I rose to dismiss the class and give them direction for the next session, fielded questions, offered praise and constructive criticism. By the time I turned back to further query Lettie, I found she'd gone. Again. And I no more educated about this foundling child.

When I rounded the side of the house and made to cross the terrace, a sheet of paper under the roses caught my attention. I bent and picked it up. It was Lettie's portrait of me. As always, her work was remarkable, and somehow familiar. I carried it with me to my studio and tucked it into my portfolio for safekeeping.

Instead of turning to my own work, I slid down in front of the laptop and tried to bring up the student registration spreadsheet, but the stupid network wasn't being recognized, so I couldn't access the document on my computer in the house, and with a cough of disgust I swivelled around to my work bench, picked up a brush, dipped it in water, and sloshed it through a congealed puddle of pigment on the palette. I tested the dryness of the paper with the back of my other hand, and when satisfied loaded another brush with clear water. From there I lay in a series of transparent washes, working with colour in one hand, clear water in the other, pulling and guiding the bleed.

Two hours later, cheeks feeling flushed, I surfaced and pulled back, watching colour coalesce into tangible form. As always, I felt a rush of amazement when a work went well. Painting was like alchemy, creating something out of nothing, gold from dross. And when it went well, it went very well. And when it didn't, I had paper for origami or collage.

I was just contemplating the fine brush detail I'd lay in later, when my cell phone danced across the table. Annoyed, I dumped the brushes into the cleaning jar, hooked the headset around my ear and said hello.

It was Ayashe Keeshig from Treasure Cove Gallery in Little Current where I was to show in a few weeks. She was going on about press releases and interviews, and I half thought she'd lost her mind about this show and was having delusions of grandeur. And blessed mother of god there were still three damned paintings to finish, all in varying degrees of inspiration and execution, or lack thereof, and didn't she realize I just didn't have time for this huge ramble of nonsense?

I glanced back at the painting I'd really wanted to work on, adjusting my headset as I turned. I lifted the painting from the floor to the easel, making meaningful noises into the headset as Ayashe kept going on, her voice rising in volume and pitch.

If I were honest, the painting on the easel was a stupid thing to start what with this show looming. I should have employed some of that good Puritan work ethic I'd earlier vilified. I should have been working on the three last paintings needed for the show, the three guaranteed, no-brainer paintings that were more likely to sell than this thing I'd started. I should have worked on paintings like the watercolour I'd just left.

Last week I'd smudged in the cool, dark under-washes on the canvas I now studied. Oils this time, not watercolours. Another bad decision. It would take weeks, even months, for the layers to build on this piece, unlike a watercolour or acrylic. Those I could push. Those were all about timing. But with an oil time slowed.

Finally, I heard: "Have you heard anything I've said, Vi?"

I blinked and stammered into the headset, "Sorry. I gapped for a moment. What was that last?"

"We have an interview with CBC! We've actually landed air-time! There's a video crew coming to your place by six a.m. on Wednesday. You know what to do? I gave them your number and someone is supposed to call to set up all the preliminary technical stuff."

CBC? Video crew? What the hell was she talking about? I asked Ayashe that.

"Really, Vi, I wish you'd pay attention. CBC is working on a piece on small art festivals and the state of visual art in Canada. You're to be one of the featured artists, being as you have a show coming up, and how we get a fair trade in US tourists here."

"But I'm in the middle of teaching a summer course, let alone finishing the work for this damned show."

"It's CBC, Vi."

As if that was the bloody Pope, or the Dali Lama, or the freaking Prime Minster of Canada. I was being bloody-minded, I knew, but I just didn't care. Too much lately. Just simply too much.

That pregnant pause expanded to cosmic proportions. Finally, "Vi? Can you do that?"

"Well it's a bit late now to ask me, isn't it? I'm obligated." Don't be such a bitch, Vi! "And unless I show up we are all mired in omelettes." I shook my head. Sometimes I felt like I had periodic Tourette's.

"So that means you'll do it?" I could hear the hope in Ayashe's voice. What this could mean for her gallery was impossible to imagine.

Of course, I'd bloody do it. This was all-encompassing, career-making CBC we discussed. I could be bloody-minded, but I wasn't stupid. "Yes."

I heard her let go of a breath. "Great. Okay, I'll email you the particulars. Talk to you soon." And the connection went dead.

I tapped the disconnect on the headset and tossed the contraption onto the table where it promptly landed in the jar of water in which I cleaned my brushes. Damn! I snatched it out, watched water drain from the piece and resigned myself to being a bigger fool than I cared to admit, and hastily made a note to buy a new headset. If Uncle Ianto found out he'd be pissed. It wasn't the first time I'd done something lame like that.

CBC? Blessed mother of god, what had I gotten myself into?

I slumped into the chair. The stupid back slid down a few notches again, and I reached behind and shoved the damn thing up.

An interview? How the hell was I going to handle an interview? I swivelled back around to the tablet and brought up the camera and stared at myself, trying to fluff up the pancake of my hair, and when it just hung there like coiled, limp floss, I wet my fingers with gum Arabic and tried spiking it to give myself a bohemian, urban vibe. That just looked completely stupid. What was a middle-aged woman doing with hair like that?

Disgusted, I shoved my fingers into those unruly curls and shook them around, letting the hair just fall whichever way it would. I tried to tell myself it didn't matter. Beauty and youth played no part in public perception. Right, and that's why women spent billions of dollars on creams and unguents, gels and peels, injections and surgery—because beauty and youth didn't matter. Ma would have said I'd let myself go, that a woman's business card was her face, and then her figure. That's when I realized the fine lines under my eyes were no longer fine lines. Somehow between last month and this there were rutted highways under my eyes. And from where had bloomed these dark circles?

I pulled the tender tissue under my eyes back toward my ears, vaguely wondering how they did that plastic surgery stuff, and then pinched the flesh on my cheekbones thinking about injections and wondering how the hell that didn't hurt.

I let my fingers fall away.

Cosmetics! That's what was needed. With enough concealer, a bit of highlighter, something to make cheekbones out of this round face, I might pull it off. Fine to be a sagging, middle-aged man, but the public didn't take well to mediocre or homely women. And suddenly I wanted the public to like what they saw. Ayashe was right. This was the bloody CBC we were talking about, not some local cable TV. And even if my segment in the overall show wasn't much more than a passing thirty second byte, it was my thirty seconds of fame on national Canadian television.

I clicked off the webcam and swivelled back around only to be confronted by the work I needed to finish and frame for the show.

So much for my glamorous debut. Without paintings there was no show. Feeling foolish for my girlie outburst, I moved the oil canvas back to the floor, retrieved my watercolour brushes, dried them, and went back to work.

When I resurfaced shadows crept across the gardens and lawn, reaching down to the shore. Satisfied with my day's production, I cleaned my brushes and plunked them into the old salt-glaze mug that had been commandeered years ago as holder. I touched the pebbled surface, traced the blue bird motif.

I remembered the day I'd purchased that mug, part of a box of stuff I'd decided I needed to have. It has been an estate sale held on the lawn of the home. Ma and I decided to go because there was a chance of some good antiques, but as usual the dealers were there and bidding went high. She said I was foolish to waste my money on a salt-glaze mug. But the irregular shape and grainy texture captured my heart, and so I brought home my ten-dollar mug, and put the remainder of the box of junk in my next garage sale, which had been when David and I divided up the contents of our lives.

Cycles is what that mug had come to represent for me, cycles and change.

I stood and stretched out the stiffness in my body and closed up the studio for the evening. Uncle Ianto was snoring in the rocker when I reached the porch. Rather than disturb him, I carefully let myself in through the screen door and set about putting together salad and burgers. It was the searing of ground beef on the barbeque that brought his snores to an abrupt end.

"Catch a good kip?" I asked, watching him shove the fall of hair on his forehead back into place. It was amazing that he should be eighty-four and still have that lush head of silver hair.

"Cocktail hour," he announced.

I waved the spatula in my hand at him. "As long as it's a mocktail, you're okay."

"I'm having a beer."

"You're having tonic water."

"I'll have a bloody beer if I want one!"

"You're on blood pressure medication and thinners. You'll have a tonic water and be happy."

"Harridan!"

"You can call me harridan, Hectate, or anything else you like, but I'm not going to be rushing you to hospital because you decided to follow your Irish roots."

He stumped over to me, pecked my cheek, and left for

the kitchen. When he returned he raised a clear glass of bubbly water into which he'd thrown a lime wedge. I smiled and gave him a thumbs-up. He lowered himself to one of the chairs on the terrace where I barbequed. "So how went the afternoon's work?"

"Good. I'm nearly finished the La Cloche landscape. Just working in some final details."

"You left that oil alone?"

"I behaved, yes."

"I heard you talking out there. You keeping yourself company, or did someone call?"

I grinned and then sucked in a lungful of air, my heart fluttering again with excitement. "It was Ayashe from the gallery."

He made a gesture in the air for me to accelerate the information.

"Seems a crew from CBC will be here on Wednesday to do a shoot for a piece they're doing on local art galleries and festivals."

He pointed at me, grinning. "You?"

I nodded. "Too strange, eh?" I lifted burgers on to toasted buns, plated them, and dialled off the burners and gas. We settled to the table.

I watched Uncle Ianto squeeze green relish onto his burger, something he seemed to do in like spirit. "You going to have some burger with that relish?"

He fired me a look and waggled the bottle at me. "It's a food group."

"Oh really?"

"Sure." He turned the bottle, gestured with the other. "There, see? First ingredient: cucumbers!" And plunked the bottle back onto the table between us. "So why is CBC interviewing you here?"

"I guess they want to interview the artist in situ." I shrugged. "I'm not sure. I guess I'm going to have to go shopping."

He laughed. "Now that I'd like to see. Just be yourself. Don't go glamming up."

"What do you mean by glamming up?" I stabbed at my salad.

"You know, getting all tarted up into something you're not. You're a beautiful woman just as you are." He wiped condiments from his chin.

"Well, I need something better than these old ratty jeans and t-shirt." I stuck my finger through the hole in the front of my shirt.

He laughed. "True enough. But don't go and buy something you'll never wear again."

"I also need to have something nice to wear to the show opening. I don't know whether to do summer dress or nice slacks."

"Dress."

"Well of course you'd say that. You're a man."

"I'm your uncle!" He grinned.

"And useless. I guess I'm going into Little Current tomorrow after class. Wanna come?"

"And watch you melt down over a bit of fabric? I think I'd rather they did another colostomy."

"Lot of support you are."

He poured me another glass of wine and himself a glass of sparkling water. "I'll make the appropriate noises when you come back."

"You sure you don't want to come? You could catch a coffee with the boys. Maybe play a round or two of euchre. Maybe it would be good for you to get out."

"As scintillating as all that sounds, I'm thinking I'd

just like to commune with the garden. Those tatties need hilling. And the last of the peas shelling and freezing."

"Right domestic darling, aren't you?"

He grinned. "Well, one of us has to be."

I put my chin on my hand, watching his face, his blue eyes, the pleasure with which he masticated greens and burger. Not for the first time I silently thanked whoever listened for the gift of his presence. Light to Ma's darkness. Compass and oracle. Father without paternity.

The sounds of the island settled around us, a pileated woodpecker drumming in the distance, a loon wailing on the water, leaves rustling in a mild onshore breeze. Together we watched the light fade, spectators to a larger theatre.

Una: October 1946

Smoothing things over with Ma has proved harder than Ianto thought. It's been made clear my situation is all my own fault. Dirty laundry is not to be aired in public, and I have, apparently, made a public spectacle of myself.

How is any of this my fault? Was it wrong of me to believe a man would love me? That I might be worthy of shelter and safeguarding? He made promises. I opened my legs based on those promises.

None of this turned out the way I thought it would. I thought there would be tenderness, just like in the novels, that maybe there might be passion. I didn't know passion could hurt you, put you in fear for your life. I didn't know it was my responsibility to disappear, be invisible, and it angers me savagely I am not allowed the freedom to think, to act, to be.

Sometimes I think it would be better to be a dullard.

But to the practical. Mr. Fraser has been kind enough to give me a position again at the hardware store. It's difficult fitting in being a mother and a bread-winner. I use my lunches to hurry home and nurse little Violet, change her, and bed her down again. But she's older now and getting to be active, and I can't leave her alone 'cause I'm afraid she'll get out of the playpen where I've moved her for the day hours. And I can't afford to hire someone to watch her, so I'm not sure what I'm going to do.

Mr. Fraser said I could bring Violet to work and keep her in the office in the playpen, check on her periodically. But what happens when she's sick? And she's sick a lot, always coughing. I don't know what to do. And as it is I can barely afford the room I rent.

I'm not supposed to cook in the room, and my landlady is Jewish and has made it clear she's doing me a favour by letting a Gentile use her kitchen, and of course I have to follow all the rules of Kashrut. That makes it hard when I'm trying to heat milk for Violet. So, I got myself a little hot plate and a saucepan, and I make things with that, smuggle in supplies and keep them under the bed in a small cold box Mr. Fraser gave me.

And as lonely and tired as I am, my comfort is that little girl. She struggles so hard to stay alive, to breathe. And if I were a better mother I would have never paid attention to a charming smile and all that brash bravado. But then I wouldn't be a mother.

Thank goodness for Ianto. Were it not for him I swear I would lose my mind sometimes. He visits when he can, always bringing gifts of necessity, for which he refuses any thanks. Just his job as a brother and an uncle, he says. He chivvies me along. Always a ready smile, a shoulder, hope cast about like sunshine.

Lettie: Abdukchon

Ma and Uncle have come to visit again, and this time Doctor Skulksomethingorother has said it would be okay if they take her outside in a wheelchair, out into the garden where she can get some fresh air. She hates the hospital, is convinced it's a castle of some sort where there are dungeons and kids are tortured with needles and poisons because there's no one here who isn't sick. The doctors are all lying, she's sure, telling parents who visit their kids are okay when really they're not. She knows, 'cause she's seen too many parents crying, and that can only mean there's a whole lot of lying and hurt going on. And the kids are all sad, not wanting to talk, lying in cribs and beds with tubes and things sticking out of their arms or their mouths or their noses, and if not that then there are casts and bandages, or metal frames that hold up legs, or arms, and lots of moaning and nurses with trays of little paper cups that hold coloured candies which are really bitter poison they make her take with sips of water or apple juice. Like the evil witch who fooled Snow White with the poisoned apple. And they watch her swallow the bitter, poisoned candies too, just to be sure she's had the right dose to make her sleep or cry and get sicker and sicker.

And then there are the cold rooms they take her into where everyone is dressed in baggy uniforms and they wear masks to hide their mouths and hair, and gloves so they don't have to touch her 'cause she probably has something they don't want to get, or they're going to give her something she doesn't want to get. And it's in those cold rooms they do the biggest evils, the real tortures, where they put a mask over her face and tell her to count, except she never gets to count and the mask smells funny, sort of sweet and sicky and sends her off to the place in the mountains with the black lake where she has to swim and swim even though she's drowning and the water is like ice, and there is no shore where she can haul herself out, only black stone and black water and the cold, white light glaring above her.

And she doesn't want to drown.

She really doesn't want to drown.

And only at the last moment, when she thinks she can't tread water any longer, and she can't feel her arms or her legs and her heart is crashing around like that bird that got caught in the house and smashed against the window over and over again, they finally hauled her out of the black water and brought her back and put her in a soft bed with soft sheets and blankets and warm air and light, and nurses with caps who have soft smiles and soft eyes and help her to suck on cold popsicles that are so wonderfully cool and sweet in her hot, burning throat.

They ask her if she can hear them, and ask how she feels, and she thinks it's all going to be okay because these are the nice people in the castle after all, the ones who rescued her from the black water.

And they're the ones who have now said it will be okay if Ma and Uncle take her out into the garden in the wheelchair. She's not supposed to walk, not supposed to get all tired out. That's okay. She doesn't much feel like walking anyway. Everything feels sort of floaty and dreamy, and it's good to sit in the chair with wheels and have someone buggy her around, a blanket wrapped round her legs and one draped like a shawl round her shoulders. Ma's asking all kinds of questions about how she feels and what she's eaten and what she's been doing. She answers, but doesn't really feel much like talking 'cause it's too hard to put the thoughts together, find the words to fit the thoughts and then push them all out of her mouth so they make sense and stop any more questions from coming. So mostly she sort of sticks to yes and no and shrugs and nods.

Uncle has parked her under a big tree where there's shade, and Ma has spread a blanket on the grass and bends down to sit. Uncle says he'll be back in a minute with some drinks. Ma chatters away at her and it's nice to hear her voice, just to look at her, her dark hair which is cut short, and her sunglasses which are like two teardrops turned up at the outside edges. Ma has on red pedal-pushers she says are part of a mother/daughter matching pair. That thought is pleasing to her and she says so, thanking Ma for this gift she'll get to have when she comes back home, which brings her to ask when she can come home, and Ma says not for awhile yet. Why not, she asks. And Ma says 'cause they all have to make sure she's really well. So she asks if she's been very sick. Very sick, yes, Ma says.

Ma's about to say something more when her face

changes and there's fear there, and anger, and her gaze is somewhere beyond the wheelchair. She watches as Ma gets up all in a scurry, her hands balled into fists, and then yells, "Don't you dare!"

It's then she feels herself lifted up out of the wheelchair, and is startled, then turns her head to look at who has taken her. It's Da. But that can't be, because Da has been told to stay away and she knows now there's a problem.

"You can't take her," Ma yells and hurls herself like one of those big black jungle cats at Da, all snarls and claws. She feels like she'll be torn in two because both of them have hold of her, and Da's yelling too, talking about blood of my blood, flesh of my flesh, and she wonders if that means she really is going to be torn apart like a joint of meat at the butcher's. She realizes she's yelling too, and it hurts, and she's crying and bubbling all kinds of words to make them stop, just stop, let her be. Distantly, she wonders if the Rose Guardian has any power here, if it can reach through the earth to this garden, this place, and send help—

— which comes in the form of Uncle who slams a fist into Da's head, and there's a crunching, squishy sound and blood, and suddenly she's moving through the air and then settled, like a chick to a safe perch, in Uncle's arms, and they're running now, bouncing and jouncing, across the garden, the lawn, into the doors of the hospital where nurses and orderlies close around them like guards and whisk her off to her room. There are cold stethacopes. Voices are loud and sounding scared, and the words police, abdukchon. Don't worry.

Don't worry, says Panda who is there and waiting in the chair by her crib.

I'm scared.

I know. It's okay.

She takes in a deep breath, manages to smile at Panda. *It's okay.*

The Rose Guardian is always watching.

"It's okay," Ma whispers, her lips moving on the top of her head.

A Student with No History

Class the next morning followed what had become routine: the boys an energy threatening gleeful explosion; the two girls as secretive and conspiratorial as ever. And Lettie my shadow. I'd transferred a copy of the student roster to my tablet that morning, and now as the children worked at the day's assignment I pulled the tablet from my pack and tapped at the screen. The spreadsheet opened. Six students were listed. There was no seventh. Lettie wasn't on the list. How could that be?

I looked up and over to where she sat cross-legged beside the white Cotter roses. I could hear her singing. I crossed to the two girls.

"Do you know her?" I asked them, nodding to where Lettie sat.

They looked up at me, confused. I pointed to the roses. "Lettie—do you know her?"

They looked at each other, back at me, shaking their heads no.

"You've never seen her in the village?"

Again, a shake of their heads, that look of confusion growing.

"Not at school, or on the bus?"

By now the boys watched us. I could see them

looking over to the rose garden, back to the girls, up to me. One of them exploded into laughter, punching his neighbour in the arm and fell giggling onto the grass.

"Stop it!" I snapped. "I won't have that in my class! Back to work!"

So, by virtue of the fact they didn't know her she was outcast. I felt the rage of that unfairness, wanting to dress down parents for allowing that sort of behaviour, wanting to berate these children for their stupidity and ignorance.

I crossed the lawn to Lettie, sank down beside her. She glanced up at me, back at the roses, her pencil scratching against paper, shading negative space.

"Lettie, I don't have any registration for you." I realized as soon as I said that how mercenary it sounded. At this point I didn't care about fees. All I cared about was the well-being of this little girl. "I need to know who to contact should there be a problem."

She looked up at me. "Is there a problem?"

"Well, no. But just in case. I need to know who are your parents."

She looked back down to her work. "I told you before. Da left. Ma's dead."

"So, who do you live with?"

"My uncle."

"And where does he live?"

"Here."

"In Meldrum Bay?"

She nodded yes. "The Rose Guardian says you're asking too many dumb questions. You already know the answers."

"This is no time for games, Lettie."

She looked at me, her small face so intent. It was like

looking in a mirror and I felt a sudden sense of vertigo, of being lost. I felt as though I'd stepped outside of time and stood here at an important crossroads, but didn't know which way to turn. Any or all choices might be the right one. But what was right? What was the destination? Again I felt my heart stutter, flutter, felt the need to cough and did that, knew panic was rising and for what reason I couldn't fathom, just that I knew I was losing control, out of my depth. And then, good the gods, there were tears blurring my vision and I found myself blinking, swallowing, cursing myself for every kind of a fool.

"You've just forgotten how to hear them, that's all."

Hear them? I said it aloud, frustration mounting.

"We used to know how."

There was a mason chipping at the walls of my heart. I was aware my hand trembled when I reached for her drawing that looked suddenly familiar, let my fingers fall short, rose to my feet in a burst of fear and pounded to my studio. There I found my first portfolio open on a table, sketches scattered. I felt as though I looked through a chiaroscuro. Nothing was clear. Brilliance and darkness. Shadows and reality. Definition scattered. I was adrift over the Marianas Trench.

My first thought was: *How dare she!*

My second thought: *Why?*

I whirled to confront her, to address invasion of privacy, of theft, only to be arrested by the imperative of a sudden burst of violence from the two girls who were screeching and thrashing. Reaching through a tangle of limbs I managed to extricate the girls into two squirming, grunting bundles, and demanded to know the cause of this outburst.

There were the usual accusations of theft and looking and touching, and once again I wondered how parents found the patience to deal with this sort of behaviour on a daily basis.

I glared at them both. "You get only one warning in my class, do you hear?" They both opened their mouths to protest but I overrode them with dire warnings of expulsion, exposure to their parents and shame.

"You're here to learn about art, believe it or not, not to attend some sort of summer day care. I'm not your sitter." I released them both. "Now go, the pair of you, and finish this assignment or else."

"Or else what?" one of them dared, puffing herself up with sudden importance. "Do you know who my Mum is?"

"Do you know who I am?" I countered. "There's no status here but that of student and teacher, with me clearly the teacher. And as to the *or else*...." I leaned in close to the girl, watched her blue eyes widen with alarm. "You don't even want to go there. I'm older. I have way more experience than you. Something you should think about." I made a shooing gesture, glared at the boys for emphasis, and then just to cement my authority turned my back on them. They'd get the message. They usually did.

It was something I'd learned very well from Ma whose presence I felt very strongly just then.

And where Lettie was—anyone's guess. Gone with my sudden burst of fear and then anger.

I should go and find her. Call someone. Do something. But where to look, who to call, what to do? I raced to the house, up the steps, and slammed through the screen door, yelling for Uncle Ianto, not receiving an answer, getting angrier and more frightened as my calls remained unanswered.

Thinking he was in the vegetable garden I pounded back outside and found him hilling potatoes, sweat on his face.

"Have you seen her?" I asked, catching my breath, feeling the giddiness of fear rising up my throat.

He leaned on the hoe, looked up, his eyes narrowing. "Who?"

"Lettie."

He frowned. "Lettie?"

"Yes, yes. The girl. The girl in my art class. The one who isn't registered."

"Violet, are you okay?"

"No, I'm not bloody okay! She's disappeared. I can't find her anywhere."

He let the hoe drop, gripped my shoulders. "I think you need to calm down."

Calm down! Calm down? How the hell was I to calm down with her gone missing, when it appeared she was a thief, a wild-child without history or background who had just shown up at my art classes?

"Violet...." He shook my shoulders. "Violet, listen to me."

I focused on him, saw the worry there, the colour draining from his seamed and kindly face.

"Lettie's long since gone, Violet. You know that."

I ripped away from his grip, not wanting to hear such nonsense, knowing I'd lost this girl and needed to find her. The only place for me to turn was back to my students whom I'd abandoned in my panic—isn't that just what you always do—and try to make some sense of this.

Lettie. No registration. No history. No background.

Lettie's long since gone, Violet.

Ma has forgiven me. I'm back home, in this big, old, stone house, with our history and our forbearers watching from the walls. She has agreed to take care of Violet when I'm working. It's hard for all of us, I suppose.

Ma's turned the old house into a guest house with both boarders and tourists, and now Ianto is home with us again, unscathed, he helps her with both the guest house and the tobacco farm. He seems to be everywhere at once. They've turned the front parlour into a reception room for the business, and the dining-room is now for guests. We eat in the kitchen with the small staff Ma's hired. There's a cook, a maid-of-all-things, a man who acts as a sort of butler-valet kind of thing. Ianto tends the grounds and sees to vehicles and luggage and oddments, as well as oversees the tobacco. Ma's energy is boundless, cleaning and cooking, and taking reservations and the like. She seems happy, as though she's finally shed her mourning and come into the light.

Where she got the money to put in an indoor toilet I have no idea, but she did, and the small room on the second floor that wasn't much more than a closet now has a bathtub, toilet and sink, and there is a second bathroom for our own personal use. Such a luxury not to have to use the galvanized tub, chamber pots, or outhouse, or stand and shiver at a washstand in the bleak chill of morning. Such a luxury to have hot water on tap, no coppers simmering eternally on the woodstove. There's a great behemoth of a boiler in the basement, oil feeding it at reasonable cost. It's strange to hear the clack and bang of pipes expanding, radiating warmth out into the house. Central heating—such a concept. Truly, it's an age of miracles, and it would seem prosperity is coming to Canada, if not overseas.

There's a cook now, who can actually cook, and guests rave over the dishes she prepares. Ma has given her two rooms Ianto built in the attic, a sort of bed-sitting room. The second floor has been transformed so that our three rooms are sectioned off with a locked door, and the other end, which Ma has taken to calling the east wing (you'd think this was a bloody manor house), has been made into four small rooms and the bathroom, with another two guest rooms on the main floor where one of the old reception rooms had been. The library room is now the parlour for the guests, and the dining-room as I said before, is now for them as well.

Ma says if things go well, we may look at also renovating the stables into a series of rooms.

And it seems now the war is over, and with all the men coming home, work and industry is wanted by not just the men, but women who have become used to the money they earned while our men were away. And it's mostly women who work the tobacco fields, as they are willing to work for less than men.

I must admit it's kind of exciting having all this change and newness around, and I'm glad the small amount I earn from Fraser's keeps me and Violet without having to depend upon Ma's help more than we do.

Ianto is making noises about how I should get more involved in either the guest house or the farm, and of the two I think I'd rather muck around in the dirt than smile and curtsey for guests. I do enough of that sort of thing at the hardware store. And if I were here, I'd be closer to Violet.

She's not getting much better and coughs all the time. It's worse in the summer I've noticed, when the damp night air sets in. Couple of times I've thought maybe she was going to come down with pneumonia, but the spells pass.

I've had her in to see the doctor, and he's talking about sending her out to Toronto to Sick Kids for tests. He says it's likely she's asthmatic. But of course, these things cost money, and I have no idea how I'll pay for all this, but then it's not as if I can just say, sorry, can't afford it, kid will have to suffer. Maybe die. How is it health, especially for children, is only for the well-heeled?

So, this has left me to think that either I'm going to have find myself a husband who is well-heeled or find a way to heel my shoes myself.

In the few moments I find for myself I've been tending the old roses on the property that Da had cared for, originally planted by the first Cotters. Hard work, but I'm enjoying rescuing beauty from dereliction.

Ma thinks it's idle work, but secretly I think she's pleased I'm doing this.

Lettie: Wolves at the Window

She has been in hospital for such a very long time, she thinks. They let Panda come to stay with her when the darkness of her room and being all alone became scary and lonely and made her cry like the sissy baby she's become, not even the comfort of Ma's lipstick kiss in her palm. But that's ended, and now she watches from her metal crib—she's too grown-up for a crib—as the lady doctor with the funny name and Ma and Uncle whisper as though she's not there, or won't understand, using words like *recovery*, and *safety*, and *danger*, along with bigger words she doesn't understand, things like *imyunsistem*, and *hemraj* and *skaartishoo*.

"But you do realize," the doctor says, glancing her way, "she'll have to be constantly monitored. At the first sign of bleeding you bring her right back."

"Of course," Ma says. "But you honestly think she'll recover better at home at this point?"

"She's been here so long I think it would do her good to take her home. It's very likely she'll rest better, recover faster. Just so long as you're aware of the risks. And you of course have my phone numbers, day or night. Don't be afraid to call."

I think we're going home, Panda says, and she nods,

hugging him tightly. He smells all auntieseptik from the bath they gave him, but she doesn't mind. She's used to the smell now, has come to know it means the *Uglies* lurking everywhere are kept away because of it.

The lady doctor gets up from the chair and smiles as she walks over to the crib and reaches over Panda to ruffle her hair, says, "You take care, okay? If all goes well I won't have to see you for a week."

She nods up at the doctor's smiling face, smiles back, thinking it will be sad not to see that face, hear that kind voice, but also relieved 'cause it will mean she's going home and can get back to the Rose Guardian who has been left to care for the Pussywillows in their Kleenex box, and Trixie and Greenie and Gran and all the others back at home. She wants to lie in bed in the evening and look out her window where the leaves of the maple shiver in the breeze, where moonlight swims in the dark of the night creating the stream that leads to the Golden Sea and Over There.

After the doctor leaves, Ma helps her into her special red cardigan, the one Gran knit with all the twisty ropey bits down the front, and the leather knotted buttons. When Uncle scoops her up in his arms, smelling of spices and Brylcreem, she watches Ma stuff bottles of pills into her purse. Ma turns toward her. There are tears in her eyes, her mouth all quivery. She looks as if she's going to say something, swallows and looks down instead and pats Uncle's arm.

They walk through the halls of the hospital, nurses and people waving and smiling as she leaves. She feels like a princess, or at least someone important. When finally at the car, Uncle scoots her onto the front seat and he slides in beside her behind the steering wheel while Ma folds herself in on the other side. She feels like the fig in the newton and clutches Panda even tighter.

All the long ride home she can hardly believe she's going back to her own place, her own room, her own things, where she can watch the staff in the guest house and kitchen, the workers in the fields, have lunch with Mrs. Hamilton and be extra careful quiet when Gran's having a nap.

By the time she hears the tires crunch on the gravel of the drive, her throat is hurting and it's hard to swallow. She doesn't want to complain and wreck this wonderful homecoming. She's afraid they'll send her back to the hopital.

Uncle carries her up the stairs to her room, Ma and Gran clucking behind like the hens they keep.

"Can I bring her something to drink?" Gran asks, and Ma replies, "Just water. The doctor said just clear fluids until we're sure she's healing. There's a risk because of the chicken pox."

"But she's not contagious?"

"Do you really think they'd let her come home if she were?"

"No. No, of course not. I'll go fetch a pitcher of water for her."

She wants to ask what contagious means. And chicken pox. Does that mean she's at risk of growing feathers and her arms becoming wings? But her throat hurts too much so she just lets Ma fuss and strip away her lovely cardigan and her shoes and her socks and help her slide under the sheets and the quilt and the blanket with the wide satin binding that she likes to rub against her lips while she's going to sleep.

Ma makes sure she's propped up on lots of pillows, the stiff foam ones, not the wonderfully squishy feather ones cause the feather ones make her sneeze and her breathing get all like cobwebs.

And at long last all the fussing and cooing and peering at her face has ended. There's a jug of ice water with a glass on a tray beside her bed, beads like dew collecting on the outside and trickling, like tears, down to the tray where a puddle forms. The door is left open half way so she can have some quiet, and a tinkling, clanging bell she can shake if she needs something and so she won't have to yell and hurt her throat some more. A vase of Ma's very best roses sits there, the white ones, spilling perfume and care into the room. There have been kisses placed on brow and cheeks and hands. And now the noises below have settled and there's only the dancing light in the maple outside her window where a squirrel is shaking its tail at something and rattling out a warning.

"I'm home," she whispers to Panda.

We're home, he says. *Sleep.*

"But my throat hurts and there's stuff I have to keep swallowing."

It's okay. Just sleep.

And she does, closing her eyes to the soft light and the clean smells and the noises of home like a heartbeat under your ear when you're scared in the night.

Except now the noises shift and it's her own heart she hears thudding, skittering, and she knows there's danger 'cause she can hear the Darkies hissing from the corners. There at the window shadows thrash and at first, she thinks there is a storm and the maple's branches are tossing in the wind, but then she looks again, gulps and flinches from the pain of it, and realizes the Rose Guardian must have sent the Darkies to protect her because there are wolves scratching at the window. Huge wolves. With dripping fangs. And claws like daggers. And eyes like the ghostly light of mist in moonlight. Even Panda's afraid, because he isn't answering her. So, she grabs for the bell and it falls to the floor, and the wolves batter at the window. She's afraid the glass will break. She yells and the pain of that makes her reach for the glass and gulp some water to put out the fire the wolves have put in her throat. They're snarling. At any moment she knows the window will break and they'll leap in all muscle and power and hunger and tear her apart. She yells again, this time for Uncle who is bigger anyway and stronger and will be able to wrestle the wolves. The Darkies will help him, just like they did last time there was danger in her room, she knows. She opens her mouth to yell a third time but another pain burns in her belly, now up her throat which is like the coals of a fire. Too late she realizes what's happening, that the wolves are tearing her apart even from the other side of the glass, that they're going to kill her. As proof of that her body heaves and she lurches forward on hands and knees, her back arching with the force of what's coming up from her stomach. The wolves howl and snarl. She howls and snarls. There's blood on the bed. So much blood! And she can't stop throwing up.

Uncle, Uncle, help me. Panda!

And then: *They're coming. Help is coming.*

She hears the voice of the Rose Guardian, sees its face in the vase of roses at her bedside.

They're coming.

Preparing for Winter

After my students had gone, I spent the afternoon lost in painting. Against all my better judgement I'd abandoned the safe landscapes and flora still life, and returned to the series of paintings I'd come to call dreamscapes. I had no idea where these came from, these wild images, these compositions of dreams. This wasn't what Ayashe expected from me. It wasn't what any of the patrons of my art expected. I'd made a modest, regional name for myself painting the lonely wilderness of Manitoulin and that land between escarpment and shield country, what every Canadian laughing called rocks and trees and water. There was a quality to that work, yes, but from a creative perspective it left me hungry. And now I threw myself into a feast of scenes that left me feeling fevered.

But maybe, if I were honest with myself, I'd found the genesis of this explosion in my Ma's journals. They'd filled my nights, bedtime reading which did nothing to soothe the mind into an Orphean journey.

Did it matter?

I touched the three hundred pound, cold pressed paper on my painting glass as I always did before beginning the next phase, using the back of my hand as a moisture guide. Yesterday I'd thrown a series of warm washes onto this sheet, strobes of light that would throb through the composition I'd create in transparent washes and later ink.

Now I took my favourite graphite pencil and sketched in the bare bones of my main subjects. Detail wasn't necessary. I just needed to set guidelines for areas which I'd mask out by carefully laying in a barrier of dry paper, allowing the transparent washes to flow where I created channels of water, sometimes flooding, sometimes the merest whisper of dampness to tease out the cooler colour and allow it to thread, dissipate like spring rain on parched soil. And then wait for water to evaporate under controlled temperature in order to determine if there would be sedimentation which would create a granular effect, or separation which would cause one pigment to halo another. And then wait again until the paper was dry enough to introduce another wash or dry-brushing without it disappearing altogether into what I'd already laid in, resulting in mud where there should be transparent layers like cellophane.

I thought of the cellophane stained glass windows Ma and I created one Christmas. After Ben. When we were a strange family living in an ancestral home.

My hand faltered, breath caught.

If I left this wash now I'd ruin the painting.

Concentrate. Focus. Distill your thoughts to only this.

I touched my cheeks and felt the hectic flush there, let my hand steady and return to the paper where I was dropping sap green into a pool of water that lay over a dry, aureolin wash. The sap green was a transparent, staining pigment which would allow the rich warmth of the aureolin to shine through yet remain fixed in place when I later laid in transparent strokes of ultramarine and then semi-opaque textures of cerulean, allowing light to travel through the layers and create the illusion of the watery depths of a pool.

And so it went, hour upon hour, working quickly with pigment and clear brushes, sometimes sponging, sometimes letting the chemistry of the medium create interesting textures.

I was so lost in the piece I didn't hear Uncle Ianto until he said, "Ah, there. I was waiting for you to lift your brushes away."

I let out a breath and smiled, looked up at him where he stood in a corona of late afternoon sunlight.

"I don't like to ask," he said, "but I've a surfeit of spinach harvested and that demon food processor escapes me. Are you at a point you might lend a hand?"

I waggled my brushes in the jar of clear water I used to clean them, ran my fingers along the hairs and shaped the ends. "I could use a break, yes," and dropped the brushes handle-first into the mug with others.

"I see you've ignored your own good advice."

I looked down to the glass where the painting was forming, smiled ruefully. "I have."

"Your Ma's daughter."

He turned away before I could retort, and I hesitated, unwilling to accept the bait, wanting only to slide from these hours of creative immersion into another form of creativity. But I sat there, staring at what was forming on the paper, thinking about the genesis of inspiration, of how we often work memory and dream, even if that dream is nightmare, into what we create. And why should that anger me? Cause fear? Did I dare go too deeply into the well? Didn't I know by now that what stared up at me from those depths was merely myself? And perhaps there lay the true source of all my fears.

Had I made this silence between Ma and me into an impenetrable fortress? Was it my fault? But blame was always so easy to assign, to absolve oneself of, or immerse oneself.

I caught myself clenching and unclenching my fists, fled the studio and crossed into the garden. I lingered a moment near my legacy roses, checking for infestation, amazed they had taken so well and were in fact sending up a bounty of new shoots. Now that classes were over I had a bit more time to devote to the garden, and I'd taken care to assure this gift from Ma survived. It mattered; almost out of proportion it mattered. She'd created these for me. A convoluted demonstration of maternal care.

I bent and inhaled the rich perfume of one of the blooms.

Whispers behind me. I turned. At the edge of the woods where ferns grew, a girl in white blouse and red pedal pushers deked down into cover. My breath caught. Lettie? Here? Now? It had been two weeks since classes ended and I'd not seen any of my students since, little say any glimpse of this mysterious child who seemed to come and go from my property like some fey spirit.

I stepped toward the trees, caught myself when Uncle Ianto shouted from the porch, "The spinach will be a wilted mess by the time you get here!"

I looked over to where he hung out the screen door,

back to where I'd seen Lettie. Gone. As always. Why that should make me feel angry seemed illogical.

Trembling with a sense of foreboding I turned back to the house and entered the kitchen.

When Uncle Ianto said he had a surfeit of spinach he wasn't kidding.

"There now, see?" Uncle Ianto wrenched the bowl of the food processor. "The blasted infernal demon of a machine won't lock into place."

"I don't know how many times I have to show you." I crossed to where he wrangled, gently removed his hands, took off the lid, snapped the bowl in place, replaced the lid and smiled at him when it also snapped into place. "The bowl has to be secured first. I've told you."

"Ack, overly complex gadgetry is what it is."

I let go a breath, smiling at his harangue. "Just get yourself settled preparing the ingredients and I'll do the processing and freezing."

"Teamwork."

"That's right." I threw a few cloves of garlic into the bowl, lemon zest and juice, chilli pepper and let that process, then started packing spinach into that fragrant mess and let it all puree while dribbling in olive oil. It had been a summer ritual with us since moving here, the annual making of the green goo, as he'd come to call the pesto we'd created in order to deal with an abundant spinach harvest.

When the batch was ready I decanted it into a freezer container, sealed it, and began the process over again. We worked happily enough for awhile, Uncle Ianto only just keeping pace with me peeling garlic and prepping lemons.

When I returned from another trek to the freezer, Uncle Ianto said, "Reminds me of the farm."

"You used to make green goo?"

"Not that."

"Then what?"

"You know, this whole thing of bringing in the crop, of putting by for the winter. You surely remember."

"I remember pitting cherries and bottling."

"And lots more besides. It was our Ma who oversaw that until she became too crippled up to handle it, and then it was yours who took over."

"And the staff."

"Aye, the staff. Everyone helped, and the guests and hands all benefited."

"The cold cellar was huge." I remembered the cool darkness of that stone space, of the annual cleaning of the shelves and the smell of bleach and lye soap, of those same wooden shelves bowed with jars. What hadn't been used from the previous year was given to the poor of the area. There were jars put to boiling, and women sweating under headscarves, their faces florid.

"We had a lot of mouths to feed." He swept a feathery mass of garlic skins into the compost bowl. "And we none of us complained."

Or dared to, I thought. It was part of the cycle, and you were glad of produce to put by for the coming winter.

"Ma says the whole concept of the inn was her idea."

He looked up at me, eyes narrowing. "Did she now? And when was she imparting this bit of news to you?"

"I've been reading her journals."

"Ah." He looked down and seemed suddenly very interested in smashing a garlic bulb.

"You know what's in those journals?"

"I can guess."

"But you've never read them."

"They were private."

"You knew she kept a journal."

"I suspected."

"She never talked about them?"

"Una learned not to talk about much that really mattered. She used to. We used to share a great deal. But after she escaped from Bannon she built herself walls."

"She says in her journals it was bad with him."

"It was." He cut the ends off the lemon he'd zested and started to cut away the membrane.

"She says he beat her."

"Something fierce. I wanted to beat him myself, but I wasn't yet home from the war."

All this history, all this story which might have explained so much. What was it about this family that refused to discuss such things? "So why am I only learning of this now?"

"It was what your gran wanted."

"Whatever for?"

"Dirty laundry and all that."

"That's positively Victorian."

"Aye, well, she was."

"But even after Gran died? Why not discuss it then?"

He looked up from his work. "What possible good could that have done?"

I wrenched the lid of the processor into place, allowing my rising frustration to show. All these years. All this secrecy. It might have done a lot of good, I thought, explained some of what I'd never understood in Ma. And Uncle Ianto complicit, knowing all this, failing to give me the map I needed to navigate the waters of growing up with Ma, little say allowing Ma a way to scream out her frustrations. But maybe that's what her journals were, her great yawp over the roofs of the world.

Angry, even more confused, I continued to pulverize ingredients in preparation of the winter to come.

We ate that evening from some of what we'd put up, linguini and shrimp drowned in green goo. Despite Uncle Ianto's best efforts to calm my turbulence, I remained silent, thinking, brooding, trying to figure things out, to come to terms with the woman my Ma was, and the woman she had been.

Late in the evening I made my excuses and left Ianto to his television programs, making my slow and meandering way back to my studio and the paintings I needed to complete for my upcoming show. In the purple shadows I could swear I saw Lettie, slinking stealthily away from the open door of my studio. The light was on. I didn't remember leaving it on when I'd left that afternoon.

For a moment I thought to call out to her. But what was the point? She was like a wild thing, uncontrollable, unpredictable, an utter mystery I'd been unable to solve.

When I opened the door of my studio I felt like I'd been slammed in the gut. Suddenly there wasn't enough air. The ground tilted.

Across the floor, the glass, my chair, a confetti of colour lay in an explosion. In denial I bent and picked up one of the pieces, knew immediately what it was, and knew also my past days of work now lay destroyed in a storm of what could only be called vandalism. And the only explanation could be Lettie. I'd found evidence before of her rummaging through my portfolio, confiscating my work. But this? Why destroy my painting?

"Because I knew it would hurt you."

I whirled around, saw her standing on the other side of the screen door, cold as winter, implacable. And then she was gone. Just like that. All I could do was sink to my knees and cry my anger to the coming night.

Una: May 1947

Ianto put forward a proposal to Ma and me, and crazy as it sounded at first, it seems it's not so crazy after all. He said I should leave Fraser's, come work on the farm. He says he needs help managing the tobacco hands, but that first I need to work in the fields to understand what that's all about.

By doing that it would mean I'm on hand when Violet gets sick—when, not if, she gets sick, it would seem. And it means the farm end of our business gets cheap labour with a vested interest. He's also proposed getting a loan based on our property's equity, which would then throw up needed cash for some improvements. But he also said if some of that money sort of got diverted to pay for little Violet's medical expenses, it could be chalked up to wages for me.

It all seemed so hare-brained it had to work, because only crazy things in life ever seem to survive. Logic seems to play no part. At least that's what I think.

And so there went my brother Ianto with plan in hand, forecasts made, figures and facts, property appraisal and he just up and convinced the bank manager our property was worth a tidy sum, completely free and clear, and now we have a mortgage we'll have to pay back, but also cash to invest, and some personal hope for my baby girl's health.

That took about a month to put together, and during that time we were able to get an appointment with specialists at the Victoria Hospital for Sick Children. What a big city Toronto is! Cars everywhere. People everywhere. Everyone in a hurry. I felt as though I would suffocate. But what a beautiful building the hospital is, all red sandstone and arches, the whole thing dedicated to the health of children.

Violet has been assigned a team of doctors who will assess her over the next two weeks. It's meant I had to rent a room here so I could come in each day to see her. She's been scared and lonely, but I leave her with a big red lipstick kiss in her palm at the end of each day, and she curls her little fingers around that and watches so solemnly as I leave. I try very hard not to cry until I'm out of sight, with the hope she'll see I'm not afraid and so neither should she be.

Ianto has been very good and set up the practical things for me. We stay in touch by phone. I cannot begin to imagine what all this is going to cost, but he's told me not to worry, that it's all in hand. Let's just get Violet well.

Lettie: School

It's cool this morning as she and Ma walk down the lane to where they wait for the bus, the leaves of the maples all orange and red, sharp and bright against the blue of the sky. She hitches herself up on the bench in the shelter that's been built because now she's going to school and everyone agreed she'd need some protection against the Elements. She wonders if that means there are Uglies even out here, or maybe other Nasties who the Rose Guardian protects her from. Maybe the Elements are another family of Things who think it's funny to scare and hurt and mess things up.

She tucks Panda onto the bench against the wall.

"Why can't he come with me?" she asks Ma again, and again Ma says school is for girls and boys, not for Panda. "But why?"

"We've been over this," Ma says. "Panda will be waiting for you when you get home."

I will, Panda says. *And then we can go visit the Rose Guardian.*

She doesn't like it, but can't see a way around this. School is lonely, full of kids she doesn't know, and kids who are bigger than her, and they do things she can't figure out. Reading is one of them. Yesterday they were called up one by one to the teacher and had to stand beside her desk and say out loud what was on the pages. She'd stared and stared at the letters and had no idea what they meant, but other kids seemed to know so she listened to what they said when they stood beside the teacher, and it was something about a dog and a ball and the colour red, so she looked very carefully at the pictures 'cause it seemed to her the words likely were about the pictures, so that seemed a safe way to figure out what to say when her turn came.

But when she'd been called to read out loud the teacher didn't seem very happy with her, even though she told a really good story about how the dog played with the ball and how the Rose Guardian watched over him the way it did her, and all like that. At the end of the day there had been a note in an envelope she'd been told to bring home to Ma which she did, and that resulted in all the grownups talking about tutors and spending time with her in reading sessions. And then Ma all angry that all this extra time was going to be a bother because of work and being tired and all the things she had to take care of, and wasn't that what teachers were for—teaching children, and if Ma were to start doing that then shouldn't she get paid what teachers got paid?

She hadn't liked the sound of that, and when she went out to play before supper she asked the Rose Guardian about that. She looked deep into its golden centre, trying to see the face there and at last eyes and a mouth unfolded from the pollen and stamens and she heard it say, *"Reading is a magic. A powerful one. If you're to meet the Guardians from Over There you must learn this magic. You must become very good at it."*

So, she determined she would, because there was

nothing she wanted more than to finally sail the Golden Sea and cross to the purple towers of Over There. Because Over There she wouldn't be such a bother to everyone.

New Clothes

After twelve solid days of painting, forgetting to eat, voiding my bladder only when my heart started palpitating, it seemed prudent, so Uncle Ianto informed me from the comfort of his plush chair, to get out, please the gods, and do us all a favour. Didn't I want to get something new to wear to this almighty big friggin' deal of a show? Wasn't I fussing over how I'd present on camera?

And then, evil bastard that he could be, he fired the final salvo: "It is national television. Didn't Ayashe herself say so?"

Which of course had the desired effect. Which is why I now sat buckled into the Honda racing along 540 to Gore Bay. Racing. Indeed yes. 120 klicks? Really? I eased back on the pedal. I felt like I'd lost all control of myself. Beneath the achy-breaky idiot music of the local station filling the cavern of the car, there was the slap and swoosh of the wiper blades, the hum of tires on wet pavement, and the hiss of rain. White noise. Hypnotic. You could forget surrounded with sound like that. Forget a great deal. Forget about Lettie and where she'd gone, utterly disappeared from my life, her bouncing old-fashioned ringlets, those red pedal pushers she never seemed to change, her oh-so-serious face and questions, and her devastating ruination of my art. You could forget about those journals of Ma's I'd drowned in, discovering secrets and windows I had no idea existed, like stepping out the door to discover the land around you had changed overnight, as though your home, your life, had been picked up and tossed across a continent onto something utterly foreign, even frightening, absolutely bewildering.

You could forget you'd spent the past two decades, perhaps more, in denial, searching, grieving, wishing.

I glanced down at the speedometer. Oops.

Not exactly a smart move to forget speed on a slick day like this. Get it under control. Focus.

But at least the painting had gone well, images and compositions ballooning out of my confusion, pigment flowing along paths of water, ink hardening detail. Sheet after sheet of scenes from dreams, landscapes of memory, oceans of fantasy. I'd painted like I'd never painted before. Gone the tourist-approved Canadian landscape, the safe botanical illustrations. I'd stopped painting for an audience. And I had no idea how that audience would now respond to what I'd created out of complete abandonment of anything commercially appealing, painting only to give definition to my inner journey. Utterly selfish. Completely insular. And yet somehow, if I were honest, a cry, a call out into the world, an attempt at communication with people and memory and actions beyond withdrawal. It was like cutting windows in the box of my life. Letting in the light. Letting out the darkness.

Dear god, what was Ayashe going to think? She was expecting the usual Vi Cotter fare. Something safe.

Something saleable. Something from which she might expect a decent commission for her struggling gallery.

Even Uncle Ianto had expressed his concern about the direction I'd gone.

I made the long arc north out of Evansville along the Burpee Road, headed out onto the causeway that joined Indian Point to the main island at Campbell Bay. I could see the grey-green rise of the escarpment off to my left, shrouded in rain. Gorgeous country really. A land the rest of Ontario forgot, or disregarded, and I wondered how much of that had to do with the fact there was such a large Anishnabe population here. I'd discovered first-hand the kind of insidious racism Canadians practiced, part ignorance, part privilege, mostly lack of interaction which was the result of over a hundred years of isolation and a type of apartheid that could fly under international radar. All of it under the guise of God and good governance.

Maybe I'd see if David were free for lunch when I was done shopping? Maybe.

At long last I made the turn north into Gore Bay on 540B. I swung into the PetroCan, topped up the gas, and swiped my debit card, punched in appropriate numbers. When I slid back into the driver's seat there was Lettie, sitting in the passenger seat. My heart gave a lurch, and I stuttered out an exclamation, demanding to know where she'd come from, why she was in my car, where were her parents. How the hell did she get all the way out here to Gore Bay? And as usual she shrugged, mumbled something about having been there in the back all along.

Had she? A stow-away? How is it I hadn't seen her?

"But, Lettie, you can't keep doing this sort of thing.

Just showing up. People are going to worry about you. I'm going to get into trouble."

She looked at me then, an old soul in a tiny body. "You know that's not true."

"But...." What was the point? What good had it done to try to find her information in my database? What had any of my local inquiries garnered? And to report her existence to Family Services seemed ridiculous in light of the fact I had nothing beyond her given name, no background, nothing. Reporting this lost child was like reporting a phantom. I could hear it all again in my head:

You say there's a missing child, Ms. Cotter?

Yes. Her name is Lettie.

Lettie....

That's all I have.

And how old is she?

I don't know. I'd say around seven.

And what association have you had with her?

She's been attending my art classes.

Is she a student?

Yes. Well, sort of.

What do you mean, sort of?

Well, she just sort of showed up.

So, she's not an enrolled student?

No.

Have you checked with your neighbours?

Yes. That's why I'm calling you. No one seems to know anything about her, or even heard of her.

Is she staying with you?

No. She just comes and goes?

Does she appear to be suffering any harm? Bruises, malnourishment—

No, no, nothing like that.

So, she's not with you now. Does she come at a regular time?

Well, not now, no. She did when I was teaching. But now she just sort of shows up.

So, no given time or schedule?

No. Like I said. She just shows up. Day or night.

Well, I'm afraid, Ms. Cotter, without something more substantial, and because there have been no other reports, there's not much I can do. I could perhaps have the OPP look into this, perhaps surveil the area—

No, no. Never mind.

And that was that. I'd hung up. Lettie continued to be a phantom in my life.

And now she was sitting in the passenger seat of my car. Dry. Healthy. Just this ineffable sorrow and searching spilling from her like the scent of old roses and memory.

Resigned, I said to her, "I'm going shopping. For something to wear. You can come if you like."

She nodded. I turned out of the gas station onto the main drag of Gore Bay, parked, gave Lettie my umbrella and walked with her along Meredith to the upstart wee boutique clothier that had opened up in the past two years. I shooed Lettie in ahead of me and shook out the umbrella, collapsed it and scooted through the door. Robert and Greg, the owners, were perched behind the cash desk and grinned when I walked in.

"Hey, sweetie," Greg said, raising his bowl of a cup to me. "We just brewed some really great coffee. Want one? You look half-drowned."

"Well it is raining some out there, in case you hadn't noticed. And yes, I'd kill for a cup."

Robert slid off the stool and set about preparing coffee, the silent support of the duo.

"You shopping or visiting?" he asked.

"A little of both. Can't do one without the other here."

He handed me the coffee. Neither one remarked about my young friend, and I left it that way. The fewer questions asked the better, given I had no answers. I took a big gulp of the coffee which was great, as Greg had said, set it down on one of the ubiquitous side tables and motioned for Lettie to sit, dumped my gear beside her and gestured to her to avail herself of the coffee. Didn't seem like such a stupid thing to do, to offer a child coffee. Lord knows I'd had my share of it on corn flakes as a kid.

"So, what are you looking for today?" Robert asked, tucking my arm under his and steering me toward some of the displays.

"I have a show coming up—"

"You hear that, Greg—"

"And I'll need something for that, probably basic black—"

"A little black dress."

"Or trousers—"

"Or dress." He pulled out a simple black sheath. "With the right accessories you'd be dynamite in this."

"Hmmm, me and my hips, yeah, and a lot of spandex."

"You could work it, woman."

"I don't want to work anything during that opening, except staying alert and charming, which will be hard enough. Let's say you show me a number in a pair of trousers and maybe a bit of a bling of top, maybe three-quarter sleeves, no darts or waist or anything like that."

"So, a black sack. You are truly no fun."

"I'm sixty. I'm done with fun. Oh, and I'll need something a little more boho but not too out there for an interview I have to do."

"Now she says an interview! You hear that, Greg?"

"I hear. By whom are you being interviewed?"

Oh god. Here it came. "CBC."

Robert's mouth hung open, the lines around his eyes crinkling up. He looked like a sparkler. "You don't say."

"I do."

"Must feel very gratifying and a bit scary," Greg said, selecting skirts and shirts and tees. I noticed there was a definite lack of trousers.

"All that. Yes."

"Well come, sweetie. I'll get you all set up in a dressing room and Greg and I will ferry clothes to you. Don't you worry about a thing."

"I suppose I should feel some alarm at the thought of two men dressing me."

They looked at each other and burst out laughing. Greg pushed some of the curls out of my eyes. "Vi, you are very dear to us, but you know very well you're the wrong flavour."

We laughed. I looked askance at Lettie, hoping this was all just a bit beyond her, and let Robert guide me to one of the curtained cubicles. The fellows certainly knew how to set up a dressing room, complete with divan, lots of mirrors, soft light. Why they decided to settle on Manitoulin I had no idea. They were better suited to some southern urban vibe. But they had adapted beautifully really, combining local talent with some of the more eccentric pret a porter available.

First up was a pencil skirt and tunic shirt with a peplum, which from the front made me look like a failed umbrella, and from the back, dear god, was my ass really that broad?

"Well?" Robert asked.

I flung open the curtain, struck a pose and muttered, "You have got to be kidding."

From across the room Lettie scowled. If a child thought it was ugly, then it was ugly.

Greg smiled and crossed his arms. "I see your point. Maybe not."

"Maybe? There's no question." And I tore the curtain back into place and tried on the next offering: a sleeveless baby-doll dress that only served to make me look like a crone who was miraculously with child. I didn't even bother to indulge the fellows with a look.

And so it went, a frustration of fabric, the fellows considering, Lettie sending censure. I wrapped a dressing gown around myself and slumped onto the divan which was draped with rejects.

"You decent?" Greg asked through the curtain.

"Yes."

He pulled back the fabric and hung several garments on the hook. "I think these might work."

"That's what you said about the last four offerings."

"Now, Vi. Give them a chance."

"I'm about ready to give up."

"No, no. Not yet. Honestly, I think we've found the perfect match for you."

Unwilling to shred his good grace, I nodded. He retreated, and once again I disrobed and attempted the fashionable. The formal offering was a pearl grey dress of simple A-line cut, gathered into a yoke at the bustline and delicately embroidered with beading and thread in a tonal variation of the fabric, employing First Nations motifs. It had simple three-quarter sleeves. Very elegant. Very understated. I actually looked like someone of substance. I turned to look at the breadth of my bottom and was pleased to find it agreeably disguised.

"Well, I never," I said.

"Good?" Greg asked through the curtain.

"Good."

"Well, let us see," Robert said, and slid open the curtain. "Oh, my, Vi. You look lovely."

I grinned. So, did Lettie. "Thanks to you two." I fingered the beautiful embroidery. "That just leaves something for the interview."

"The trousers and tunic we just gave you are by the same local designer."

Pleased, I retreated behind the curtain, tried on the next offering, found it equally perfect and stepped out to show the fellows and Lettie.

Who was not in the chair. I pushed past Greg and Robert. No Lettie.

"Where did she go?" I asked.

"Who?" Robert said.

"Lettie."

"Who?"

"The girl! The little girl who was sitting right there!" And I pointed to the chair where my bag and umbrella were still stowed. I stepped out further into the store, looking around displays. By now I'd drawn the attention of two young women near the door, pawing tees.

"What little girl?" Greg asked. "There was no little girl."

"There was! Of course, there was! I came in with her. She was sitting right there!"

The girls bent to one another, whispering, likely some disparaging comments about seniors losing their crackers.

"Vi, sweetie—"

The girls burst into laughter.

"This isn't funny!" I pushed back to the dressing room, flung out of new togs and into old, and shoved my new acquisitions at Greg. "Ring these through. Hurry. I have to find her."

Greg threw Robert a glance. I caught the concern there, the beginning of alarm. Whatever was the matter with the pair of them? How could they not have noticed Lettie? I made a gesture of haste and Greg moved to the till.

"Are you feeling okay, Vi?" Robert asked, guiding me forward as though I were some frail old woman.

"Of course, I'm bloody okay. I just need to find Lettie is all." Yet it occurred to me I needn't be so alarmed. Lettie was always appearing and disappearing at whim, seemingly hale and hearty. Maybe she'd gone back to the car? I said that.

"Maybe she stayed in the car?" Robert said.

"No, no, she's likely gone back to the car. Not stayed there."

Greg handed me my bill and I passed over my debit card without glancing at the amount, which is what I should have done were I paying attention. But we often overlook the signposts along the journey of our life, and thus find ourselves lost.

I punched in numbers, hit okay, fidgeting, worrying. Where the hell had she got to? When I flung out into the street, rain was coming fast and hard, and I was drenched and gasping within moments. Lettie was nowhere to be seen, the street deserted but for a few shoppers seeking shelter under awnings and in doorways. Even at the height of the shopping week you couldn't call Meredith a hustling avenue of commerce, so you would have thought locating one small girl in bright red pedal pushers an easy target.

It was then I latched onto Robert's thought—she was in the car. She had to be in the car. Clutching that thought I pelted to my bland little Honda and flung my purchases inside, scooched into the driver's seat and found myself alone in a bubble, the rain thundering on the roof and sheeting down the windows. Gone. Just gone. And for some reason her presence today shredded all my carefully stitched artifices. My tent turned out to be flimsy after all. I hung onto the steering wheel as though it might anchor me. The tears came then, hot and fast, great gulps heaving my throat.

From somewhere beyond someone said, "Call David. He'll know what to do." And then there were strong, gentle hands tugging me from my anchor, the sound of rain hissing all around me. Quiet then. An office chair under my rump, a towel on my head and a coffee in my hands. I sipped. Sugar. There was sugar in the coffee. I decided I liked that, drew a long, shuddering breath, sipped again, and again, until the cup was empty and still clutched in my hands.

David then, crouched into my field of vision, worry there, his lips moving. "Vi. Hey. What's going on?"

I looked at that face I knew so well and felt if I spoke I'd never be able to stop, never be able to contain all the tears there were yet to shed, never be able to come back from the place that would take me. So, I shrugged instead.

"You want to go home?"

I nodded. Meldrum Bay. Uncle Ianto. The gulls crying at the dock. Yes, I wanted to go home, over there at the other end of the island where things were safe, where I knew my world, and the world at large didn't intrude.

The concept of Violet getting well doesn't exist, it seems. I've been told this asthma is something she will live with the rest of her life, that there will be new drugs to help, that I will have to make a lot of adjustments in her life to prevent allergies from triggering.

I near came to a full-blown hysterical fit when I saw her after one battery of allergy tests. She's such a little thing, and they used her like a pin-cushion. One hundred and seven needles down her little back, her arms. And she cried. Of course she cried. I would have cried. But I was so proud of her because she didn't make much noise at all, just those huge tears streaming down her little face.

And then of course she went into an attack and couldn't breathe, and there was oxygen and nurses and doctors flying around, and I got pushed out into the corridor where I was told to wait. And I waited and waited while carts and machines and people bashed into and out of that door where my girl was faring who knew how well? And I wanted so badly to have someone, some shoulder, to lean on, to break down and cry, because I could do nothing, felt so helpless.

Finally, after what seemed hours—I think it was

hours—one of the doctors brought me a cup of coffee and sat down beside me and we talked. It was then I learned my baby girl had died. But they brought her back. He said what a little fighter she is.

Such bald statements. I didn't know how to react. I didn't know if I should mourn. Or celebrate. Or all of it all at once, which would be just too much emotion for one person to put out, like a stove with too much coal, overheating, and boom, there you go, explosion and fire and mess everywhere.

So bank the coals, I decided, let it all out in small amounts like letting steam off a pressure cooker, and so I answered the doctor with small words, small gestures, keeping the engine of my thoughts and emotions in check, all the while wanting to bash through that door and scoop up my little girl, cuddle her, whisper cooing noises to her that it would be okay, that Ma is here and loves her.

And it was then, in the middle of these thoughts the doctor explained to me some of the effects of asthma, and how I would have to change Violet's world in order to help her control this problem with her lungs, not just physical things, but emotional ones as well. He told me I had to give her stability and order and structure, and there in his comments were underscored judgements about husbands who are fathers and how no household can be secure without the strength of a man to balance the softness and emotion of a woman.

I near came to smacking him then I felt such a burst of anger, his saving of my daughter's life quite aside. I wanted to shout at him about my knowledge of the safety and security of a home with a husband, how fists are neither safe nor secure, and what did he, in his privileged world know about trying to survive, especially as a woman.

I think, though, I learned in that moment about the advantage in keeping your mouth shut at certain times. I wanted Violet to get the best care. And in order for her to have that, I needed to make sure this man not only liked my girl, but liked me.

It would seem women have been prostituting themselves from the beginning, because too often it's the most powerful card we have to play. So, who is the wiser, I wonder, the woman for using her sexuality to achieve her purpose, or the man for requiring that specific coinage?

Lettie: Deceptions

She clutches her rosemary tightly in her fist, tucked under her chin, the covers pulled around her head like a hood. Gran has told her the rosemary will protect her, will give her the ability to talk to God. She's not quite sure how it is a string of white beads can do that, but Gran is old and knows about these things. It's a kind of Gran magic, she's sure. And Gran seems to share it with Father Murphy. They certainly do seem to talk about those sorts of things a lot, about how water can turn to wine, and the intersection of the saints, and the Blessed Vurjun Mary—with that thought she sketches the holy magic gesture to keep away evil spirits. She's not sure why every time Mary's name is spoken she's supposed to touch her head, her heart and her shoulders, how it is Mary's name is powerful enough to make the bad things wake up and pay attention. If Mary's supposed to be so good and stuff, then why do the bad things stir? Wouldn't it make more sense for them to lurk about and then hide when Mary's name is spoken? It's not like they're actually ever going to see Mary. She knows she never gets to see Mary except for those statues and paintings, but they're not real, not like a living person.

One bead....

Hail Mary, full of grace.
Our Lord is with thee....

But now she's not sure, because maybe those things are real. Panda talks to her. So does the Rose Guardian. So why not that really big statue of Mary in the church? Or the picture of Our Lady of the Secret Heart that hangs over her bed since she's come home from hopital?

Maybe it's just that it's been so long since she's been here, and the house smells funny, auntispekic like the hopital, and that can't be good.

Blessed art thou among women,
and blessed is the fruit of thy loom, Jesus....

It's those doctors, she's sure, who have sent Ma and Uncle home with their secret poisons. Even Panda doesn't smell right. They've given him a poison bath, she knows.

Holy Mary, Ma of God,
pray for us sinners....

"Are you hurt?" she whispers to Panda.

Not now. But it did when they pinned my ears to the line.

She could just imagine what torture that would have been, water streaming from Panda's feet as he was hung by his ears to dry in the sun.

They're cruel, cruel horrible beasts, she thinks, to do such a thing to a perfectly innocent Panda. And if they'd do that to Panda, what more would they do to her?

now and at the hour of our death.
Amen.

She feels the beads of the rosemary in her palm, five groups of ten Hailmarys, then the bigger bead where you pause for the Lord's Prayer or a Glorybee.

Why did Gran think she needed help to talk to God? She didn't know why she needed help, or why she'd want to talk to God when she had Panda and the Rose Guardian. But maybe the Rose Guardian was God, 'cause Gran said the rosemary was the garland of roses which was the Blessed Vurjun Mary's. Or maybe that made the Rose Guardian a kind of a saint?

Next bead....

Hail Mary, full of grace.

Our Lord is with thee....

And why did she have to use all these special prayers? Why couldn't she just talk? And what happened when she fell asleep in the middle of the rosemary praying? Did that mean she'd be punished 'cause she didn't finish sending up her prayers?

Blessed art thou among women,

and blessed is the fruit of thy loom, Jesus....

But maybe tomorrow she would sneak outside and sit in the rose garden and ask the Rose Guardian about all this. He would know. She's sure he will.

Holy Mary, Ma of God,

pray for us sinners....

Why was she a sinner? Gran had said it was because she was human and even worse a woman who was the cause of all mankind's suffering, all 'cause the first woman ate an apple. But she liked apples, picked them up from the windfall in the orchard, loved the way the juice ran down her chin and squirted in her mouth all tart and sweet and crunchy at the same time.

now and at the hour of our death.

Amen.

Next bead.

And she was walking out in the garden, her feet wet

with dew, and the Rose Guardian blinking long golden lashes furred with pollen. She curtsied to him, and he nodded back, white petals gleaming in the moonlight.

Are you a god? she asked.

Not a god, no.

Then what are you?

I am your guardian, your spirit guide.

So, you're like the Holy Spirit?

More like the garden spirit.

But Gran says that's stuff and nonsense, and pagan evil.

Gran is allowed to think what she will.

But are you evil?

Have I ever done anything evil?

No.

Then our actions speak for what we are.

And then her palms hurt as if there were nails being driven into them, and when she looked she was in her bed and a snake glowed with a sickly green light in her hands, coiled and slithering. It was poison, she knew. Gran had gotten this from the doctors. Why else give it to her when she came home from the hopital?

She screamed and tore at its segmented body, ripping it apart, throwing it across the room where each tiny glowing green part of it scattered and rolled and hissed across the floor only to become a smaller snake. And so now instead of one there were fifty-nine.

How to kill them? How to stop all those snakes? She could smash them with one of her big wooden blocks, bang, bang, crunch, crunch. On went the lamp by her bed. She hung over the edge and pulled out the box from the nightstand, leapt up and out fully armed, growling and crazed with fear....

Only to find the snakes were just the beads of her rosemary. All pulled apart. All without magic. Just beads that in the light were pale and white.

She sank to the edge of the bed and turned out the light and there they were again, all glowing and eerie and evil looking. With a jolt of fear she again turned on the light, and there were only beads. Off and they glowed. On. Beads. Off. Glowing. On. Beads. Off. Glowing.

Summoning her courage, she stepped across the slick surface of the wooden floor, toed one of the beads and watched it roll and turn lazily in a circle and come to rest beside another.

Just a bead. A glowing one. But just a bead.

She went back to her bed, hoisted herself up and sat on the edge, legs dangling.

Not everything was what it appeared. Not everything was exactly as explained.

Very good, she heard the Rose Guardian say.

A Semblance of Normality

There had been a great deal of fuss, as far as I was concerned, about my state of health little say mind. Seems a person couldn't have a wee bit of a meltdown without everyone getting into an almighty hullabaloo about it.

"I really think you should see a counsellor, Vi," David said. He'd been a constant figure around the house this past week, driving out every evening after work to make sure neither Ianto nor I needed anything.

I looked out over the garden to the shoreline, watching light spark and shatter on the waves. A cool breeze tightened my skin, the air damp, portending rain. *Summer's waning*, I thought. Winter to come. Cold and bleak, a landscape of white and frigid pastels. A loon wailed then, and already I felt the loss of them, fully prepared to mourn. Easy to mourn for a bird. Not so for a Ma long-absent before her death.

"Afraid I'm going batshit crazy, are you?" I said finally, realizing David expected an answer, that the atmosphere on the porch was one of anticipation.

"Vi—"

"I know, I know, I'm being difficult."

"Your Ma's daughter," Ianto muttered.

I shot him a glance, wishing him to silence. He sat

there in his cushioned chair, a reminder of secrets, of sorrow; of conflict and crisis.

"Look," I said. "I've just been working too hard. There's been a lot to deal with. Ma's death. The whole bequest thing. Her journals. This show. Now the threat of CBC looming."

"Exactly why I think you might need some help in organizing yourself, in prioritizing," David said. I looked back over to him, unable to see him clearly in the gloaming, only his eyes which caught the sunset and seemed preternaturally bright. One could wax poetic, when looking at him, about native lore and power, and therein lay another tragedy.

"No," I said, softly, firmly, careful not to strike too strident a tone.

"Vi—"

"Give it a rest, David. Honestly, I'm okay. I just need to slow down, get some sleep, drink less coffee." So much for diplomacy.

"You might as well talk to her as an ass," Ianto said.

"Oh, so now I'm an ass." That shot it. No retreating from this confrontation now I'd created it.

"Vi—" But I wasn't giving David any quarter, which was simply gruesome of me, unfair, loathsome. He was only trying to help. Always caught in the artillery fire that was my family, and my nature.

"Then at least let me make an appointment for you to see your GP. Might not hurt to have a checkup."

"Give you some hormones," Ianto muttered.

"Oh, so it's a *female* thing is it?" I snarled. "I am more than my ovaries. If I had any."

He made a derisive sound.

"You're not helping," David said, firing a warning look at Ianto. "Shit, what is it about you Cotters?"

"The fighting Irish," I said, trying to gentle my tone, to alleviate David's growing frustration. How was it I'd always had to defend him from my family? From me? "Okay, yes, you're probably right. I should see my doctor. At least do the annual thing."

He let go a long, shuddering breath, bowed his head. "Good. That's at least a start." He looked back up at me. "You know I'll call you tomorrow to make sure you've made the appointment."

I smiled. "Yep. I get that."

"Good. And I'm going to tax you further. I think it would do you good to come to one of our healing circles."

"Healing circle?" Ianto said, derision sharp as a blade in his voice. "What—all that banging of drums and wailing and smoke?"

I watched David master anger, saw the bulge at his jaw and knew he chewed on retorts that could utterly destroy my uncle.

"I think it would do you good to be in a loving community who come together to find a path to healing."

"But I—"

"You don't even need to say anything. Sometimes being quiet is as effective as hollering."

Oh, brilliant man! Lovely David. Always had a way of firing sage salvos at multiple targets.

"Yes. Okay. I'll come, if for no other reason than to test the efficacy of Uncle Ianto's blood pressure medication."

"Harridan!"

"Curmudgeon!"

"Enough!" David rose to his feet. "Thank you both for dinner. I'll be back Friday to pick you up, Vi, and we'll head out to Wiki. Make sure Ianto has everything he'll need for overnight, because the circle will be late and you'll be staying."

I nodded and walked him to the door and out onto the porch where I wrapped my arms around that broad back, felt the tight muscles there, his tension, and once again let regret wash over me. I was the cause of his distress, had the remarkable knack of making this very calm, reasonable man into ball of conflict. We had been happy together. So briefly. All shattered under the Cotter conflicts.

I watched as he climbed into the cab of his pickup, listened to the roar of the motor, loud in this quiet bay where neighbours were distant and careful of disturbing the ebb and flow of things older than memory. I could still hear the engine long after the red tail lights winked out amid the cedars of my lane.

It was easy to linger there in the twilight, to settle on the steps after Ianto had gone in, to let tension spill out across the lawn and slide into water. My loon wailed. I shivered, breath caught. Tears were cool on my face and I let them come without sobs, without dissolving into the darkness descending. I should go in. I should check on Ianto, make sure he was okay. But there was that horizon on the water, an incendiary sky. You could almost imagine another world in those gold and crimson clouds.

I wondered if Ma had sat like this on the back porch of that old stone house, if she'd tried to weave together a new fabric from which to cut her life when her old had frayed. I wanted to hate her. Wanted still to feed that rage that had been fuel and focus for most of my life. But how could I now? I'd read what was in those journals, saw the life revealed through the cracks of her writing. Not easy. Not fair. What was fair? Life happened. You dealt with it or you didn't, and Ma certainly did—deal with it. How she survived all that and gone on to carve out the life she had truly required recognition, at least my grudging respect. I could see now why the staff of her greenhouses had been courteous, if cautious.

And realizing that required recognition that I too had changed, evolved, stepped through a doorway into a new understanding. That landscape wasn't comfortable. It required a continuation of that adaptation, and after sixty years of nurturing granite epaulettes I felt as though if I shed them I'd float away, lose my moorings, perhaps sail off into that distant horizon. Over there.

I wiped my cheeks, inhaled to steady myself and rose from the stairs to check on Ianto.

March 1950

Seems I've found need to return to my journal, a need which surprises me. Why is it so easy to organize and speak my thoughts here, and yet when confronted with family or friends I'm as mute as stone? It's not as if I don't long for companionship. Just that I'm sure they'll find much to ridicule in the thoughts and hopes of a woman. And I'm tired of being marginalized, tired of passion being confused with illogic, of ambition interpreted as arrogance.

So, here's the thing. The farm's done very well these past few years, but I've been at Ianto about diversifying our crop. Right now we have most of the thousand acres under tobacco, and there's pressure to start ripping out hedgerows so we can plant even more. And now there's movement toward newer and supposedly better varieties the buyers prefer and for which they'll pay premium rates, and none of that encompasses the trend toward companies buying out the farms and putting the land under corporate agriculture. I'm not sure about the wisdom of that, but then I've been called old-fashioned.

Those modern initiatives sound very promising, but I keep worrying about what happens when we have a bad year, when the weather doesn't cooperate—when does the weather cooperate with a farmer?—and about needing more and more expensive fertilizers dumped on the fields because we're not rotating crops the way we used to. I mean, isn't weather and a one-crop farm part of the reason we Cotters fled Ireland in the first place? All those fields of flax and potatoes, neither suited to the constant wet of that green isle, so that when weather ceased providential cooperation, and disease crept through the soil along with the rot, didn't matter how old your ancestral estate might be, how puffed your pedigree, a debtor was a debtor and all left was to sell up and migrate with the thousands of others in search of hope and the promise of relief.

Or what about the disaster of the Prairies in the 30s? All that land under one crop, year after year until the rains failed and crops failed and the land blew away, buried houses, buried people, buried hope and livelihood.

And here we are preparing to repeat the same disaster. Too many acres under one crop. If one summer should follow another and another with too much rain, or not enough, or blight or infestation, on what will we fall back? To where would we migrate this time if we lose our land and this home which has now moved into the domain of ancestral?

So, I've suggested we keep our woodlot, because that throws up periodic income if we manage it well; we need to also consider if we make sure the trees remain that provide cover for the owls and hawks that keep the rats and mice in the fields under control. I can't help but feel the hedgerows do the same thing. I wonder if using what's there in nature to our benefit, instead of manufacturing a replacement, isn't the wiser course. Not a popular view these days. I'm being told I have to pay attention to modern technologies. Well, sure, but you don't adopt a practice, or product, or machine simply because it's modern. You study it, consider all the ramifications of its use as best you're able, and then decide whether it's a prudent addition or not. I'm told I'm thinking irrationally, like a woman. Oh, for fuck's sake!

Ma would faint if she saw what I've just written. Ladies don't say such things.

Guess I'm not much of a lady.

I've gone on to suggest we should revitalize the old fruit orchards. There are so many varieties of apples, cherries, pears, plums and even peaches. The trees have been let go. But all that's needed is a good hard pruning and we'd be back in business. I've even suggested we consider investing in greenhouses dedicated to growing spring bedding plants. Seems to me with everyone making a little more money these days, they're also fixing up their places and planting ornamental gardens, and that means nursery plants. So why shouldn't we be part of that growing trend? That's one, at least, that isn't creating a one-crop farm, or one basket for all our eggs.

Most of this, however, has been ridiculed by the new hired foreman Ianto has brought in to manage the farm, a Mr. Macafferty thank you very much. When I asked why I needed help, Ma said women didn't go around being managers, especially not of farms. That was a man's work, and I didn't want to spoil my prospects for landing a new husband, did I?

Land a new husband? What talk is that? You'd think I was reeling in a fish, getting ready to net him and gaff him and serve him up on a bed of greens with a side of Escoffier sauce.

I've had a husband. Didn't like how that tasted, thanks. Violet and I will do just fine without.

And why the hell can't a woman manage a farm?

The other side of the Cotter enterprise remains brisk. Throughout the year the guest house is full on weekends, and come the good weather we book throughout the week. It's nigh unto impossible for a guest to stay with us without a reservation. That's mostly thanks to the clever cook Ma brought aboard some years ago. And the people who travel here from Toronto and Hamilton seem to like a taste of farm life with an edge of elegance, have taken to punting around on the Grand River which borders our property. Ianto had a private dock built and we keep a few small boats in good nick.

Violet, amid all this industry, has fared pretty well. I refuse to coddle her, as I won't see her made an invalid in spirit. Bad enough we have to shelter her from so much in the way of the physical. Ianto says I'm too hard on the child, and Ma disapproves of most everything I do, so there's no redemption there.

I'm concerned how Violet will manage come the fall when she starts school. She doesn't have playmates, being as we're out here. She plays well enough on her own, talking to the stuffed toys with which Ianto showers her. Well, she'll have to learn to cope. We all do.

Flesh of My Flesh

Da's gone. That's what Ma says. He's gone and isn't coming back. Good riddance to bad rubbish, says Gran. Uncle says he'll thrash Da if he shows up again.

She watches Ma sitting at the kitchen table, a cup of tea clutched in her hands, steam spiralling in front of her face. She watches Ma's lips tremble, sees her wince and touch the purple smear beside her mouth. But the purple stays, and a tear slides down beside her nose. Ma sets the cup down, fetches a hankie from her apron and swipes away the wet.

All the grownups are hetted up. Gran tells Uncle not to get his knickers in a knot and settle down, there'll be no thrashing in this house. We're all to go about our business. She'll not have an uproar.

"There are guests who have paid good money for rooms in this house, and I'll not have it broadcast about that we're bog-trotting Irish who speak with our fists instead of our heads."

"For the love of God, Ma," Uncle says. "You might show a little compassion for what your daughter's experienced."

"Aye, well maybe if she'd watch that impertinent mouth of hers, and not go mooning after every swain that walks down our lane, we might not be having rows and bruises at the breakfast now would we?"

There's a crash and Ma's chair topples over. She's standing now, shaking, her face like snow it's so white. "So, I asked for this, did I?"

"No woman asks to be beaten, but every woman knows well enough if we show enough of the lamb instead of the lion we can make putty of men."

"Are you listening to the shite your flinging about this kitchen? Are you really hearing yourself?" And with that Ma bangs out the kitchen door to the porch, down the stairs, and off across the lawn.

Gran makes a face, all pinched and fierce, moves around the table but Uncle catches her arm, his blue eyes like pools of water in the light from the window. It's like you could swim in them.

"I wouldn't, Ma."

Gran tries to shake her arm free, but Uncle holds tight, his other hand now reaching for Gran's shoulder, gently, and he turns her toward him, looking at her with such fierce attention it's like you can hear his thoughts.

"Ma, let her go. You know you had no right to say the things you did. She'll be sore at you for awhile, with justification, but let it be. That excuse of a man is gone now, and we need to think about her and the child. This is no time for laying blame. This is a time for us to close around our own and take care. If I know anything about anything he'll be back. He'll try to find a way to hurt her, whether with fists or other means remains to be seen. But he'll be back. And we must be vigilant."

Gran glares at Uncle. "So, what, we're to be prisoners on our own land?"

"Hardly that. But we must protect what's ours."

She shook him off then. "Leave off." Beyond the room there was the tread of footsteps on the stairs, one of the maids calling out a greeting to a guest. "Do what you must. But keep this scandal from our patrons. I'll not go seeking charity when ruin is brought down upon us." With that she pushed through the doorway and closed it solidly.

Uncle let go of a long, shaky breath then, shook his head and looked out the kitchen window. "Are you ready for school?"

She looks down at her toast. "Yes, Uncle."

"I'll be driving you in and picking you up."

"I'm not taking the bus?"

"Not for the next wee while. I'll be letting the principal know." He looks over at her and she doesn't know what to make of the look on his face, whether it's anger or hurt or worry or what. "You're not to take the bus, do you hear? And you're not to take a ride with anyone but me or your ma. You understand?"

"Yes, Uncle." But she doesn't.

"It's important you do."

Why, she wonders, but is too afraid to ask, because she wants to ask about Da, about why Ma has bruises and why she's so mad and sad, and why Gran's so hetted up. So instead she stuffs the last of the toast into her mouth, gulps the last of her milk otherwise she'll hear about the sinful waste of food when there are children dying somewhere in the world for want of what's on her table, picks up her satchel and looks up at Uncle.

"Off with you then," he says and snatches up his keys as he follows her out the door. He tells her to get in the car while he has a word with Ma. She does that. As she's sitting there on the cold leather she's wishing she had Panda. But she's not allowed to take Panda to school. He has to stay home and be lonely.

But I'm always with you.

She looks around. That wasn't Panda. Panda didn't talk to her from so far away.

No, he can't.

"Who are you?" she whispers, a little afraid, looking around. There's a white rose on the seat beside her. She doesn't remember it being there before.

Tuck me in your satchel, in your handkerchief.

"Rose Guardian?"

Of course.

"But how did you—"

Doesn't matter. Quick. Uncle's coming.

She unbuckles her satchel and slides the rose into a space between the canvas and her scribblers. The driver door creaks open and Uncle throws himself behind the steering wheel, kicks at pedals and pushes and pulls at keys and knobs, then the engine roars to life and she feels a little thrill of fear because the car is like a beast growling to life. It backfires like a shotgun exploding the air. She ducks down. Uncle laughs and pats her leg.

"Gave you a start, did it?"

She nods.

He kicks again at pedals and shoves the stick thing, and they lurch into motion with another crack of sound and Uncle laughing, his blue eyes alight with mischief and just the joy of doing.

"It will be a'right. Don't you worry. We'll get you to school and you'll soak up all they give you, and we'll fetch you home safe and sound. Mind your manners. Don't accept a ride from anyone but me or your ma. D'you hear?"

"Yes."

"If your da shows up you're to go right to the principal's office and wait for me there. Under no circumstances are you to go with him."

"Has Da done something wrong?"

"Aye, he has. Beyond pardon."

"So, is he not my da anymore?"

"True enough, that. A sinful man he's that."

And she wonders about Uncle's mad and what Da could have done that would make it so that not even Jesus nor Mary nor any of the saints could forgive him. And if she were not to go with him he must be very dangerous.

When Uncle pulls into the school drive and stops at the big front doors she's feeling very alone, very frightened. She fingers the side of her satchel where the Rose Guardian hides. Uncle pats her head and shoos her out the door. She pauses at the school entrance, looks back, sees Uncle watching her. He gestures for her to get a move on just as the final bell rings and with a start she heaves on the door and enters the big, echoing space of the school. It smells of stinky shoes and antiskeptik and bodies.

Kids are still putting away sweaters and jackets in the cloak room when she pounds in. Margaret shoves her and Kevin with the freckles laughs and rolls his eyes. They start chanting *fatty, fatty, two-by-four, couldn't get in the bathroom door....* She hangs her orange and green sweater on her peg and walks around Margaret and Kevin who are now into *so she did it on the floor, licked it up and did some more....*

She wants to yell at them, but remembers the last time she did that they'd come at her with fists and feet and when Sister Angelica found them on the schoolyard pavement she was blamed for the ruckus. So, she keeps her head down, her tears for later, and pushes her way into the classroom.

For the rest of the day she struggles with sums and the songs they say about vowels and numbers, recites the lines she memorized for memory work and the hope of winning a bar and that book on Sister Angelica's desk. She hangs near the school doors when recess is called, and sits near the back of the auditorium when it's lunch and eats bologna and mustard sandwiches wrapped in wax paper from a red tartan lunch pail of tin. Ma had given her milk in her flask from their own cows, and it's still cold when she gulps it down. She can feel it spilling down her throat and cooling her tummy.

Mostly, though, she stays away from the other kids who all say things they mean to be nasty about her ma and her, and how her da isn't really her da, and what can you expect from Irish who think they're all grand what with their farm and their guest house, and all these new-fangled ideas that are sure to bring ruin and regret.

In class she stares out the window at the trees beyond, and beyond that to the horizon where clouds float. If she's lucky she'll be able to see the spires of Over There, maybe later on the ships that are coming to take her away to their land of music and birds and where the Rose Guardian rules with kindness and wisdom, to where das and mas don't fight and grans smile, and uncles don't look so worried all the time.

When finally four o'clock comes she goes with the others to the cloak room and shoves her arms into her green and orange sweater, flings her satchel over her shoulder and amid the screeches and rough-housing of the other children bumps her way to the main foyer and the principal's office where she's supposed to wait for Uncle.

But Margaret and Kevin find her, their smiles like the wolves who had come to her bedroom window that awful night, and now the Rose Guardian whispers to her *run! Run! RUN!* And she does, slamming out the doors and round the corner of the school and pushes her way into the scratchy cover of the cedar hedge.

She waits there for what seems forever, listening, listening, her breath catching like cobwebs in her throat. Then there's quiet, just the sounds of traffic and people walking by, and in awhile the sound of her name being called, and so it must be Uncle, and she shoves her way out of the hedge and finds instead of Uncle her da, and now she knows she's in danger all over again, because Uncle and Ma and Gran have all said how she's not to be with Da, and so he must be a very bad and horrible person. But as much as Rose Guardian tells her to move, to hide, to get away, she stands there frozen, the way the lambs do before slaughtering, and Da's face works through emotions so fast and horribly she doesn't know what to think or do, and this is Da, but he is trouble, and when he takes her arm in the huge paw of his hand and closes the steel of his fingers she feels the rawness of what he feels. And she is afraid.

"You're coming home with me," he says.

She cries out. The Rose Guardian is shouting at her to *run, run, get away* and her breath is now coming in short gasps and it is hard to get enough air into her lungs.

"I can't believe you're afraid of me!" he says, all in a groan and there are tears in his eyes. He shakes her then, tightens his grip on her arm and now it hurts. "But you are my daughter as if you were flesh of my flesh. Don't let them tell you otherwise. Come. We'll be happy. You'll have toys and the best of everything."

But she knows it can only be a lie. She's seen Ma with bruises and heard what Gran and Uncle had said about the getting of them, and now Da has his hand closed so tightly around her arm she thinks he'll snap it in two and there just isn't enough air. She gasps, feels her face wet with tears that are gushing and then she's up in the air and in Da's arms and he's pounding across the lawn of the school toward his car.

Then a roar, a shout and the words: *Let her alone, you bastard!* Then more hands, strong hands, and she's being torn in two, pulled and yanked between two men, and her screams filling up her mouth with not enough air to push the sound out and into the world to tell them all to let her go, she is afraid, she hurts, she can't breathe, she just wants to go home, go home, go home....

And then home, and evening light in her window, and the smell of roses in the garden.

We must be more careful next time, she hears Rose Guardian say.

She nods and closes her eyes on the sunset, exhausted, wanting sleep, to forget, to go somewhere safe. She pulls the covers up around her head, makes a hood of them, clutches Panda and the rosemary, and begins to recite the first of her prayers.

An Invasion of Intimacy

Dr. Frost was on the phone when I finally found the right entrance for the extended services of our community hospital. There was no receptionist, just an unkempt hallway with worn plastic chairs. I'd looked up and down the hall, checking doors to see if I was mistaken about the absence of a receptionist. Nope. A janitor's cupboard, a turn to the right where there was a door that took you into the hospital proper. I walked back down the hall through dim and a strobing fluorescent light, past the door a bit so I could read the sign. Dr. Frost. Yep, this was it. Door wide open. A middle-aged woman sat behind a tired, metal desk, an old black phone receiver to her ear. There were teetering mountains of files on her desk, one open in front of her, stacked atop sheaves of print-outs—people still used continuous stationary?

I glanced in the other direction, thinking there might be a wall with a door, surely something that indicated a doctor's office beyond. But no. Just more space which was sparsely appointed: a worn shag rug which might have been green, a chrome and upholstered sofa that looked like either a pack of dogs or a clowder of cats had used it for nesting material, and two armchairs I'm sure were sprung.

I looked back at the woman. She swivelled in her chair, waving me off with the curt comment: "I'm on the phone." *No kidding.* "I'll be with you in a moment." *I'll just bet you will.*

This was not an auspicious start. I could already feel my feet beating a retreat to my car. But I reined myself in, nodded to her, turned and planted my butt into one of the molded plastic chairs in the hall. I could hear her going on about one of her patients. Or was that clients? Zoloft had been prescribed. Responding well. Two children, single mother. Needed to connect to social services. Perhaps a home assessment done. *Really? Did this doctor not realize I could hear every word?*

In the next ten minutes I learned more than I cared about her client, knew all her personal history, all the medications that had been tried, how many times she'd been into and out of psychiatric evaluation.

My bum was getting numb and I found myself fidgeting, then pacing. That my anger was reaching ignition caused some anxiety.

At twenty minutes I'd given up trying to control anger and frustration, was convincing myself I'd be doing us all a favour if I just bolted.

By thirty minutes I heaved my bag over my shoulder and was heading for the exit when Dr. Frost finally stood in her doorway, all smiles and apologies and waved me in. I stared at her for a moment, chewing on retorts, instead just grunted an acknowledgement and entered the seedy space she called an office; then garnering a look of surprise from her, I closed the door firmly and definitely. The hell with my session being public broadcast.

That would be going in her notes, I was sure. She

gestured me to the sofa. I took one of the chairs. Yep, it was sprung. I was sure my ass was on the floor. Again, she looked surprised, and I knew I'd set off a whole system of analysis and biases.

Uncooperative, confrontational, anti-social....

Yeah, well, bite me.

She wound a kitchen timer, set it on the coffee table in front of her. So, we're watching clocks. Tick Tock. "Hi, Vi. I understand you've been having some difficulty."

Oh, dear god, why had I ever agreed to this? "Apparently."

She waited. I wasn't responding to that stare, the way she looked over her reading glasses at me, a cultivated attitude, I was sure, to appear professional, professorial. Maybe a smoking jacket and pipe? Too socially unacceptable. Finally, after I met her expectancy with the rebuff of my silence, she glanced down at her notes, said, "Your doctor prescribed Ramelteon. So, you have trouble sleeping?"

"Yes."

"To both?"

"Yes."

"Why do you have trouble sleeping?"

"Doesn't anyone over sixty?"

"Have you been under stress lately?"

"Not particularly. My Ma died. I have an art show coming up. I'm taking care of my elderly uncle who is a spirited handful." *I'm being visited by a little girl no one else seems to know anything about.* "You know, life"

She looked up again, aware her bait had been taken. "That's a lot to deal with."

I shrugged, unwilling to nibble further.

And so it went. Question. Evasion. It was easy to manipulate my responses to garner a specific response from her. I wondered, vaguely, if I weren't in fact exercising some sort of socio- or psychopathic tendencies? Was this how a monster was born? Someone just soaking up experience and knowledge until one day they toed that line, just a little, just enough to taste, until the next time and they'd taste some more so that they'd find themselves deep into alien territory and the path back to the other side of that line had all but disappeared.

"Let's get a family history then, shall we?"

"Sure."

"Parents?"

"Yes." *Like as if I was bloody hatched. Of course, I had parents.*

"They both still alive?"

"I just said my Ma died recently." *And clearly she wasn't really listening.*

She looked up over her glasses again, pulled out a mask of sympathy, uttering the words. I shrugged.

"Father?"

One, like most. "Also dead."

"Were you close?"

"With my father?"

"Both."

"Not particularly."

"Why was that?" Ah, there the hound is on the trail. Abuse? Dominance? A genetic predisposition to disorders?

"Why don't most children get along with their parents? Differences of opinion. Paradigm shifts. I dunno. Why not ask Socrates?" *You just fucking don't like their shit. Sacred trust shattered. Get the hell out of my life and my head.*

And so, our riposte and parry continued, and were I honest I was enjoying baiting her. How was my childhood? Was there violence? Stability or lack of? Reveal to me, Vi, why you're so screwed up.

It was a relief when that kitchen timer jangled. I was getting too old for this nonsense.

"So, Vi, would you like to set up another appointment?"

"Not really."

That garnered a raising of eyebrows and that look over the glasses again. She really needed that smoking jacket and pipe. "You feel comfortable without any follow up?"

"I'm a tough old bird. I can negotiate my path." *God, I sounded just like Ma!*

She nodded, scratched her pen across the yellow paper. Did the woman not even know how to use a tablet?

I rose, unwilling to engage in further discussion, and signalling an end to this charade. "Thank you for your time, Dr. Frost." And I stepped toward her, stuck out my hand in a gesture aimed at placation. Clearly caught off guard, she raised her hand to mine, shook it limply, gave me a matching smile, and I made sure to make my response firm and definite.

When I closed the door behind me, I knew she was still sitting on that ragtag sofa, staring.

The long drive home I berated myself for an arrogant wretch.

1950

So, it would seem Mr. Lord High And Mighty Macafferty thought it would be a good idea to revitalize the orchard. Huh. Imagine that. Took a hired foreman, a man, to figure that out? Couldn't possibly have come from some woman, because the female sex is incapable of comprehending the mechanisms of business. Same reason we were denied the vote. Look how that worked out.

So, we spent most of March in the freezing cold, pruning trees. Branches fell along with the snow. Day after day of saws and raw hands, tea lukewarm from a flask left too long out of doors. A soak in a tub of steaming water at night after Violet was snugged up under quilts, easing the ache and chill from my bones.

Ma's been minding Violet and the guests who frequent our little guest house, while Ianto and I have tended to the farm. I'm no good with the guests. Not much at small talk, the deference and charm that's required. Suppose if I were back in old Ireland I'd have been lousy in service. At least that's what Ma says. Not enough respect for people's stations, she says. *That,* to stations.

We've taken to hiring the vagrant men who wander through in search of work, and a meal, and the hope of a warm, dry place for the night. My idea. We pay them pittance, but we feed them well from kettles of soup at night, and bowls of boiled oats in the morning. Bread and onions for their break at noon. They sleep in the barns, warmed by the heat of hay and the cattle murmuring from stalls, and the warm musk of men wearied by hard labour in the fields.

Out of earshot of Macafferty, I've suggested to Ianto we turn the old horse stables into quarters for the labourers, given the success of the extra guest rooms created from the carriage house. I've run some numbers, and figure we can maximize the labour force we're using if we house them. That will allow us to retain workers, thereby ensuring people who are familiar with our needs and routines, build a bit of loyalty and reduce turn-over and training of new staff by offering up bread and board as part of their employment. And by using the converted stables as quarters for labour instead of paying guests, we won't have to invest in renovations of such high spec, and we'll reclaim yet another building on the farm and turn it to good use.

Ianto thinks it's a good idea, and together we've told Ma what we're going to do, leaving her little room for protest. But my biggest triumph is the plan has been presented to Macafferty for implementation, who is none too pleased to be carrying out the designs of someone younger, and worse, female. Digest that, Mr. High And Mighty Macafferty. Pity such a handsome fellow has to be such a boor.

In what little spare time I have, I continue to rescue the flower beds on the grounds, and have given new life to the old roses planted by the first Cotters. I was surprised to find the canes responded so well to harsh pruning and a little help from the fish heads and bones from our Friday dinners. I've had blooms of bounty, and in the evenings the fragrance is enough to make you giddy.

Violet, I've noticed, has taken to playing near the roses.

August 1950

Looks to be our best harvest yet, if the weather holds out. Always at the mercy of the weather. We cut back on tobacco this spring, sewed some of the fields in a good hay crop to let the soil rest and rejuvenate, and plan in three years, when the hay won't be worth cutting anymore, to pasture sheep. I figured the flock would manure the fields, and we could diversify by selling off fleeces, and perhaps lambs for meat. We brought in our first ewes in early summer, just twenty to start, and spent the money for a good ram, and a jenny to warn off dogs and coyotes. And, of course, the obligatory collie we've named Spark, comes of a good bitch who is a prime herding dog. Spark, it seems, has taken to herding not only the flock, but Violet. Funny how that dog knows when I call Violet. He sets to gently nudging her along until he's herded her to me, and of course Violet has come to think of this as a game and shrieks with laughter. It's good to see her laughing.

Even Macafferty has cracked a smile watching Spark work his flock and little mistress. Could be I've misjudged the man.

September 1950

Dinner and a movie in town. I've agreed to that with Macafferty. How many times can I say no?

Violet has started school. She's being bussed into Paris, as the small rural school has been closed. Ma, Ianto, or I see her on and off. She doesn't like it much. She's wanted to take one of her stuffed toys with her, but I've told her no, that big girls don't need that sort of thing, that she must be brave and strong. Best to teach her early girls need to be stronger than their male counterparts, because we have larger battles and greater risks. I don't want her to grow up a crier.

November 1950

The weather was providential, and the harvest munificent. We've made enough to make a serious dent in what we owe the bank.

Macafferty and I have done dinners and movies, and more besides. It's the more I should be concerned with, I think. I'd sworn off men, their sweet words, a drug to numb the brain, but now I've given up caution and opened the gates to invasion. A heart made a fortress is cold comfort.

I would talk to Ma about this, but she has no idea how to scale the walls of silence, to discuss things no proper woman would discuss, not even behind hands with flushing cheeks and the wisdom of old wives. It's been made very clear to me women of repute don't discuss what happens between the sheets, between the legs, between the boards that bookend our lives.

So that would leave my brother. And although I love

Ianto unquestionably, without reservation, he, also, is a man, and cannot begin to understand what it is a woman vouchsafes a lover. What she risks. What the opening of her heart and her sex can set into motion.

What I fear has indeed been set into motion.

Oh God, what will I do?

December 10, 1950

I asked Ma for the recipe. She refused.

December 20, 1950

I asked Macafferty would he do right by me, and after a long pause he said yes. Under condition. He wants our own home to be away from the farm and guest house. Privacy, he says. A place Violet and our child can grow up without the influence of Ianto and Ma. We Cotters, apparently, have provincial notions, and he is a modern man.

But, apparently, doing right does not extend to financing my divorce from Conner Bannon, who last heard from was drinking his way to oblivion. So, there is to be a ruse, says Macafferty, a small holiday for the two of us and the fiction of a private ceremony, rings exchanged for the sake of appearances and to make an honest woman of me. What does that make him?

And it's Christmas. I will put on a game face for the season, if for no other reason than to make it pleasant for Violet.

Balor

She's not supposed to be outside at night, she knows, and it's taken courage more than she thinks possible to gather up her picture in her satchel where the Pussywillow family live in the tissue-box house, and the white bloom from the Rose Guardian tucked beside it in the handkerchief. Panda's in her other arm. Her heart feels like its bouncing around inside her chest as she crosses the hall in the river of moonlight. Danger enough in that because she could get swept away in the current at any moment. But she doesn't, and now she's past Gran's door, and then Ma's, and last Uncle's, and she's at the head of the stairs—the servant's stairs Gran calls them. Are they servants?

Hurry, hurry, Panda says. *Hurry, hurry,* say the Pussywillow family. And she hurries down the stairs, feeling each tread beneath her feet, sliding heel to the edge and then down, one by one, carefully so as not to fall in the deep dark of the cave of the staircase, and then she's down into the kitchen and now the back porch where her wellies are stood side by each and cold on her feet when she slides into the them. There will be dew on the grass as heavy as rain. For a moment she pauses because she remembers Ma's warning that she must do everything possible to prevent the damp from getting into her lungs, so she sets down Panda and her satchel and stretches up and up, feels the soft-scratchy wool of her cardigan, jumps and pulls at the same time to unhook it, then yanks it over her arms and shoulders and does up the buttons from bottom to top to make sure she has them all lined up properly. The collar sits around her neck like a scarf.

That's good, says Panda. *That's good,* say the Pussywillow Family.

The satchel sits heavily on one shoulder when she again tucks Panda under her arm. She's careful to be quiet when she unbolts the door and pushes open the screen and lets both snick back into place. Now she's down four steps and out on the lawn where the moon makes the wet grass silver. She cuts a path across it like a small coracle on a moonlit sea, and heads to the rose gardens, past the red and the yellow and the pink where their perfume blankets her, and then to the tall shrub of kingly white blooms which are the Rose Guardian.

Kneel on me, says Panda.

"I won't," she whispers back, horrified at the idea of using him in such a way.

But the grass is wet and it's okay if I get wet, but not if you do.

And she understands the sense of that, aware the bottoms of her pyjamas are already wet and to invite the damp further up her legs would be to invite the cobwebs back into her lungs and the anger of Ma and the worry of Uncle. So, she gives Panda a big squeeze for a hug and a smooch on his nose and lays him out carefully beside the garden, kneels on his tummy and bows deeply to the Rose Guardian who then wakes up and shivers. Drops of dew spill down the Guardian's leaves like ribbons of silver, and one huge bloom nods toward her. As always she feels a thrill shiver down her skin when the golden eyes within the white petals stare at her, pollen thick on lashes, and a voice in her head: *What brings you out in the soft of this night?*

She carefully pulls the Pussywillow family out of her satchel, arranges their front door to face the Rose Guardian, and then sets her picture on the ground in front of her. She can hear the Pussywillow family stir, feel their fear, hear Panda's sharpened breath. They're all afraid. She's drawn her dream.

The Beast King, says the Rose Guardian.

She sucks in a breath, the hairs on her arm stiff and prickling.

Balor!

What is this? she wonders. Balor? Is this the one-eyed and one-legged beast who steals her sleep and makes her afraid even into the promise of dawn?

Maker of Death, says the Rose Guardian, and they all feel the stillness of the night, the dangers that lurk beyond the gardens, out in the fields, sneaking and slithering in the byres with the cows, and the coops with the hens, and pounding the fairy rings round the fruit trees into dust.

She stares at her drawing, the dead in heaps at his gigantic foot, his eye now closed and death awaiting his awakening.

Do not awaken him! Balor!

Balor drawn in charcoal which is the death of trees, and in doing so a small defiance from her because she would make creation of this death, this destruction, this dream which has stalked her for days and weeks.

"What must I do?" she asks, and wishes she had not. Despite the dew she pulls Panda out from under her knees and clutches his damp body to her, feeling the familiar nap of his fur, his smell, his softness. Beside her she senses the Pussywillow Family scuttering in their house, hiding behind cardboard doors and under cardboard beds. Wise creatures. Hide.

You must wear the sacred rosemary the next time he comes for you.

"But it's broken."

But it's not.

And she feels the smooth, slick, glowing pearls against her skin, reaches to the neck of her pyjama top and finds them there, eerily pale and green in the night.

You have seen what the rosemary can become.

Snakes! But they must be evil because Sister Angelica said it was the snake in the Garden of Eden that made women fall and bear the weight of sin. So, all women were evil just as all snakes.

But the rosemary will save you. It will make you invisible in your time of greatest need.

A Dangerous History

It wasn't until several days after my aborted immersion into counselling, Uncle Ianto made inquiries. He'd wandered out to my studio with a flask of tea, tottering unsteadily.

I could feel him bristling with questions, concerns. Sidelong, I watched him ease into the battered Windsor chair in the corner by the window. The light there was soft, tempered by shade from the woods that bordered this cleared bit of land by the bay. I heard the flask clunk on the side table. A groan. I looked again. Pain there in his face. I remembered him as a young man. He seemed to fill all the space around him. Both he and Ma.

I drifted my rigger through the umber puddle on my palette, stroked away the excess on the filthy excuse for a rag I kept near my work, and continued to feather twigs into the hair of my subject.

The need to talk swirled around him like pigment in water, nebulous and uncertain until interfered with by the hand of the artist. I should be kind. I should exercise compassion. Ianto was no longer a young man, staggering at times under the cruelty of age and a failing heart. But I was my Ma's daughter, and

I cultivated my anger carefully. I knew what this visit meant.

And then the first salvo.

"So, you think you're fit enough to continue to work."

Good ranging shot. Let's see how near the mark we can come with that. Too near, if I were honest, which I didn't wish. Truth be told I'd manipulated that counsellor. It was so easy to spin those answers, to delude her into thinking I was holding it all together. But I was, wasn't I? No more hysterics. I'd learned to take Lettie's visits for what they were. To accept that she came and she went and I had no control whatever over her. She just disappeared that day at the shop. Gone in the rain. Left me soaking wet, weeping, and terrified about her well-being. Somehow responsible. And no one could help. It was as if she didn't exist, had not entered the shop with me, had not fingered clothes and made inquiries and prattled on about her own enchanted world.

But then I still had come no closer to finding out anything about her. She just showed up on the grounds, in my studio, talking to the Cotter roses, confiscating pencil and paper and sketching scenes like distant memories.

"You've not been right since you started reading your Ma's journals."

That gave me pause. And I did, looked up at him. "What?"

"She's still in your head, stirring you up. I'm not sure it's a good idea you finish reading those things."

"How would you know what's in those journals?"

His mouth became a rigid line, and then: "I don't."

"Then how can you know they'd bother me? Maybe

they aren't much more than gardening journals, for all you know." But they weren't, were they? This was Ma exposed, raw, uncensored, the mycorrhiza of her existence.

"Then why would she leave gardening journals to you?"

"Maybe to teach me something, to share something."

"The only thing she ever wanted to teach you was how to build armour."

"How can you say that? She was your sister."

"And I loved her. But I also knew her."

"Which means what?" He pushed the hair out of his eyes, and I noticed how rheumy they were, how tired. I should stop baiting him. I should be kind.

"Una had to control her world, and I can't help but feel this is her way, from the grave, to be sure she wins this last battle."

Apparently, I wasn't going to be kind. "You're talking nonsense."

"Am I now?"

I dumped the rigger into the jar of water. "Okay, I'll admit Ma had a way of trying to haul me back onto the rails she'd laid for me. But to think her bequeathal of journals was meant to somehow manipulate me after her death makes no sense. To what end?"

"Because she liked to mix up people's heads. It gave her a sense of control, of power. Do unto others before they do unto you."

I looked away from him, unable to deal with the complexity of his sorrow. Truth to tell I was having enough difficulty with my own. I wanted to weep for loss. But what had I lost? Ma and I hadn't exchanged anything in years. I'd done my grieving. I'd learned to live without her. And any loss I might feel was for things never known, never done. Regret. Not loss. My true regret and loss was Ben, but that was a relationship long-ago drowned under the weight of Ma's manipulation. I was not his sister, she'd told him, not really, only half, and half of anything was inferior. The words never said, but always there.

It was then I realized for my uncle the loss of his sister was profoundly different.

I looked back at him, at that face so like brittle photos in the cigar boxes where Ma kept our family history. He had a strong, square jaw, jowled now with pale, parchment skin; apple cheeks that flushed when he was excited; a large nose like the profile of some Romanesque cameo. And those blue Cotter eyes, duller now than they had been. It was the male version of Ma's face I looked at. Same temper. Different demeanour. With Ianto it was all summer squalls and sparking sunshine. But I'd always known he was the bulwark.

"I tried to protect you," he said at last. "Even though I watched Una go to heroic lengths to ensure your well-being, I tried to protect you. That's all I'm doing now."

I reached over and touched the back of his hand where he gripped his cup of tea. He watched me intently, an apprising stare I had to meet.

"When you went away I was glad," he said. "I thought, finally, you'd be free to live your own life. I wanted to see you and David happy. Wanted you to have what Una never managed to achieve, what she always drove away before it could hurt her, and being hurt all the same because of the vacuum left in the wake of her destruction.

"It was the hardest thing I ever did when I told her

I was coming to live with you on the island. She told me I'd betrayed her, betrayed all the Cotters had tried to build. That I was encouraging you in your defiance.

"I wanted her to understand. But all she knew was the hurt of it. And I'm worried now she's retaliating through her journals. You don't need to know what's in them. Best leave the past where it is and deal with the living."

Leave the past where it is. There was wisdom in that. If I'd heed it. But the past was like a scab for me, something that itched and needed picking, knowing full well there would be blood and an open wound.

I'd lied to that counsellor. I'd lied artfully and well. Painted a picture of illusion not unlike what lay drying beside me, what filled this studio. Artifice. And so wasn't I very much Una Cotter's daughter? She painted with plants, created a growing, burgeoning Eden around her while still courting the serpent. Unable to stop herself. Without the will or ability to prevent the disaster she always invited.

"I'll pack them away," I said, knowing full well I only meant to ease Ianto's worry. Another lie. A benevolent one. But a lie nonetheless, landmine planted for future detonation. "It's all okay."

I removed my hand and picked up the flask, poured him another cup of tea. "Here, look what I've been doing. A whole new direction." And I steered him into discussion of my new tack in artistic vision, the possible risk in losing my current client-base, but the freedom there was in this new venture. All the while I knew I had to go carefully. There was crisis yet to come.

1951

May

A son is born. A father is cast out.

June

Ianto fired Macafferty the day Bennet was born, threw his raggedy ass out the door for showing up soused as a pig with his floozie on his arm. Ianto tells me Macafferty has sworn to sue for partnership in the business, says he was promised a share in Cotter Farm.

Bluff and bluster.

But it occurs to me to be afraid. I remember fists underscoring demands, whether rational or not, from Conner, and Macafferty more than once hinted at similar outcomes, although the reality remained latent.

How is it a woman should live in fear of violence, of every decency and rationality extended to men but denied a woman? Why is that? I begin to feel communion with our sheep, a ewe guarded by the all-important ram. Is that what this thing of love is in actuality? Is this all about breeding rights? Am I a ewe to be coveted and bred? And if I don't bleat piteously enough, prettily enough, does that give the ram license to ram? Are my body and my mind not my own?

Ma would indicate this is fact. She says a woman of propriety knows her place. Apparently that place is silence. Obedience. Open your legs to the rut. Carry his seed to term. Raise it. Accept it and all it entails. Whatever pleasure we find must be in the things small, insignificant. Don't draw notice.

But I wasn't the one to throw out Macafferty. It was Ianto who charged in. Somehow that makes it all okay, that my brother should have taken charge, that I didn't.

I've been moved back to the great stone house and its pioneer acres. Again. This may become habit, it would seem. Ma has said little, only watched me with what I take for silent despair. I was out in the garden the other day with Bennet in a basket beside me, Violet off in the roses, when Ma joined me where I tied tomato vines. All was quiet between us for awhile, and then she said: "You need a father for those children."

I felt my breath catch, anger and surprise quick on my tongue, suppressed, and finally, civilly, I managed: "Ianto and I did well without."

August

Apparently not to be this thing of peace. Macafferty tried to kidnap the children. Broad daylight. Their own garden where they played among my roses. He came with one of his cronies. We were right there! What am I to do? Ianto came running from the field when he heard the racket, a couple of the hands in tow, and set upon Macafferty like a man deranged.

There was enough muscle to make Macafferty think twice, and Ianto wasn't backing down, threatened to kill Macafferty if he showed up again. Probably not a smart move, but I am grateful.

At Ianto's insistence we called the police, who were sympathetic but made it clear they could do little. This was a domestic dispute. The father had a right to see his children, and the law would not look kindly upon a single mother, one estranged from her husband. I imagine the law would look even less favourably upon a mother who bore children out of wedlock.

So, we've opted instead for vigilance.

The children were scratched harshly when they ran through the roses. I've determined to start selecting for thornless canes.

October

I heard rumour Macafferty's hired on as a Great Lakes merchant sailor. Maybe he'll drown.

Poor Banished Children of Eve

She has watched the seasons slide through colour. Red, orange, gold. Soft yellow sunlight. Woodsmoke like a grey haze where it drifts over fields harvested and brown. Winter then, and white and blue and pink at sunrise and sunset, and the woodlot purple in the distance. Everything pale and still. The Rose Guardian an iron-coloured crown of thorns, a voice like cloud and whispers, there in the closet of her thoughts.

She's practiced with the rosemary, said the magic prayers, knows them by rote now as easily as she knows how to read and write and do sums which are perfect. It's important to get it all perfect. Only then can she conquer Balor. Only then will the ships arrive from Over There and take her away to where there are no more worries, where they are all safe, and they laugh, and no need of guests in the house, and workers to plant and hoe and harvest. An end to Ma's anger, and Gran's tears, and Uncle's worry. A place the Pussywillow family can live without hiding in their tissue-box house.

And now spring and the pale colours like chalk on the board, pink and green too shy to hang heavily on branches and make deep shade. Pink in the canes of the Rose Guardian. Pink in the buds of the fruit trees. Pink on her nose in the damp, fresh air of morning where she waits again for the school bus.

She can hear a woodpecker drumming in the woods. Such a sharp, drilling sound. Over her head, in the umbrella of the willow, goldfinks trill and titter: *Are you there? Are you there?* And then she can hear the stuttering warning of an oriole: *my-i-i-i-i tre-e-e-e, my-i-i-i-i tre-e-e-e,* but the goldfinks ignore the brash, bold oriole and continue to call to one another: *Are you there? Are you there?*

I am here, she thinks. And the goldfinks answer. The Rose Guardian answers. They're all there in the morning sun of spring. A breeze stirs down the laneway, bringing the scent of roses. She touches her satchel where the gift from the Rose Guardian remains tucked in tissue. She touches the rosemary around her neck, pausing over the lump of each bead.

She looks down the road where it dips down through woods and rises up again to the fields of her farm. There's a dust cloud out there. Probably the bus coming, but she's not so sure when she hears the growl of an engine. Not her bus. Not the right sound. She watches down the road now more carefully, wondering if it's one of their neighbours' trucks, then sees it isn't. For a moment she sees a navy-blue car. Her heart kicks hard. She blinks. Not a car. A beast. Lurching and catapulting at speed up the hill, dust rolling like fire in its wake.

Run!

And she spins on her heel and starts to pound away from the one-leg, one-eye beast charging up the road toward her. Away. Away! *Away!* But it's no use. Balor is there, bounding beside her, now in front of her, the beast's horrible chest opening, gaping, now a cave and she's being drawn in, Balor's breath hot on her face *you're mine, you're mine, you're coming with me* and all she has is tears and fears and pleas to not take her, leave her be, she's not Balor's, not Balor's, not, not, not.

Use the rosemary!

Yes! She remembers now, and yanks the holy white beads over her head and throws them into the cave of Balor's chest, screaming, "Leave me be! Leave me be!" She watches as the rosemary flies apart, hissing, each part a snake, each snake a strike, and Balor's face white with shock as he sinks and slides down under the weight of the magic of the rosemary *to thee do we cry, poor banished children of Eve.*

To thee do we cry.

Poor banished children of Eve.

The Unspoken

From Meldrum Bay to Wiki was a drive of two hours, an astonishing fact that often baffled tourists. Manitoulin was an island, fergawdsakes. A freshwater island. How could it take so long to cross a freshwater island? As if the geographic distance and temporal fact were a deviance created by Haweaters to confound those from away.

I'd made that trek today, in grey overcast and muggy air, watching forest and water and rocks slide by. There had been that promise to David, one I couldn't break, because I'd broken enough promises to him over the years. One more, no matter how small, would be too many. So, it was I'd squirmed in the knowledge I would soon be part of a circle of people seeking healing, respite, closure; people I'd been convinced I would only insult with my own meagre whining. What were my hurts compared with theirs? And I'd also considered the fact I was an outsider, a descendant of the usurpers who had heaped such misery upon an unknowing society. But David, gentle soul, would have none of it. Be more positive, he'd said. That was my problem, he'd said.

And, in a way, he'd been right; because I'd expected it to, the entire experience had gone less than perfectly.

Standing on David's deck, looking out into maple and birch bush, I was convinced I'd embarrassed him, or worse, hurt him deeply. And what about poor Mary Nishkigwan there in the house? David had settled his mum, brought her tea, spoke to her softly while I'd looked on for a moment, feeling lost and disconnected, a pariah. Mary had only ever shown me kindness, let it be known her son was a good man and deserved happiness.

Didn't we all? Didn't Mary? Gawd, the things she'd said in the circle. All with patience, measuring out her life's story with careful words. Seeking acknowledgement, but never retribution. Seeking understanding, but never condemnation. Seeking closure, but never harm. Such grace.

In the face of that I'd felt small, petulant.

Because people didn't just walk out on sessions like that. People didn't just deliver another blow in a lifetime of blows, by turning your back, by tacitly saying with that action: *You aren't worth my time. My presence. My empathy.*

And especially not when one of the people speaking had been Mary Nishkigwan., She'd spoken sotto voce about the things that were horror. Memories of residential school. Memories of betrayal, and hurt, wounds both seen and not. An attempt to find a way to forgive, a path to peace. A warning against, and an explanation for, actions and behaviours that perpetrated despair.

And I'd walked out, drowning in unshed tears, my throat tight in an attempt to stop the words and the yelling that would start and not stop if I were to let go. And a knowledge that my pain was a paltry thing compared to Mary's.

Mary with whom I used to laugh when David and I were married. Mary who taught this stumbling pilgrim a few phrases in Anishinabek.

I'd stood there in the cool September sun, looking up to a sky like a Turner masterpiece. And cursed myself for an arrogant fool.

When finally the community centre spilled out the circle's people, I'd regained my composure and was leaning against the fender of David's pickup.

"I'm really sorry, Mary," I said when she reached me, shuffling behind her walker.

She didn't look up. Instead: "If you hang on to that knife long enough you'll have butchered everything."

Fair enough.

I opened the front passenger door for her, pulled out the stair, and helped her in while David stowed the walker, and shot me a few incendiary glances. It all seemed a little surreal surrounded by the chatter of people, the palpable emotion in the parking lot.

I slid into the cramped confines of the rear seat, buckled in, and tried to be the invisible cargo.

All the drive down to Beach Road, and David's house, we listened to Mary talk about the circle. How important it was. How now, after these years, she knew there was true healing going on. How there was hope.

The sky had closed over by the time we pulled into David's drive, mist rolling in off the bay. We did the whole disembarkation thing. Mary begged off, seeking a nap, and retreated to her room, leaving me standing there in David's living room with his anger banked.

"Tea before you go?"

Ah, so he really was furious. No invitation to stay for dinner, to linger. Just tea and go.

I nodded.

"I'll bring it out to the deck."

I glanced out the window to the drifting fog, nodded again, and stepped out the door. Through the screen, I could hear him say something to Mary, his footsteps, water running—he actually had water, unlike so many. After that were only the sounds of his movements.

I was waiting for David to say it, if not yelling from the kitchen where he made tea, then certainly when he joined me in the damp and mist. Which he did—join me, tea in hand, but with a neutral face, that mask he could bring down and hide his thoughts just as surely as any False Face mask. Wrong culture. Right analogy.

When he said nothing, only leaned over the railing, staring out to the bush, I gave up and admitted guilt. "So?" Which was about as close as any Cotter would come to an admission of guilt.

He gathered in a lungful of that fragrant, fecund air, but kept his attention on the waterline. "So?"

"No chastisement?"

He let out a grunt which might have been a laugh, or might have been a sob. "Oh, you'll do that well enough for yourself. But for what, I'm not sure."

I chewed on that, wanting to argue, wanting to vent and unburden myself of responsibility. *Don't be your Ma.* But it was so tempting to go on the offensive. And rather than step over that cliff, I chose to hang on, to grip the rail of David's deck, and try to let all that fury slide out and away into the mist. To borrow from David's gentle spirit. From his mother's grace.

So the sounds of the land settled around us. We

sipped tea. We watched steam spiral from our cups and our mouths, from the woods and the bay beyond which was curtained in grey. Chickadees piped in the trees, one and then two, three, four dropping in to inspect the platform feeder at the corner of the deck. They paid us no mind, hammering seed to break it open, and then doing it all over again.

"I'll have the new dock and boathouse finished before freeze-up," he said.

Where did that come from? "That's good, I guess."

"Then I can winter the *Gayaashk* here."

"There's no rush, you know."

"No. I know. But it does make sailing her a bit difficult when I have to drive to the other end of the island."

"I thought it was a good excuse to visit."

"It is. But then sailing gets forgotten."

"True that."

"Funny how that happens. You start out to do one thing and end up doing something completely different. All best intentions aside."

Ah, David. There it was.

I tossed the cold dregs of tea out into the scrubland he called a lawn. "You're a sneaky bastard, you know."

I caught the slightest twitch of a smile when I glanced at him sidelong. "Used to drive you insane."

"I'm sorry, David."

"I know." He turned to look at me. "And somewhere in your not too distant future, you have to learn to stop being sorry for living, for Una's shortcomings, for yourself. If you're at all honest with yourself, you'll realize the things you're bitter about, the things you miss, are the things that never happened. It's like saying you had a meal, you didn't starve, but you wished it had of been ahi tuna instead of tinned. You were lucky, Vi, and you can't see it. You keep clinging to the confused child. Let her go. In two years you'll be officially a senior citizen. Don't you think it's time you let her go?"

And that was too close, too much the surgeon's scalpel that could cut out the cancer. So, with the utmost care—because at this point if I made any movement that wasn't carefully considered, there was a fuse that was about to ignite—I set my cup on the rail, and said with precision, "Thanks for the tea, David. Please do let Mary know I left because of my problems, not hers." Turned on my heel and retreated from it all, and David, for the fortress I knew so well.

He didn't call after me. He didn't berate me for my continued bad manners, for my inability to talk about that gulf of turmoil I looked into every day since Ma died.

I slid into the driver's seat of my pickup, started the engine, and pointed myself to the other end of the island.

December 1960

So it's coming round to Christmas again, snow to the waist, a profit turned, and the mortgage gone. Nine years since last I wrote. Violet in high school. Bennet in primary. A strange and unorthodox family are we: a grandmother, an uncle, a mother, and two children.

I have given up on society, because I'm apparently unfit without a husband and father to manage my life and children. Which is fine. The paying guests who visit us know little of the privacies of their hosts, care only for the quality of their stay, nor do the buyers of our crops, our meat, and our fleeces care. The indifference and anonymity of commerce has become my fortress, and the roses I'm cultivating my refuge.

Somehow, I've found myself mortared to these stone walls, an integral part of the seemingly haphazard meshing of glacial fallout. Ma has said little since our brief conversation in the garden when first I came back, and steadily she's been retreating into her own world; we now have a nurse on staff to oversee her days. Figured it was less expensive and easier on Ma to have staff hired in, rather than shuffle her off to a nursing home, which seems to have become the growing trend.

We hired yet another manager for the farm after I conceded all the various functions of it were more than

Ianto and I could handle on our own. After Macafferty. I've come to calling this period: AM. Ma would fetch a fit if she heard me. Such blasphemy. It's bad enough I don't attend church like the good Christian woman I'm supposed to be.

No time for reaping of souls. I have enough to do with the land. And the children. And my roses. In those few spare hours at dawn I steal out of the house to the beds of roses I've developed. It would seem I'm having success with a strain I've been nurturing through careful cross-pollination so the changes will eventually be permanent, rather than through grafts which can fail. What I'm getting is full fragrant blooms, thorns definitely diminishing. They're susceptible to rodents because of that, but the offset is they're casting heavy canes with considerable clusters of blooms and are proving winter hardy.

Beyond that, the shift to market-gardening and small herd animals for the mainstay of the farm goes well. As always, one thing seems to lead to another, and we ended up buying the family farm across the road from us, another heritage hundred acres. We installed the new manager, Louis Harris, in the farmhouse, figuring adding a house into the package of his employment and purchase terms might be an enticement. He and his family were fresh out from Scotland a few years ago, bully beef stockman of Highland beasts, working some laird's land and wanting a fresh start. But his fresh start ended up a financial quagmire when he couldn't make a go of it here, found himself having to sell. So Ianto and I stepped in. They get to stay on the farm they worked so hard to have, and we get another hundred acres of prime land to add to the Cotter enterprise, and experienced people into the bargain.

So, we've added a small herd each of prime Angus beef and Jersey dairy to the menagerie. Hoping to open our own retail outlet on the farm next year, from which we'll sell our own cheeses, beef, lamb, and chickens, along with the produce from the farm, and of course the nursery I'm anxious to develop. I suppose a bakery might be a good idea eventually, but I'm getting ahead of myself. First, we need to build that abattoir.

Mrs. Harris has proved a blessing, watching over Violet when she was younger while I was studying horticulture and economics with the hope of bringing science and modernity to the Cotter enterprises. Some of these practices I agree with, but some I question and don't recommend for the farm. I'm told I'm an idiot for not buying into the new science of farming. But it strikes me as pounds foolish to completely dismiss farming practices that have served very well for hundreds of years. I remember what drove the Cotters to Canada, what caused this old stone house to rise, the forest once here to disappear. I remember failed tobacco crops, and now watch neighbours struggling with soil exhausted from the greedy tobacco and the greedier cigarette manufacturers.

So once again I'm heading the family charge against common practice. It is reassuring to hear Louis Harris add his solidarity to the policies Ianto and I institute here.

He's a man of few words is our Louis. He talks to the stock more than he does people. Kind enough though. Kind to his wife and boy. A few years ago there had been a problem with the Harris' boy, Leslie, something

Ianto and Louis dealt with and wouldn't discuss, and shortly after Ianto made arrangements for Leslie to study at a private school that would prepare him for military life. In Ianto's words, it would either make a man of Leslie, or break him, and he wouldn't much care either way what happened.

I've been given a Christmas present by the fates, it would seem. Conner Bannon died last month, dropped dead of a heart attack apparently. It all sounds rather grisly. When he was found he was on the floor of his kitchen, wedged into the corner of the cupboards, dead some few days. He'd been living alone, I've heard. And the only reason anyone came looking was because the landlord hadn't been paid and was trying to collect.

So, it would appear I am free of him. A widow. Till death do us part.

Joy to the world, and merry Christmas to all.

Cost

Then summer, and the leaves heavy on trees, shadows like secrets, and the air cool and damp along the hedgerows where she grazes on wild blackberries. They're so dark and juicy when she bites down on their knobbly, pulpy flesh. Her fingers are stained purple and she licks at them, knowing Ma will be angry that she's a mess, and has spoiled the fine frock she was supposed to keep clean until the spectors from the Childrensade have been and gone.

There have been arguments again, and words building walls of bricks, mortared in place with tears and fears, and she spends more time with Panda and the Rose Guardian, talking about ways to get to Over There. She's wandered farther than she's allowed, but she keeps it secret, down to the lake where it lays like an emerald in the woods, and butternuts ring the outer circle, and willows the inner. These willows don't cry. They are huge and spreading, with clouds of leaves rustling cool words over the water. Ducks all brown and green, and black and white drift along, the fluff of babies bobbing behind.

She wonders if the lake is big enough for the ships from Over There. She watches them every evening when the sky to that promised land opens and wonders more how that sea and her lake are connected. Is it the river that joins them? It's a big river. George Mason drowned in it last winter, falling through the ice when he was skating too early in the season. She wonders if his body will wash up on the shores of Over There? Will they take him up, put him in a box in the ground where he'll wait until he's raised from the dead and all the sorrow of the world will end?

Or are the people of Over There like the Irish king Uncle has told her about? Will they bury George Mason with a ship and treasure so that he'll be able to live well when he wakes up in the After Life?

Is the After Life like Heaven?

And if the ships do come, does that mean they will all live Over There where everything is good and kind and no one yells? Where there are no threats from beasts and monsters and things that creep in shadows, or charge in daylight, or who are tricky and make you think they are one thing when they are really another. Bad things. Hurtful things. Things like Balor.

Is it gone now? Did the rosemary really get rid of it?

She settles under the old apple tree. Uncle says it was planted by their four bears from across the sea, and because of that she's sure the Ambassadors from Over There are four bears, coming to take her back to the land Gran's ma and da left behind. It's a grand estate Gran says, with a big house and acres of land.

But they already have a big house and acres of land, so she's not sure why she should go. Surely, though, it must be a place of peace.

Ducks rise in a clatter and squabble and she flinches, alarmed. She hugs Panda tighter, takes a deep breath. The air is filled with the scent of roses from those which have gone wild beside the apple tree. Their blooms are pink and heavy, nodding with the breeze that kicks up and then dies. Her heart hammers again when a figure unfolds from the brambles, a huge bloom atop the thick cane. The bloom swivels, turns toward her. There are eyes in the thick yellow pollen, thorny fingers on the ends of branches.

"Rose Guardian?" she whispers.

I am.

"But how did you get here? You were in the garden by the house."

The creature shuffles toward her. The scent of roses is overwhelming and she feels her lungs filling with cobwebs, feels the air become too thin. She gulps like a fish out of water.

Do you want to go to Over There so badly?

"I do," she whispers.

What would you give up for safe passage?

She feels the danger of the question, knows it's bigger than she can figure, a tricksy question.

Would you give up your little brother?

"No." She shivers with the horror of that idea.

Then who?

"Why do I have to give up someone?"

Because that is the cost. It is not for you to argue or negotiate.

Negotiate. A word she's recently learned. It means both sides have to agree to a deal, the cost of it, what each person receives. *This* is worth *that.* And sometimes it isn't, because one person needs and the other wants. And which, she wonders, does she?

But it isn't a case of her needing to get to Over There. She doesn't need that, not like she needs air and food and Ma and Uncle, even Panda. So then it is wanting. But why?

Wanting to feel safe? Wanting to have peace and quiet and her family laugh, and smooth away the lines of worry and the harsh words, and freedom from the creatures that stalk her. No more need of rosemaries and magic words.

She watches the Rose Guardian carefully, the way its eyes blink and shower yellow pollen like gold dust, the way its thorny fingers curl and uncurl as though longing to grip something.

Careful, Panda whispers.

She hugs him tighter.

Would you give up yourself? the Rose Guardian asks, and then steps back into the briars and is only a wild rose once more.

The elegant and thoroughly bohemian outfit I'd put together lay tossed upon the bed, and I stood there looking in my closet's mirrors at the shabby and perhaps questionable jeans, tank, and shirt that were my working uniform. Buttons were missing on the Hawaiian shirt. A few alizarin splotches remained on the tank despite washing and spot treating, the result of getting too deeply involved with staining pigments. One might think I'd committed a dismemberment. And the jeans were a saggy, baggy, worn, and faded comfort.

No makeup. Just my jowls and wrinkles. And that ridiculous mop of hair. I ran my fingers through those curls, attempting to rake some sort of respectability into them, then realized there was absolutely nothing respectable about how I'd present today to Banee Kaur Aulakh from the CBC.

But I'd reached a point I didn't want to be shoved into someone else's preconception. I was an artist. Just a backwoods, small town artist who for some reason got caught in a larger net.

Downstairs I found Uncle Ianto deep in surveillance mode. All he needed was the box of bits and cold coffee and you'd swear he was on a stakeout. He made a tempting target, but mindful of his age and his dicky heart I made sufficient clatter to pre-warn him of my arrival, and then served him with: "Pass inspection there, Sergeant Cotter?"

He fired back with an sharp glance, and motioned me to silence. I fully expected to find myself in my eight-year-old body.

"They could have knocked and introduced themselves."

"They will, Uncle Ianto. I'm sure that's the crew. The journalist is likely...ah, there," and I nodded out the window. "She's making her way to the door now." I waggled my finger at him. "Now look, you. You just set yourself down on the porch, or wherever you like," I saw his face spark with interest, "but not my studio. It's crowded enough in there with just one. A crew, reporter, and you would be too much."

He made a disgusted noise and slouched out to the porch, grabbing his old grey cardigan on his way out. I watched as he shoved and poked his arms around in the sleeves, looking for all the world like an albatross trying to launch. The perennial bachelor, too caught up in taking care of everyone else but himself. It was a reminder to myself.

By the time I made sure he was settled with tea to hand, a throw for his knees should he need it, that knock finally came, metaphorically speaking. I felt my heart kick. Then came the smile; I looked up, turned for a greeting: action.

"You must be Banee." Hand thrust out to shake as she ascended the stairs, action performed, hand withdrawn and gesturing to the porch in a moment of perversity. "It's such a lovely day, I thought we'd start out here," a look from Ianto of wild humour, "if that's okay with you. The light's soft. Can I get you tea, coffee, something else?" Good the gods, would I never shut up? "Here, why don't you make yourself comfortable," indicating a chair near to Ianto, back to a corner—prudent that, "I'll just—"

"I'm good, thanks. The porch sounds like a great idea—" a quick look to the camera person, who nodded, "so let's just get you mic-ed, and then we can start, maybe make our way from here to your studio? That good with you?"

I nodded. Relaxed a little in the presence of someone who plainly knew her craft. While I was being made ready for sound, Banee ran through the type of questions she'd be asking, assuring me this wasn't going to be an in-depth personal exposé, but rather a feel-good piece to celebrate artists across Canada, a grassroots sort of look at the creative process. And like the professional she was, we slid softly into recording and easy, lively banter.

It was going swimmingly well until she asked me: "Who are you, Vi?"

I opened my mouth to answer, a flippant remark ready, when I saw Lettie race toward the trees and disappear into their gloom. That brought me up short, my smartass quip fizzling.

Who was I? What kind of question was that? Were we going to get all philosophical now? I realized I could answer with the obvious: daughter, niece, wife. Well ex-wife. Did any of that define me? Was my existence made real only through my refection in someone else's lens? What made me who I am? What defined any of us? Were we all destined to be merely reflection? Or was there a source somewhere? The subject of the reflection. How far down did you have to drill to find that?

"I suppose," I said after a moment, looking back at her, taking in her cool demeanour, her complete poise, "you'd have to find that out for yourself. I am, after all, not entirely unbiased."

She smiled at that. From there she guided me through questions almost metaphysical, well-researched, incisive without being confrontational or sensational, but I felt the confrontation, the spin and manipulation. She was an expert sapper, but I was an expert mason.

Uncle Ianto, to his credit, morphed into the furnishings and remained as silent.

Having abandoned my personal walls, she asked if we might see my studio. I consented, picked up the jar of water for my paints. We left the porch, and in an attempt to retain defenses, I chattered to her about the property, the bay, the history of the hamlet, anything but myself, and then we were at the grey board shed I called my studio, honeysuckle fragrant and wantonly drooping from the eaves. A hummingbird zoomed by, scolded us a moment, and then as that brazen bird wooed the blooms, I stepped into my studio. I stood there stunned in the gentle light, unable to comprehend what I was looking at. I tried to say something witty, found myself instead stuttering incoherently. The water jar was shaking in my hand, I realized. But no, it was my hand that was shaking. That was my breath that was coming in short gasps. I looked up, startled by something I couldn't identify, my gaze searching out the windows only to find who I knew would be there, red pedal pushers, ringlets and all. And then she was gone.

"I'm sorry..." I managed to get out. "This is.... I mean to say...." I waved to the muddy water pooling across a work in progress, the brushes on the floor, the finished work flung around the room in a spray of destruction.

"It would appear you have a vandal." I caught her motioning to the videographer, watched the camera lower, that telltale red light wink out. "Who would do this? Do you have any enemies, detractors? Do you want us to call the police?"

Enemies? What the hell was that? Enemies? You'd have to be involved in the community to have enemies, and I'd followed the Cotter inclination to disassociate, that whole *it's no one's business* rule.

Which brought me crashing into: *police?* Why? I said that, and added, "There's really nothing of value here."

"You don't consider your work valuable?"

"Well yes. But how do you attach a value to something like this?" I gestured wildly to the detritus of what had been my work, aware my voiced was harsh. "It's all so subjective."

She looked at me, considering, and then I likely doomed myself by saying, "I'm sorry, but we're going to have to reschedule, or cancel." *I can't possibly do this. How can I do this interview now?*

Why would Lettie destroy my work?

"I understand," was all she said, nodded to her crew who melted away. She extended her hand, to which I responded appropriately. I watched her leave, watched them all pile into their SUV, and slowly navigate the long lane. I turned back to the wanton destruction of my work, wanted to let my frustration explode.

In an attempt to answer my question of *what now?* I finally set down the jar of water, listened to the hiss as it contacted grit, sank to my knees and gathered shreds of colour into piles, a kaleidoscope of memories. There were some pieces that survived, some of the canvases, a few of the larger watercolours. It seemed ludicrous when I wondered what my interviewer had thought, if she'd only seen the destruction, if she'd seen any of the untouched work. And if the journalist had, over the course of the interview on the porch, and then in those few charged minutes in the studio, seen behind the face. Had I revealed too much?

As I paused, sucked in air, trying to still my rampaging heart, I realized all of my wonderings were moot, because of what was too evident in the work. It was all there. My loves and fears, my joy and grief. Just as Ma had always chastened me, my heart was there for anyone to see.

So much for defenses. So much for pretense.

That was when I realized Lettie stood beside me, a drawing dangling from her small hand.

"You know you can't hide," she said.

1965

May

Tomorrow I'm getting married.

I know I said I'd sworn off men, sworn off love. All I knew of love was betrayal and bruises. I have to believe it can be otherwise. Surely in this life there is some happiness, some refuge two people can find in one another. Sanctuary. It is that I seek, I admit. And it may be perilously naïve of me to believe sanctuary can be found in a man's company, let alone in life. But I do feel so alone.

Bart is a wonderful man. I think we could be happy. He's funny, handsome, a builder. He's the one who has been in charge of building our greenhouses and the retail store on the property. A man who takes pride in his work. No puffery. The children like him.

We're having a small, private ceremony. Ianto will stand up for me. Bart's brother is standing up for him.

Ianto approves apparently. Even Ma. We've talked about this between ourselves, moments meted out in the twilight hours when the farm settles down, and the guests are retiring, Bennet and Violet chasing dreams.

Ma says a good marriage is teamwork, likens it to horses pulling in tandem. Such a bucolic metaphor, but I suppose it is fitting, given her background, what her parents left behind in Ireland, the social conditions she's experienced. I asked her about Da, whom I never knew, dared to tread upon forbidden territory. She carried her grief with Victorian conviction, a man lost to influenza. They'd been married so very young, had Ianto and me in the first two years, lived with the very present knowledge of the Cotters' loss of the land, a title without meaning, barely the means to make the passage to Canada with thousands of others.

Influenza didn't much mind if you were descended from lord or lackey. So it was Ma found herself the outsider in the Cotter clan, raising two children in Irish Protestant censure among people deceptively foreign. She'd said although the language was familiar, all else was not.

She'd sounded so lost in the darkness of the porch, swept back into memory and her own struggles. I wondered how it had been for her in this big, old house, indentured by marriage.

It was then I'd lit the kerosene lamp, to bring some light to what we three shared.

After a moment Ma said, "I outlived them all. It's on my shoulders the Cotter posterity rests. Now yours." At that she'd turned to Ianto and waggled a bony, bent finger at him. "At least Una's trying. You? Not so much as the whisper of a lover." The blue of her eyes seemed very bright in the lamplight, the creases of laughter there, her white hair escaping from the chignon she always wore. Square-jawed, broad-mouthed, the ghosts of youthful beauty there. She had been a stunner, there was no doubt of that. But never another love in her life.

I could feel Ianto's discomfort. His lack of romantic interest had always troubled me. He wouldn't discuss it. And in the lengthening silence I knew he wouldn't discuss it now. Instead he said, "This is Una's night." His gaze shifted to me, and as I watched him I saw the Cotter lines there, the same square jaw, large mouth, the startling blue eyes. His looks could turn heads. He never seemed to notice. "I wish you joy," he said. "And if not joy, at least contentment."

It occurred to me later he should have wished me luck.

September

Why is it the heart is so fickle?
Or is it simply biology?

October

I've been taking horticultural courses at the University of Guelph. Bart is not pleased. We've had words. Ianto says I should stop thinking with my cunt. I was shocked!

December

Ma has gone. She died in her sleep. Cotter farm now belongs to Ianto and me.

God, I miss her. It's odd. We rarely spoke, shared very little, and yet her absence is large and loud.

April

Ihave thought for some time now life is like a garden, and you had best tend it or it will escape you. To my relief, Bart agrees, and figures a little shit periodically can only improve the soil. It occurs to me he demonstrates greater understanding of grace than I. I shall have to amend that. Certainly, I am not deserving of his grace. But I am grateful. I think I have been given a rare reprieve and opportunity. Best not squander that.

Beware the Claws that Catch

She is here because Rose Guardian said if she were to find the Stone of Light, she could use that as a beacon. It would be like a flashlight, she's been told—to let the Ambassadors from Over There know where she is, and where to sail.

But the sacred telein won't be easy to find. There will be old trees who do not like little Marys. They remember the old gods.

Rose Guardian uses funny words. She's thought about them a lot. She's asked Uncle about a sacred telein. He looked at her strangely and was silent. She asked him about the old gods. He looked at her strangely again, asked how she knew about old gods. She hadn't been sure she should tell him about Rose Guardian, about the Ambassadors and Over There. So instead she'd said they'd been learning about old gods in school.

"We didn't have gods in Ireland," he'd said. "We had heroes and villains, and sometimes they were the same. But mostly we had the blessed bloody Virgin."

Which doesn't help her much either.

He'd laughed then and said, "Beware the Jabberwock, my girl! The jaws that bite, the claws that catch!"

She remembers shuddering when he'd told her the whole poem. She'd taken that information to the Rose

Guardian, but Rose Guardian wasn't listening. She'd been given her quest. Get on with it.

So, now she stands amid the saplings at the edge of the woods, where bracken grows and sunlight streams, clutching Panda. She wonders if the brilligs and slithy toves gyre and gimble in the wabe. She wonders if she'll see them. And if she does see them, will they help her to avoid the Jabberwock? Because surely there is a Jabberwock in these woods, little say a Jubjub bird and Bandersnatch. Maybe if she finds the vorpal blade that will help to defend her until she finds the Stone of Light, the sacred telein.

Don't be afeared, Panda says.

She kisses his head. "I'm only a little afeared." With her free hand she touches the rosemary around her neck, feels the smoothness of the beads, closes her eyes while she gulps in a deep breath, opens them, and looks down to her feet. There, in the bracken she sees a rusty bit of metal, toes it, finds it's bigger than she thought, bends toward the damp ground and wiggles her find free of its grave. A blade. A curved and wide blade, pitted and nicked, heavy in her hand, a handle mostly rotten wood and damp from the earth. Is this the vorpal blade? Is this what she needs?

She slashes at the bracken, is immediately sorry to have beheaded them all.

If she needs a blade, does that mean she's going to be attacked?

Let's go, says Panda.

She looks up to the gloom of the woods, steps out of sunshine and into the cool and dampness of trees. To find the Stone of Light. To find a way to call the Ambassadors from Over There. Maybe, just maybe, she can get passage for her and Baby Brother Ben. Maybe Ma will be happy. Maybe Uncle will laugh. She likes it when he laughs, the way his blue eyes sparkle, the way that curl of white hair bounces down across his brow.

She looks around, unfamiliar with this place. She's never been in these woods. Ma and Uncle and Gran all say never to go here. But she has to. Rose Guardian says this is where she'll find the Stone of Light.

So, she takes another step into the trees, and another. Her trousers are wet with dew from her walk through the meadow, her sneakers squishing. She wiggles her toes around as she steps, feeling water slide between her toes. Which are cold. And why she wiggles them.

Branches clatter and chatter overhead, trees talking with the wind.

I don't understand what they're saying either, says Panda.

She trips, catches herself, is mindful to watch where she's going. She's not sure where she's going, where to find the Stone of Light, just that her quest has to take her into these woods, to a pile of rock. She looks around and feels herself shrink. There are so many trees. So many piles of rock. There are ferns and baby trees, and flowers like tiny stars everywhere. Which pile of rocks? How will she know? And as she peers out into the stretches of the woods, she realizes the farther she goes, the more sound seems to shrink, so that there is only the scrunch and squelch of the dead leaves under her feet, the clicks and whistles of birds overhead. Way off in the distance she hears the drum of a woodpecker. Uncle told her you could hear one from miles away. She wonders why the woodpeckers don't have headaches. She's tried hammering her head against a tree and never did it again.

Now the woods are different, darker, greener. She looks up and up the tall trunks to where yellow light smacks and stutters across leaves, up to where birds squabble and then are silent. There are other sounds now, deeper, and a smell so sickly sweet. She gags, eases to a fallen log cushioned with moss, sits Panda down in the duff. What is that smell?

"I'm afeared," she says to Panda.

Me too.

She listens carefully to the new sound, breathes that smell so thick in the air it's like syrup, sticky and catching in her throat. She pushes up off the log, her bum damp, and pulls at the wedge of her panties, picks up Panda again. What if she walks toward that sound? Will she be safe? Should she go away from the ruckus ahead of her?

There's no way she can see what's ahead. Trees close around her, no longer welcoming.

Go back, Little Mary, they say.

Keep going, Rose Guardian says.

She steps, carefully, placing her foot just so, mindful of twigs and things that crackle and betray her. She holds up her blade before her. Steps again. Trees part. A path opens, winding and narrow, ferns and deadfall to either side, grey rocks like rotten teeth and that smell like nightmares drifting in the air.

Now she makes sense of the noises, sees in the distance a mound of rock, a moving wave of black feathers, red faces, beaks stained and sharp as Ma's pruners. She doesn't want to go nearer, hears Rose Guardian demanding she does. Her heart feels like it's going to pop right out of her chest and she sucks in a gulp of that rotten air, feels her lungs start to close with cobwebs. The birds stop as one. Heads turn. White-rimmed eyes stare, at her, and she wonders if these huge black birds are going to eat her the way they're eating whatever that is on the mound of rocks.

It's a little Mary, one of them says.

Will she taste good?

Not ripe enough.

Blood's too hot.

Most turn back to their feast. She sees antlers, bone sharp and white against all that meat, and maggots like foam. She can't help it and starts to cry, afraid, her feet wanting to leave but her heart determined to stay and see this quest finished because in all this death there has to be hope.

Several of the birds watch her, their eyes like yellow beads. One of them skips clumsily away from the feast, waddles closer to her. Another joins it, then another.

I think she won't last, the first says.

She wonders what it means by that. She edges away, threatened by the way they watch her, their heads bobbing, almost like they are sniffing her.

I think we could have this one. Ripe or not.

"Go away," she says, feeling her voice thin, knowing she's shaking and yet mustn't let them see. Maybe she should just go back. Maybe she could try another day.

But there was Rose Guardian's insistent demand in her head, and then: *I think you are not brave enough.*

The First steps nearer, its wings tented, its red neck stretching. She steps back, the blade coming up and pointing toward the bird. The blade trembles at the end of her hand.

Not brave enough.

But she is. She's commanded The Darkies. She's defeated Balor with the rosemary. She is so brave enough, and she leans forward now, jabs the blade at the bird. It backs up, spreading its wings wider. Second and Third lunge toward her and she slashes out at them both. They skip backward, rising off the ground and then down.

"I am so brave enough," she says. And slashes again. Now the rest of the vultures are interested, gulp down what they'd torn off the dead deer. They watch.

There are more of us, First says.

Her blood's even hotter now. And still not ripe.

But she won't last.

"I will so!" And because she's been told she's died before, when she spent all that time in the hopital, she knows she is brave, that she can fight death, that she can find the Stone of Light. With a shriek, she slashes out at the wave of vultures, driving them back, out, away, screaming her fear and rage so that the dead deer can find its own way to Over There. The birds hiss, rattling anger. She won't be defeated. She will find the Stone of Light. And she will drive back these birds of death. The blade is heavy in her hand, but she hacks, looses her footing, the blade clanging hard against stone. There is a crack. The vultures rise up through the trees, roost on high. She's falling now, down onto the rotten deer. The blade cracks, then shatters. She pushes away from the stink and the mess, rolls hard against stone, bumps up against the rock that wrecked her blade and there, split open like an egg, is the Stone of Light, two halves of sparkling, purple crystals inside a black shell.

She clutches them to her breast and weeps.

A Complexity of Relationships

When David drove up in his battered pickup, I was surprised to see his sister Dottie with him. That could only mean he needed her assurance, which could only mean he expected confrontation. So, this visit wasn't going to be all friendly banter. It was about a question David likely found uncomfortable, a request or action he was about to make of me.

It was early and I'd been wiping down the kitchen counter, eliminating toast crumbs from breakfast. Uncle had gone to shower and dress. I'd already been up and working, unable to sleep after closing the cover on the last of Ma's journals. That was enough to set me on edge. *Don't go looking for trouble*, I told myself.

I watched him out the window, felt that familiar ache in my gut, that detonation. How could I have thrown that relationship all away? *He's such a good man.* And I'd allowed the dysfunction between Ma and me to infect his life.

I went out to the porch to greet both David and Dottie, listening to the clack-thump of the wooden screen door behind me. It was a fine day, cool portending autumn. Dew was heavy on the lawn, a cardinal flashing by in a burst of red. I wondered how such an idyllic setting could host the turmoil I felt. Was I completely beyond redemption? I did need redemption. Wished it.

David had his hands in his pockets when he strode to the porch, then took the rail in one hand and scuffed his way to where I stood. I managed a smile, a greeting to both him and Dottie. She looked as if she were ready for a fight, acknowledged my hospitality with a barked reply and a nod, eased against the railing, no pretence of accepting hospitality. If I'd a mind to analyze that I could deduce so much. But then I always analyzed things and found myself suspecting shadows where there were none.

My Ma's daughter.

"Tea?" I asked.

They both declined. David now took the chair next to where Dottie leaned. And again I wanted to dissect that choice, and again cautioned myself against it, instead easing myself to the loveseat where I'd have my back to the drive, which of course left me feeling exposed.

How was it I'd come to this, to calculating the most defensive positions?

"So, what brings you to the ass-end of the island?" I asked. *Oh, that was great.*

"Thought I'd sail *Gayaashk* into Gore Bay today."

"Sounds great. The weather's fine. You going to moor her there for a few days?"

He nodded, glanced nervously at Dottie. "Yeah. Until I get the boathouse finished."

Ah. "I see."

"I think it's better this way."

And so my mooring lines had been cut. Which brought me to: *it's always about me. Your Ma's daughter.*

What about David? Maybe he needed to be cut free, to be absolved of his never-ending sense of responsibility to me. Maybe he needed to finally move on with his life, let the hope of a hopeless love die and at last find peace in these his senior years. "Of course."

"I'm sorry, Vi."

I laughed, and found I couldn't stop for a few moments, glanced out to the garden and found the white roses, let my thoughts settle there in a suspended moment, watching vignettes from childhood. The laughter stilled, and I managed grace, turned back to David, saw Dottie ready to be the warrior for her brother.

"You have nothing to be sorry about, David. *Gayaashk* is yours. She brings you peace, something I was unable to do because I have none myself. So, this is good. You need to do this. We do, if I'm honest."

There was silence after that, his steady gaze upon me. So much regret on his face. Then: "You were the love of my life."

A hitch in my chest, a bird caged. *Were.* He'd moved on. He was finding his own healing, his own closure. Hence the circle he'd taken me to, the attempts to reconcile a different relationship. I hadn't seen that. "And you were mine," I said, and meant it, letting that whispered confession hang between us. A loon cried at that moment, adding mournful ellipses to what we didn't say. "But that doesn't mean two people can necessarily live together in harmony. It's I who owe you apology, for so many things." And a hard will to still my own tears, to refuse to let emotion clog my words.

I watched tears pool in those dark eyes of his,

watched the bulge at his jaw, knew he fought the same battle. He rose suddenly, stepped toward me as though to bend and gather me into his arms, checked, turned like something wooden and scattered down the stairs to the boathouse.

"Thanks for not fucking that up," Dottie said as she made to follow David.

I snorted a laugh, said, "Sure," and watched her retreat to help David make *Gayaashk* ready to sail.

Myself, unable to watch, I sought the only refuge I knew, and crossed the lawn to my studio where light filled the clutter of this domain. Here there was only my life's work. It was both a curse and gift that colour and form took all my attention, that the demands of knowing when to push, and when to wait guided time, an irony that I could understand so much about this metaphorical relationship, and so little about the real. My world distilled to the demands of the medium and the composition. It wasn't until I became aware of the shift of light in my studio, of morning become late afternoon, I realized I truly needed to move, to find the loo and deal with a bloated bladder. I'd shut out any of the sounds from the boathouse, and I stilled for a moment, listening, and received only the sounds of water and birds, a breeze shifting through trees. So Dottie had gone. David had sailed. I felt the vastness of those departures, saw it in the painting I'd created.

Just as I waggled my brush through stained water, Uncle thumped into my space and groaned when he took the rocker in the corner. Apparently that pee would have to wait, because the look on Uncle's face said I had better sit still and listen.

"They've gone. You can stop hiding," he said.

I ran my fingers over the golden bristles of my brush, smoothing the edges into a taper. "Who says I was hiding?" He snorted a laugh, which likely meant he was in fighting temper. "They had work to do to get *Gayaashk* under way. And so did I. No point me hanging around getting in the way."

"Lending a hand at something you know something about, being hospitable." I heard the sarcasm in his voice.

"They didn't come for hospitality. They came to get the boat."

"He bringing it back later?"

"No."

"I thought not. The boathouse is all sealed up as though it's never to be used again."

"Well, you know how David likes to keep things organized."

"He could have said goodbye."

I looked up at Uncle then, heard the loss in his voice, saw it in his face. "He was having a hard enough time. I don't think he meant any disrespect."

"Of course not. You're a fool."

"I know."

"He gave you every chance to make a life."

"I know."

"For twenty years he's hung on." *I know, I know, I know.* "Why, Violet? Why could you not make that work?"

"I don't know." Because of Ma. Because of me. Because I had no idea how to share myself with anyone without fear of reprisal. Fear of living. Fear of never being good enough.

"You don't need to do penance the rest of your life for not meeting up to her expectations."

And I was. He knew that. Even reading Ma's journals left me feeling that if somehow she had found a way to abort me her life would have been less complicated, that she could have achieved so much more than she did. It was there in her precise script, in the truncated phrases, more written between the lines than in them.

Which of course was completely pathetic to think at my age, and I wondered if we ever stop being our parents' children? Do we always seek their approbation?

"You should never have read her journals," he said, slapping the arm of the rocker. "Mistake. Always a mistake to get into Una's head. It's a mess in there. Was. Apparently still spilling out everywhere."

"Violet, you have to know she did love you, watched over you, that love and acceptance for her were complicated."

"You making excuses for her?"

"Yes. No. She was my sister, and life bent her, and while she learned to survive, she never learned to recover. You can't be your Ma's daughter in that regard. It's not too late."

"Oh dear god, Uncle, I'm a senior citizen. You think I can change now?"

"Who said the will to change is defined by age?"

I looked away from him, down to the scene of dreams I'd been painting, layers of washes, glaze over glaze, hidden faces, hidden movement, a subtext beneath the obvious. A deviation from my usual landscapes which spoke of environment and elements. I didn't want to study that now, so sought the familiar, the cobwebs in the windows, the shelves of bric-a-brac, the cabinets where paper and pigments were stored, pencils, pens, and canvas. Organized but weedy. Like me.

"I don't know how," I said at length, sotto voce, letting the admission slide out like all my ghosts in this studio.

"Then maybe you need to put aside that Cotter hubris and see that counsellor again. Or find another. Or talk to me at the very least. I'm not going to be around forever, you know, and I'd like to depart knowing you're going to be okay. That my life's work hasn't been for naught."

"Is that what I've been to you? A life's work?"

"The daughter I didn't have. My dear niece."

I cleared my throat of emotion, looked at that face of his, the jowls around his mouth, the rosacea in the apples of his cheeks, and always that recalcitrant lock of silver hair that fell over his brow. He would have been a catch for anyone. "Is that why you didn't have a family of your own?"

He looked away. I'd prodded something tender. "Never wanted one, not after you were born."

"You weren't a closet gay, were you?"

He laughed then, looked back at me. "Your Ma asked me that a long time ago. No. Not gay. Why does everyone think that because a man doesn't take a wife that he's gay?" He waved a hand dismissively. "No. I had a love. So did she. But by the time she was free it was too late, or somehow not the right moment, and friendship had evolved where once passion had prevailed."

"Mrs. Hamilton."

"The very same. I'd not do injustice to her good man, nor to her. I found them a place here, made sure they were secure, and I married the farm. And raised you along the way."

So he had. It would seem we Cotters were full of surprises. "So why tell me all this now?"

"Because you need to know you're not the only one who knew heartbreak." He levered himself up. "I fancy a bit of fishing off the dock. And you need to think about what I've said. And box up your ma's journals and leave them boxed." He patted my head as though I were still his wee girl, turned and tottered out the door to the dock, no tackle in his hand, fishing for peace.

I didn't want to think about what he'd said, didn't want to poke at it and find out where it all fit. Instead I heeded that now urgent call of nature, and then frittered away the rest of the afternoon prepping a treat for our dinner, my tacit way of showing Uncle my gratitude for his forbearance.

We dined that evening in the garden, letting the sound of the bay and the trees engulf us, citronella burning in the lamps I lit upon the terrace.

After Uncle retired for the night, I lingered for awhile, walking around the rose bed where Ma's legacy thrived. The petals were soft as velvet when I fingered them, the fragrance a delirium. On impulse, I fetched pruners from the garden shed, snipped one of the blooms and brought it into the house, to my room, where the last of Ma's journals lay on my bedside table. I carefully closed the back cover over the rose, and then took the book downstairs to the living room where my library covered the walls. There was just enough room for this last journal on the shelf where I'd given them a place. And then to remind me of the strange relationship we'd had, I found an old, framed photo of

Ma, Uncle, and me standing in front of her now famous roses. There were happy faces in that photo. And that was a rare moment I wanted to have as a signpost to what lay behind the image.

March 1970

It's been raining all day, a bleak, cold, sleeting rain that seems to have pervaded this old stone house and dampened all warmth, all light, all life.

I buried Bart today.

My heart, like the stone of this house, I think will never warm again.

Oh, for God's sake he'd been fine! And then the other morning he was putting on his shirt and said, "Una, look at this," and pointed to his throat where the vein throbbed erratically, noticeably. His colour wasn't good, and when I suggested perhaps he should call off work today, let Louis manage on his own for once, and maybe see the doctor, he seemed to recover himself, laughed, and kissed my cheek. I still remember the feel of his lips on my face, warm, full, both strength and tenderness in the man. "I'll be fine," he said. "Just a little flutter." And then his shirt was buttoned and he was down the stairs, out the door before anyone else stirred.

It was Violet who found him sitting on a stump outside the dairy barn. She'd gone to fetch him in for breakfast as is her wont when she comes home to visit. He told her he wasn't feeling well. And then died. Just like that. She came crashing in the kitchen door, wild-eyed, hiccoughing with weeping. We brought him home, laid him in our bed. The doctor said it was likely a massive coronary. And so, then the seemingly endless litany of rites and procedures to perform, paperwork and forms, the legalities of death, the heart stilled until a more convenient, private time to shatter. Ianto shepherded the children while I saw to details. He'd wanted it otherwise, but I told him I needed to do this.

I can hear Ianto murmuring with my grown children down the hall, the soft snuffling of Violet trying to be as strong as her Ma, of Bennet who is trying out the trappings of a man. I need to go to them, to share our grief, to console each other. I need to be a Ma to these young adults I realize I barely know. I need to help them navigate this grief over a man who has been their only father. A kind man. A dear man.

How is it you are given love after such heartache, only to have it stolen? I think there are no fairy tales, no happy endings. We live. We die. And that's all there is.

How will we find the road from here? How will I?

Dust to Dust

She's standing in the aisle of the church with her classmates, Derek in front, Maggie behind, nuns watching them. It occurs to her the nuns are like those vultures, hissing and pecking as they're all shuffling up the aisle.

There's a priest up there mumbling something, his voice like rain against the walls.

She looks up at Sister Elizabeth, the white cloth around her face and forehead, the way she always seems angry at everything around her. Sister flicks Derek's shoulder when he gripes about having to stand in line. She wonders if the nuns are herding them the way the vultures tried to herd her, if there is something not very nice at the end of the aisle.

She watches one of the bigger girls as she walks back to her seat. There's a dirty smudge on her forehead, right over her nose. The boy behind the girl turns down the outside aisle after her, the same muck on his face. Had they been marked with the holy ashes?

Sister Elizabeth said yesterday the ashes represent the dirt from which God makes us, and to remind us of our sin and mortality, which means we're all bad, and nothing but dirt, and we all die.

She shuffles forward, ducking Sister Elizabeth's

constant swats, as if they're all flies. She thinks about the ashes, about dirt, and making clay. She's found clay in the river bank, all grey and slimy and squishable. She's shaped it into pots and bowls and left them to bake in the sun, serving up grass salads and dandelion tea to Panda and Rose Guardian.

But she's never made a doll, never thought such a thing was how she started. How does the clay doll end up in Ma's tummy, and how does Ma make it live? Does that mean Ma's actually like God? Or an angel? Do angels make clay breathe?

She doesn't remember there being a clay doll of Baby Brother. Maybe if she wants a sister she can make a clay doll and leave it in Ma's bed. Maybe somehow the doll can crawl its way into Ma.

That thought makes her shiver.

She watches as other kids file away, marked with ash. Marked to die.

The line is closer to the altar rail now, Sister Elizabeth daring any of them to misbehave. The way Sister's glaring at them, she's sure nothing good can come of what's about to happen.

Just four people ahead of her now. She doesn't know what to do. She sees kids kneel at the railing where a priest in purple keeps saying, "Remember, O man, that you are dust, and unto dust you shall return," and then dips his hand in an ashtray and smears ash on the kid kneeling in front of him. "Get up, get up," he hisses when the boy remains where he is. The boy rises from his knees, a tall boy, one she's seen on the school yard shoving smaller kids around for their milk money. But he's afraid, this boy, and she watches as he slumps away. So there must be something very powerful happening at the railing, something that would make even a bully afraid.

Now it's Derek's turn at the rail. He kneels. The priest mutters out the magic words again, makes the death cross on Derek's forehead. Derek gets up, his hands pressed together in prayer in front of his chest, and walks away.

She steps forward, afraid, because she doesn't want to die, doesn't want to be marked. There's no way out. If she bolts for the door one of the nuns will catch her and she'll end up back at this rail where she'll be marked for death. She wishes she had Panda. She wishes the Rose Guardian were here. She clutches the cross of her rosemary—*to thee do we cry, poor banished children of Eve*—falls to her knees and watches with growing horror as the priest dips his finger into the ashtray and makes a cross on her forehead—*Remember, O man, that you are dust, and unto dust you shall return*—and feels relief wash over her. She's not a man. The priest says that men are made of dust. She remembers very clearly Sister Elizabeth teaching them that God made woman from Adam's rib, so that means girls are made from bone, not dirt, and it's men who are marked for death, not women. She smiles. She feels it push her cheeks. She whispers, "Thank you, Father," and gets to her feet, and knows this magic can't touch her, that she's free. For the first time ever, she's glad she's a girl.

Through the Glass

Wind buffeted my car when I made the turn onto Range Street, bypassing the long, winding, albeit picturesque drive into Gore Bay. There was sure to be a November storm slash through the island today. Clouds piled grey upon slate, the light remarkable. In the distance, I could see a line of squalls cutting across fields where incongruous alpacas grazed. I'd learned that first year here that come November, these kinds of squalls could turn nasty in a hurry, leaving you isolated, even stranded. Great day to be travelling. But I needed to get this last load of paintings to Ayashe Keeshig and her gallery. She'd been more than patient. First the aborted interview. Then the cancellation of my participation in the summer show. And her final capitulation to my entreaties to let me hang a one-woman exhibition, never a wise thing for a gallery owner to do, especially with an artist without a name or following. But it was November, and Ayashe was hoping for some early Christmas sales, and maybe the cachet of a one-artist show might draw in customers if not for my work, then perhaps for some of the smaller sculptures and pottery which were from a collective of other artists.

By the time I pulled in front of Ayashe's gallery,

the snow was thick, streaming mostly horizontally. I called Uncle, heard his familiar bark on the other end.

"Hey. It's just me."

"Hey yourself. You just arrive?"

"Yep. Just sitting out front. Thought I'd let you know I arrived safely."

"Good. Thanks."

"It snowing there?"

"Yep. There?"

"Yep."

"You be careful."

"Of course. You too. I'll let you know when I'm leaving."

"You do that."

And we rang off.

By now Ayashe was at the door of the gallery, waving and approaching, a huge cardigan enveloping her. We embraced. The fragrance of smudging herbs drifted from her. I inhaled, smiled, stepped back, and looked at her.

"You purging the gallery of evil spirits?"

She huffed a laugh, looked away to the window of her shop. "You carry spirits with you the way the sky carries weather." She gestured to the load in the back of the car. "That the last of them?"

I nodded and popped the hatch, got out and hefted a painting under each arm, as did she, watercolours all but one, and then we struggled to extricate the last, large canvas I'd wedged between the front and back seats. I hoped the canvas' stretcher hadn't bent. This was the anomaly of the last group, oil instead of watercolour. It was likely going to be the focus of this series, a strange exploration.

There was a steady howl of snow by the time we were done unloading, standing in the warmth of Ayashe's gallery, mugs of hot chocolate in hand. She looked up from the huge mug, a moustache of brown on her upper lip. She grinned and licked it away, then laughed.

"I love chocolate," she said. "Forget drugs. Just give me chocolate and I'm good to go."

I hummed an agreement, swirled the dregs and tossed that off, then set my mug on the antique glass and wood counter she'd kept from the original shop.

For the rest of the day we propped paintings against the walls, shuffling, commenting, rearranging until we felt we had a cohesive and logical flow to this exploration I'd taken. The easy part was the actual hanging on the click rail system.

By mid-afternoon we paused for a break and I called Uncle to make sure he was okay.

"It's howling here," he said. "Like a banshee gone wild."

"Make sure to keep that fire fed."

"Well of course. This isn't the first early storm I've weathered."

True enough. And because of that I'd made sure to have lots of split wood on the back porch for him, given the frequency with which power died out there, and the caprice of November. "I'll be home as soon as I can."

"Or maybe you'll be smart and stay put until morning."

"I'm not going to leave you alone."

"What? You're afraid I'll trip going to the loo?"

"Oh, for god's sake, Uncle."

"Be smart. Watch the weather. I've lots here and can

manage. The old jackass isn't going to up and hike off into the back of beyond."

And after a few more assurances, I rang off and ducked out to fetch tea and sandwiches from the eatery down the street. I'd come back and settled down with Ayashe on the stools she kept behind the counter, enjoying melted cheese and crunchy bread, tea hot and strong enough to pucker your cheeks.

"I had my doubts, Vi," she said after a moment, studying the work both hanging and not.

"But?"

"But you've proved them unfounded."

I smiled, admittedly relieved. "You think this show will fly?"

"Well, it's hard to tell, but I think this is your best work. I had no idea you were going to do a study of childhood and its secrets."

That gave me pause, and I set down my cup, looked from Ayashe who seemed thoughtful, even bemused, and out to where, for the first time, I was actually able to look at the body of work I'd created. While on the surface there were landscapes, images of lakeshore and woods, of roses blooming in cascades of disarray, of windswept coasts and abandoned buildings, there were figures and oddments, a face where there shouldn't have been, a whisper of an arm from behind a tree, shadows incongruous with what was being illuminated. There was a sinister bent to much of what I saw, of subtext. And throughout many of the paintings I saw Lettie, arriving unknown and unwanted from my unsettled thoughts to the irrefutable truth of my paintings.

It was then I turned to look out the window, to what

I expected to see of an early squall, only to find her there, that changeling child who had beleaguered my days since Ma's death.

Lettie. The oval of her face there in the window, ringlets pulled into dark ribbons by wind and snow, and I lurched off my stool, a cry in my throat, with Ayashe concerned at my side, "Vi! What's wrong?" And by the time I'd taken a step, then two, Lettie was no longer there. Just gone. As always.

I hesitated, not knowing whether to pursue her, whether to stay, whether to admit I'd seen the girl that had precipitated my faltering sensibilities this summer past, decided it was better to let the moment bide.

"Vi?"

"I thought.... Never mind. Just had a moment." I turned back to her, smiled. "I'm relieved you think this show will be good."

She watched me a moment, assessing, and I knew she could see things there I didn't want to reveal, my increasing sense of instability, of feeling disconnected and unhinged. I'd grieved for Ma a long time ago, for the things we never shared, never did, never said. I'd mourned a childhood bent and broken, a relationship stillborn, and wallowed in self-pity and recriminations. Did Ayashe see that on my face, in the way I hesitated there at the window, caught between what I thought I'd seen and the reality of what was on this side of the glass? "I said your work is good. Whether the show will be good is another thing. Not sure how Joe-public's going to react to this. This isn't exactly an urban mecca of art, you know. People here like safe—"

"Pretty pictures."

She smiled. "Exactly. And these may be pretty—well, not pretty exactly—but most certainly not safe."

I looked over at her, that seamed face and strong lines, those dark eyes, her dark hair bobbed and spiked with blue tips. She'd told me she decided on blue because it was a sacred colour, and she needed all the sacredness she could find in her life. She had a flutter of silver feathers tinkling from one ear, and one of Patrick Hunter's pride t-shirts over jeans.

Not safe. I wondered how much of that statement applied to me? Certainly, I brought to my work my own sensibilities, but were those sensibilities about what was safe and what was not? Is that what I'd been doing all these years—exploring sanctuary? Was that Ma's real legacy to me?

1980

April

So that daughter of mine is to marry tomorrow. Foolish girl. It will end in misery. How could it not? He's a damned Indian, for the love of god. She met him on an artists' retreat on Manitoulin, fancying herself a painter. I don't know what's got into her these past years since Bart's gone. She won't listen to common sense. Won't have anything to do with the farm, the nursery, any of it. Says she wants to carve out a life for herself, free of the Cotter shadow. Now what in hell is that supposed to mean?

As to that man she's marrying, David Nishkigwan, I don't know. The odds are stacked all against him. Who hires Indians? No one trusts them with their soft, hesitant speech, the way they won't look at you directly unless they're pickled and then the only thing you can expect is trouble. So, what does that leave her? Life on a reserve? That?

I've told her I won't attend the wedding. She said that wouldn't be a problem because they weren't going to have a ceremony, just an official attendance upon the local Justice of the Peace up there.

You love them, raise them, sacrifice, and what? You get this.

August

Two letters of import in the mail today. One from my daughter, a photo in an envelope, that man David Nishkigwan in a white shirt, dark tie, and trousers, she in a dress of blue and a bouquet of white roses. I remember I wore blue. *Married in blue, always be true.*

I thought to myself what a handsome couple they make. I wish her better fortune in love than mine.

The other envelope contained the University of Guelph's transcript of my successful completion of the horticultural courses I studied, and my official certification as a Master Gardener. I wonder what Ma would have said about higher education for land husbandry? I'm not even sure what I think.

The Danger of Gifts

It's Auntie Alice who sits perched on the sofa beside a huge package all tied up in newspaper and string, sipping tea, the cup barely touching her red lips. Ma says Auntie Alice is a witch, that her red hair is the cause of her wild and wicked ways. But as she watches Ma and Auntie Alice she wonders about that, about why red hair makes Auntie Alice wicked and a witch. Do all witches have red hair?

And if Auntie Alice is a witch, then why is she so nice to her? Is she being sneaky like the witch that tried to eat Hansel and Gretel?

Auntie Alice laughs when Ma asks what's in the big package, and Auntie Alice says it's a gift for her niece, and looking at her, says, "Will be better than your silly pussywillow dolls."

But they're not dolls. They're a family, and she likes them even though they're getting old and starting to shed their soft, silky hair the way Greatgran is, who lets her sit on her bed and read aloud from books with strange words even though Ma and Gran don't like it, especially when Greatgran lets her have one of the bug candies in the jar on the bedstand. They've never hummed for her, even though Greatgran says they're humbugs. She's tried eating other bugs, but none are sweet like the ones in Greatgran's jar.

Still, she is curious about the package Auntie Alice has brought, about what might be better than the little family that lives in the tissue box. She's a little unsure about Auntie Alice, the way her aunt has a way of looking down that long nose at people, tilting her head back, her gaze sharp and hard.

Auntie Alice sets down the cup and saucer, motions for her to come close and open the package. She does that, remembering to fold her dress under her the way Ma has shown her, but hating the way her crinoline scratches her legs. She feels like a stupid doll, the kind you have to set on a shelf and not play with, never get dirty.

She pulls the ribbon on the package which is as red as Auntie's lips and the bow comes free, then works the knot, and it all slides away. The newspaper wrapping tears and drops, and as it does Ma says, "Really, Alice, you couldn't have wrapped it in decent paper?"

"What's not decent about newsprint?"

"It's so common."

Auntie Alice laughs that big horse snort of hers, says, "And we're not?"

"Don't start."

The wrapping reveals a window of cellophane through which a doll's blue eyes stare. They have lashes, those eyes, and as she reaches and pulls the wrapping completely away those eyes jiggle and move, and she sits back with a start. Her heart jolts.

"Oh, she's beautiful," Ma says.

She's scary. She has black ringlets under a smart straw hat, big gold earrings, a red, rosebud mouth. Her dress is blue with a tight bodice and puffy sleeves, a skirt that's huge and flowered and fills the coffin of her box in layers of foam. The doll is bigger than she is. Panda's almost as big as she is, but that's okay. She's not sure about this doll.

"She will look lovely on your bed."

Which means this doll is not to be played with. This doll is something else, and what's the use of a doll if you can't play with it, talk with it, share all your secrets and be friends? This doll won't be like Panda, won't be like the Pussywillow family. This doll is something else for sure, and she's not sure what yet.

She doesn't know what to say to Auntie Alice, who sits there pursing her red mouth, looking as though she expects something, as though she's going to eat her alive if she doesn't come up with something proper to say. Perhaps she should say thank you, and does, but she's not sure she is thankful. The doll's eyes follow her.

"You can take her out of the package," Auntie says.

She shakes her head no.

"Oh well fine. I will." And Auntie heaves the box up onto the sofa beside her and shakes the lid away, lifts out the doll, and sits her on the sofa between them. The doll's skirts splosh out around her legs, the eyes opening and then closing.

She wishes she had Panda. She wishes she could talk to the Rose Guardian.

"Where did you find such a beautiful thing?" Ma asks. And Auntie Alice answers. The rest drifts away in a buzz of chatter while she sits there beside this huge doll she's sure isn't a doll at all. Carefully, she slides her hand toward the doll's white-stockinged legs, feels the warmth there, is sure now this thing is alive, like one of those clay creatures Sister Elizabeth has said the Jesus-killers can make. Sister Elizabeth called them golums.

After awhile Ma tells her to go and take her new doll to her room, that she can change out of her good clothes and play, but not to get dirty. She's never supposed to get dirty.

So, she slides off the sofa and struggles to lift the doll into her arms, totters away and up the stairs to her room, going carefully because she has to peer around the huge doll she carries. One step, two steps, up the rest, down the hall, finally to her room where she sits the doll on her bed, up against the pillows, because she knows Ma likes it when pretty things are arranged like this. The doll watches her as she undresses and pulls on pants and blouse, socks and sweater.

"Why are you staring at me?" she asks the doll, wondering if she should name her, if that would make the doll want to be her friend. But the doll says nothing, only continues to watch. It occurs to her it might be a good idea not to give the doll a name, because then that would make her alive, and if the doll were alive that might give the doll power. There is magic in names. Of this she is sure.

She lays the doll down so the eyes will close, knowing Ma won't like it that the doll isn't sitting up in a pretty pose, but even lying down the doll's eyes flip open every time the bed jiggles.

"It think maybe you're not my friend," she says. Doll says nothing, only stares, and it is the steadiness of that stare, the way Doll follows her movements that convinces her this is no gift of love from Auntie Alice.

Doll is something else, something probably not to be trusted.

With that thought she stuffs Pussywillow Family into her satchel where she keeps the Stone of Light, slings the satchel over her shoulder, tugs Panda under her arm and slides out to the hall, watching Doll as she goes, watching Doll watching her. She closes the door, wanting to keep Doll where she lays, away from her brother, who she checks on in his nursery to make sure he's okay. He's sleeping, his cheeks pink, his red hair like a crown of curls. She pads quietly out of his room, hears the latch click, turns and treads down the back stairs, into the kitchen.

"Out for a wander?" Mrs. Hamilton says, who now cooks for guests who come to stay in the extra rooms, and she nods, accepts the chunk of hard cheese she's offered and bites down into the sharp, salty treat. She remembers eating pea soup in Mrs. Hamilton's kitchen, remembers her singing, and on impulse hugs her around her apron, to which Mrs. Hamilton laughs and scoots her out with a peck on her head.

The screen door bangs behind her, and she's into the cool shade of the back porch where morning glories wink and hollyhocks nod. *Hello*, they say. "Hello," she replies.

Sunlight is harsh and bright after the dimness of the porch. She hurries off to the rose garden where the ruler of roses lives. She needs to talk to Rose Guardian, to ask it about Doll. She wonders if Rose Guardian is a boy or a girl, and thinks maybe a girl because of the way its voice sounds in her head, because of the white petals which remind her of The Blessed Mary. She touches the new rose petal rosemary around her neck, thinks of the Stone of Light, and wonders about all the powerful magic she now holds.

It's a lot, Panda says.

You must be careful, Ma Pussywillow says.

She agrees. With all of it. And she wonders about the use of these things, about what is ahead for her. Her heart skips and she inhales sharply, stops a moment to let her breathing settle. Always good to do that, to stop the spiders in her lungs spinning cobwebs that choke her breath.

She settles down at last beside the bed of roses where Rose Guardian lives, pinches away the sticky glob of cowbugs that always plague the roses. Ants scramble to rescue them. She's sorry to rob the ants of their food, but knows there are other places they can herd and harvest. She makes Panda comfortable, sets the Pussywillow Family's house in a safe place so they can take part in the conversation better than from her satchel, and waits for Rose Guardian to appear.

It's taking a long time, so she gathers the white petals that have dropped, making a pile of the silky things. By the time she's given up on Rose Guardian appearing, she has a large pile of petals. She wonders if Rose Guardian has died because so many of the flowers have shed their petals, or if Rose Guardian is maybe sleeping, if that's what the roses do when they lose their petals, or if maybe they've had a clay rose put inside them to make the fruit that appears later, if the hips—that's what Ma calls them—are baby roses. The way Ma treats the hips she's sure they are baby roses. Only Ma takes away the rose babies and dries them, and then either stews the babies into tea, or crushes them when they're dead and buries them in little pots.

Are the pots graves for the dead baby roses? Do they rise again like Jesus? Or are the pots of earth like ma-tummies for the baby roses, and maybe when they're dry they're not dead but only sleeping, waiting to grow into a growedup rose? Did she start out as a hip? She thinks about that and decides that's wrong, because Sister Elizabeth said woman was created from Adam's rib, so that means she started out as a rib. But from whose rib was she made?

None of it makes any sense, because if Eve was created from Adam's rib, that would make Eve Adam's daughter. But Eve was Adam's wife. So how could Eve be both Adam's wife and Adam's daughter? Did that mean Da was also her husband? But which Da? And why would Ma and she share a husband?

"I need to talk to you," she whispers to the roses, confused and feeling that sick hollowness inside her. She doesn't know what to do about Doll. She doesn't know what to think about hips and bones and being borned.

But Rose Guardian isn't answering. She would like to cry, but she's not a baby anymore, and only babies cry. Instead she sweeps up the rose petals and lets them fall into her satchel, keeping one behind which she runs over her lips because it feels smooth and makes her feel better the way running her fingers over the satin binding on her blanket makes her feel better.

She thinks that maybe if she made clay roses then maybe she could make more Rose Guardians come alive. Maybe it would be better to have lots of Rose Guardians, like lots of angels, watching over all the people she cares about. And now that Doll has come to live in her house, she's not sure any of them are safe, because Doll doesn't talk. Doll just stares. And if she's learned anything at all she's learned that people who stare usually cause hurt. Like Leslie. Like the kids at school who shove and push.

She fingers her rosemary, the new one made from rose petals and clay, and realizes she has exactly what she needs to make more Rose Guardians, that the magic she's been told the rosemary has is in its power to create more Guardians.

She feels her heart bump when she pulls the rosemary over her head, and with a grunt pulls apart the silver loops that join one bead to another. When she has a small pile of them, she sticks her finger in the dark earth, inhales the old smell of it, and carefully pushes one of the powerful beads into the hole, pats the dirt back into place like a blanket. When she's done she's planted twelve of them. A good number, she thinks, like the number of apostles Jesus had. These Rose Guardians will be helpers to the old Rose Guardian she knows, like all those angels with names all ending in *iel*.

By now the shadows are growing long, and she knows the spirits of that other world will be stirring. Some of them are helpful. Some of them are not. Some of them don't much care.

She goes in for dinner when she's called, stows her satchel and Panda in her room, avoids looking at Doll who watches her every move, and washes her hands. When back downstairs she speaks when spoken to, listens to Ma and Auntie Alice, Gran and Uncle talking around the table, listens not so much to their words but how they say the words, how it's like music sometimes, like rain falling fast then soft, thunder then not. They're eating with the staff in the kitchen because there are guests in the dining room. Brother gurgles in his high chair. He's spitting out mushed peas as fast as Ma spoons them in. And later they retreat to the back parlour where the guests don't go. Mrs. Hamilton and the staff don't follow. There's more talk once the parlour door is closed. Now she listens to the words instead of sounds, because Auntie Alice sniffs comments about how there's no da to take care of Ma and Brother. She notices how she's overlooked in that comment, and wonders if it's because she's taking care of herself just fine, or if girls don't deserve the care of a da. As she watches Ma's face get hard with anger and listens to the way Auntie Alice talks about how boys need a father's strong hand when they get older, she remembers the Bible classes at school and how Eve is responsible for all the sins of the world, and because of that all girls are sinful, and bad.

"Mind your own business," Ma says, and her voice is low and hard. She realizes she listening to something she's not supposed to hear. Uncle says Auntie Alice has gone too far. And at that Ma puts Brother to bed. She stays small in her corner of the sofa, like chippie in the garden when there's something to be afraid of. When Ma comes back she glares at her and is told she can go to bed too, even though it's not nearly her bedtime. But knowing better, she slides off the sofa, kisses each of them goodnight because she's been told it's what she's supposed to do and hates it because she doesn't like getting that close, having lips pressed to her cheek, and smelling smells she doesn't like. Finally, she's free to go to her room. Where it will be safe. Where there aren't growedups being all angry and firing words like arrows.

She presses her back against her door when she's inside her own space. But it's not safe.

Doll is watching in the last of the evening light, like a shadow on her bed, those blue eyes like lamps. She doesn't want to touch Doll but has to so that she can get into bed, setting her on the floor in the corner beside her dresser.

She snuggles down between Panda and the Pussywillow Family, feels her satchel below her feet, under the covers.

"Stop staring," she whispers to Doll, but Doll ignores her, doesn't answer, just keeps staring. Afraid, she turns onto her side and pulls the sheet up over her head like a hood, clutches the cross from the now-destroyed rosemary into her palm until it hurts, and tries to stop her eyes from closing.

But her eyes do close. And for a time, she is safe. And then not, because Doll is in bed with her, those hands on her chest, those eyes bright in the moonlight. She can see the gold hoops of Doll's earrings in that weird light. Doll's hands are heavy, and pressing, and with a cry she shoves Doll out of bed, hears Doll crash onto the wooden floor.

"Go away, go away, go away!" she yells. Doll stares. Her bedroom door crashes open, Ma there, a dark shape in the opening.

"What are you doing? You'll wake all the guests!"

"But Doll!"

"Oh, stop your nonsense and climb back into bed." And Ma lifts Doll from the floor, dumps Doll onto the bed beside her, and says, "Not another word!" Turns and shuts the door behind her, firmly, like an ending.

But she's not going to lie in bed with Doll. She's not.

So, she gets up and drags Doll out of bed, sits her up in the hall outside her bedroom, closes her door and climbs back into bed, pulling the sheets and blankets to her chin.

It was the right thing to do, says Panda.

She nods in the darkness, wishes the Darkies would come to her rescue, wishing Rose Guardian were here. But they are all silent and absent, and there's only herself, Panda and the Pussywillow Family.

When morning comes, Doll hasn't come back into her room.

Something's changed, she thinks, when she washes her face and brushes her teeth. Rose Guardian hasn't shown up. It's been a long time since she's seen the Darkies. She has the Stone of Light which is supposed to be something powerful, something that might help her to signal the Ambassadors from Over There, and if they come in their ships she and Brother can go away to where there's no parade of das, no anger. She can protect her brother Over There. She can make them both safe.

She's thinking about that when she goes down to the kitchen for breakfast. Ma isn't there. Neither is Gran or Auntie Alice. Just Uncle, who pats her head when she sits down, and he slides toast over to her. He's pouring tea for them both. Mrs. Hamilton is punching dough at the other end of the long table.

"Where is everyone?" she asks.

Uncle looks up at Mrs. Hamilton and then away out the window. "Gran's on the porch. Ma's out in the fields."

"And Auntie Alice?"

"Gone home."

"She didn't say goodbye."

"That's okay. She was in a hurry and didn't want to wake you." He looks over at her. "I've put the doll in your ma's room. I'm thinking you don't much like her."

She watches Uncle carefully. "I think Doll doesn't like me."

"Oh?"

"She's always staring at me, and wouldn't stay where she was put."

Uncle nods, then says, "Well, no need to worry now." He sets down his cup. "I'm working out in the orchard today. You're with me."

She smiles at that, glad to spend the summer day with him.

"But Panda and the Pussywillows must bide here."

There's a trill of panic in her chest, and she takes a deep breath to quiet that, knows there's no use arguing and just nods. She scrapes butter over her toast, then marmalade, and bites down. She really wants to give some to Panda and the Pussywillows, but knows that wouldn't be a very good idea right now, so she chews off the crusts and leaves the squooshy centre on the plate, hoping her friends will be able to manage that without her help after she's gone. She looks up at Uncle when she gulped down her tea, and he nods, pushes back in his chair and stands up.

"Mrs. Hamilton," he says.

Mrs. Hamilton smiles and nods.

He turns and stumps out of the kitchen to the back porch where she follows Uncle to the old jalopy of a pickup. The step is too high for her to climb up, and Uncle boosts her in. He lets her hold the gear stick when he hauls himself behind the steering wheel, his hand over hers, and he clutches and turns the key; the engine whines, roars to life, black smoke spewing out the back. He shoves the gear stick forward and they lurch in the same direction, and then bump and jostle their way to the apple orchard.

All day they work with the other hands under the trees, scything grass away from the trunks, out into the path, where other workers fork it up onto a wagon. She has her own scythe that Uncle has made just for her, the handle short, the blade smaller than the ones the adults use.

"It's wicked-sharp," he's warned her, and to prove it he shaved some of the hair from the back of his hand with the tip of the curved blade. "That'll take your finger off it you're not careful, or cut your leg to the bone, so mind where you're swinging."

She thinks she should have had this scythe when she'd been hunting the Jabberwocky and finding the Stone of Light.

She swings the scythe like the others do, and eventually finds the dance, legs wide, knees bent, swing, swoosh, turning from her waist and letting the blade slice the grass. She's been given the task of cutting around the base of the trees, while the workers clear the paths. She does her best to make Uncle proud of her, to do well with the responsibility she's been given. She likes it when he says she's done a good job. There's never any feeling that she could have done better, tried harder, somehow been a disappointment. For a brother and sister, Uncle and Ma are so very different. She wonders if she and Brother will be that different. She hopes not. She doesn't really want to be like Ma, except not so lonely as Uncle who never seems to have anyone in his life. Just this farm. And her.

That thought strikes her as very important, something she needs to poke about at for awhile, study, because there are all kinds of things attached to that thought. She'd like to ask Rose Guardian about that, but begins to think Rose Guardian isn't going to come back.

They pause from their morning's work when lunch arrives from the house, baskets with bread still warm, cheddar that bites back, pickled eggs in jars that glow in the shade of the trees. There are bevers of water and beer, but she gets the water. The young lads who work with them laugh and share stories of being in town, the girls they're eyeing, and Uncle says, "Mind now," and they all look toward her. Some mutter, "Sorry." And their conversation stills, then rises again, slowly, like water in a summer spring.

After lunch, the baskets and bevers are stowed into Uncle's pickup. They all pick up their scythes and go back to work. She's tired by now, but tries to keep up, gives up, and stands there under an old apple tree, just staring up into the branches where balls of green blushing red hang. The harvest for fall, some to be saved for the family, some to be sold, some to be turned into cider—the kinds she can and can't drink—apple butter, jelly, dried and bagged in paper for the small store they run on the edge of the farm.

She sinks down under the shade of the tree, pulls off her straw hat and rests her head against the rough bark. Beyond her she can hear the workers, their scythes swishing, the hiss of grass as it falls to rows behind them. It's like a lullaby. She hums to that rhythm. Drifting.

And then she's jostling about, opens her eyes, finds herself in the pickup and evening light upon the land.

"I'm sorry, Uncle," she says and sits up.

"You did well, my flower. There's no sorry to be said."

And so she's content.

Once home she washes up for dinner, sits at table, and devours everything on her plate. She reaches over from time to time to spoon mush into her brother's mouth when Ma's arguing with Gran, and Brother grins at her, gurgles, and the talk of her elders disappears in the contentment of being home, with her brother, of sharing the end of the day around the table in their kitchen.

There's the cleaning up after, and she volunteers to help Mrs. Hamilton. That takes them past her bedtime, so she quickly says her goodnights, does her personal washing up, and then climbs into bed. She hugs Panda fiercely, strokes each of the Pussywillows, and sings night songs to bring on sleep and dreams, and complete the happiness that's been this day.

But Doll would have it otherwise, for she's there in the night, clawing into her bed, those strange clay hands around her throat, teeth bared. She screams and hurls Doll from her, down to the floor. She hears a crack, and with that she knows there's only one solution to the problem of Doll. She hurls herself off the bed. Doll clutches at her ankle. She reaches for her pack and finds the holy ash she's made from the rose petals she dried and saved, hurls it into Doll's eyes. Doll hisses and rubs at the ash. In that moment, she finds what's left of the Vorpal blade in her pack, hopes the rusty, broken shard on the end of the wooden handle will be enough and with a cry of rage leaps upon Doll, afraid like she was when the Balor tried to take her, crying and whispering fiercely, "You won't, you won't, you won't," and hacks at Doll until Doll is only a doll, broken and shattered.

In the stillness that follows she feels sick. Her arms are shaking, and now her whole body, and she's telling herself to be still, to be quiet, to think about what to do next, because there's always a next, always things to tidy, to put in place, a path to figure out toward the light. She knows Ma will be mad because she's destroyed Doll, won't understand that something so beautiful could be so evil, that gifts can be dangerous. And because of that she also knows she has to make it look like Doll was never in her room, never attacked her, never was anything but a doll and something to be admired. There is only one answer she can see: break Doll down into tiny bits, bury those bits with more of the Holy Ash near Rose Guardian so that Doll can never be put back together, never be found, never cause harm to anyone again. And it all has to be done now, quietly.

Carefully, she opens her door, lets her sight get used to the darkness of the hall, and when she can see well enough goes to the linen cupboard, finds a pillowcase and returns to her room, closing her door. Piece by piece she puts the broken bits of Doll into the pillowcase, and with each bit added uses the butt of the blade to crush each piece to pebbles, and more Holy Ash, put in another bit and does it all over again.

Ashes to ashes, dust to dust.

When she's done she hefts the pillowcase over her

shoulder, makes her way outside without drawing any attention, finds a trowel in the garden shed and with the grass cool and damp under her feet she makes her way to the roses, to Rose Guardian, and digs. It's hard because the roses scratch, but she knows she must do this, and keeps digging, wincing, careful not to disturb too many roots, and finally the hole is big enough. She pats the pillowcase into its grave, pulls dirt over the white cloth, smelling the earth, smelling the roses, pats it all down and then lies down herself in the cool grass. She's not afraid of the cobwebs in her lungs, of the fact her breath is short and hard to find. She just stretches out, being calm, breathing as deeply and slowly as she can. It's all okay. It's all fine.

And then there's warm morning light on her face, and Ma over her, tears on her face, saying, "Lettie, Lettie, what have you done?"

The Show

Uncle joined me in the kitchen in the afternoon, an inquiry spoken, an answer caught in my throat and left unspoken. I continued to take the frozen stew out of the freezer and set it on a plate on the counter, and scribbled a note as to how many minutes his dinner should nuke.

"I'm thinking you're in no fit state for this fete," he said.

I continued to take out bowl and spoon, hot mats, trying to make his bachelor night as easy as possible. And avoiding his comment.

"What is it ails you, Violet? I'd think you'd be excited."

I know, I know, I thought, wanting to spill the metaphorical stew of my thoughts. But couldn't. Wouldn't. He didn't need his niece to fall apart once again. He needed to know I was okay, that he could spend his last years in contentment, not having to watch over me as he had all these decades.

"Just pre-show jitters," I said at last. "You know how much I enjoy crowds of people."

He barked a laugh. "Then why you keep doing these things is beyond me."

"Because it's part of promoting your work so you can pay the bills."

"I should never have given you those paints."

I turned around then and looked at him, his electric blue eyes, the apples of his cheeks. "What, and rob me of the obsession that ended up my therapy?" I smiled at him, giving him that much of a physical assurance, a small thing, a needed thing. "This has been my life's journey, Uncle. How could that not be good?"

"I'll come if you want."

"You'll stay tucked up here with your war movies, stew, and stout."

"You're sure?"

"Yes, yes. Besides, the only thing that could make me more nervous about this show, is wondering how my uncle who loves crowds even less than I is faring. I wouldn't do that to you."

"And you'll check in of course."

"Of course. And you can text me anytime you like just to ease your worry, 'cause I know you will—worry."

"Can't help it."

"Then we make a good team, worrying about each other."

"Isn't that what a husband and wife are for?"

"I've had a husband."

"And lost him."

"So, what, I'm defined by a husband? I know exactly where he is. And he's better off."

I watched frustration twist his face, felt a jerk for doing this.

"Your Ma's daughter."

And he stumped off. I continued to set things out for his evening, and left a note on top of the container of frozen dinner to say what I could not.

I spent longer than I should getting dressed for the show opening, frittering away time, studying my ass in the mirror, both the posterior and anterior. In the end I succumbed to Greg and Robert's choice of ensemble.

Uncle was sitting in the living room, watching some streaming documentary. I pecked the top of his head. He sighed and patted my hand where it rested on his shoulder, and I left the house.

The roads were clear. In fact, it was a fine day, sharp and cold, snow on the land. I kept thinking of how I'd paint this field, this barn, this rise of escarpment. Ultramarine for shadow, good paper left untouched for snow, sepia and Prussian green for cedars and pines, a touch of red madder and Winsor blue for the distant woods of maples, birch and ash. Soft washes. Dry brush work. Yes. My raison d'être. And so, the kilometres melted away, David Francey softly buzzing over the sound of this old Honda's engine and the burr of the tires. My thoughts stilled and focused on the intake of sights and sounds, a meditation of sorts which took me through to Gore Bay.

When I walked in through the back entrance of Ayashe's gallery, the scent of patchouli hung on the air, Johnny Whitehorse's music a totemic pulse in the background. She looked up from where she arranged glasses on a sideboard, smiled broadly, and crossed to enclose me in an embrace.

"This is going to be a good day," she said.

"You're sure about that, are you?"

"Just look around you, Vi."

I did. It was a good exhibition, some of my best work. "And we open in an hour?"

She nodded. "Here, come help me finish with these

glasses. I finally got the special event license so we could have a bit of wine. And Jeanne up the street put together the cheese and fruit platters for us. Even had her husband bake us some of his fabulous pastries."

By the time we'd put the final touches on the nosh and slosh, the local reportage was there, taking pictures, making digital notes, grabbing sound bites for broadcast. Despite myself, I was enjoying talking about what I did, the impetus behind some of the paintings. Talking about my craft. It was surprisingly easy. Phrases spilled out of my mouth without apparent need to carefully hedge and craft what I said. There were no agendas here. No politics.

And that free exchange of ideas and banter simply flowed into the rest of the afternoon and early evening as locals arrived. Ayashe's staff had been well-briefed, as always, and as I was drawn from one group to another, I was aware of red stickers appearing on exhibit labels, while I said, "That storm? Yes, I canoed through that. Kept thinking about Tom Thomson's ghost rising up to take me down with him," and "Sure, yeah, that was a remarkable morning, the way the mist rose out of the spruce bog. As I recall there was a loon wailing." And I remembered the frisson of wonder chasing across my skin.

When the last of the guests left, the bell over the door ringing like a Buddhist prayer, I just stood there in the open space of the gallery, a little overwhelmed, drained but buoyant somehow. I thought I would like to sleep. I thought I would like to go walking in the clear, crisp night.

I looked over to Ayashe who grinned like an idiot. I laughed. So did she.

"All but three sold," she said. "And I think there are people who are going to come back for them after the holidays."

I stared at her, more than shocked. And in that moment, I wished Ma knew about this, would find it somewhere in her mind of penury to wish me well, even speak of pride. But she was gone. And everything that could have been, might have been, were but ghosts and wishes, ashes on the wind. Tears pricked sudden and sharp. I blinked.

Ayashe said, "Oh now, Vi," and I knew she thought me overwhelmed by the success of the show. I let the lie remain. Easier that way.

I looked down, spoke thanks, apology for not accepting her invitation for dinner, and looked up and turned for the door where there in the glass I saw Lettie's face. And then not. I felt a shard slide through my chest, the yin to this day's yang.

"Thanks again, Ayashe," I said, more to chase away my dread, and headed for the back entrance, my car, and a return to the sanctuary of Meldrum Bay.

She hung up on me. She said she'd had enough of my judgement, interference, disapproval. She screamed. She hung up.

They say fathers and sons have a hard time communicating. I think so do mothers and daughters.

I fear I've lost her. And now I wonder what I should have done differently. To enumerate, I think, would be a life's work.

So, I've successfully registered the patent on my fragrant, thornless white rose, now known as the Cotter Rose. An award-winning rose. If I've bungled everything else in my life, I have not bungled that.

In the evening, sitting on the stone bench in the rose garden, I watch their luminous blooms, inhale their old Damascus perfume. I guess we each seek out our own anodynes.

Just when you think you're done with tears, you discover you're not. Ianto has informed me he's moving to Manitoulin. Violet, it seems, has contacted him, in a bit of a bad way. She and David have divorced. He won't give me details, only says he's of limited use now on the farm, that the corporation it's become does very well without him, and he would like to be of some use to someone in his dotage.

While there was a great deal I wanted to say, what was I to actually put out there between us? That I was sorry? For so very much. And that regret is utterly useless yet inescapable and necessary. That I didn't want him to go. I wanted Violet to come home, here, to this stone fortress we Cotters have made. I wanted forgiveness and to forgive. Life is all about grey and truths which are multi-faceted, complex, and ambiguous.

But I said none of this, just nodded, asked when and what I could do to make it easier.

Perhaps our greatest fears remain so because they are inescapable.

Spells and Promises

She's made a promise to Ma to never dig around the roses again, to be careful not to get hurt, to think about what she's doing. She's kept that promise. She realizes it's important to take care of herself so she can take care of those she loves, and while Ma doesn't realize the harm she allowed to happen to herself was because she was being responsible, it also doesn't matter. Scratches from thorns would heal, only now she realizes sometimes what hurts inside is just like a scratch, and sometimes that scratch stays hurting.

Now, however, she's concerned that not only has Rose Guardian stopped talking to her, stopped appearing, but Panda is no longer talking to her. She doesn't know why. She's always taken care of Panda, and Panda's taken care of her. Maybe Panda's upset she's spending so much time with Brother and doing schoolwork? Maybe Panda's upset she no longer takes him with her on her walks? This summer has been different. For the first time she's aware time is something to be measured, and cared for, because there is only so much time she'll have to herself. She'll be out in the fields with Uncle or Ma, with only a few hours to herself. School will start again in the fall. And then there will be all that study, which is wonderful to discover all those things she doesn't know, but it also means less time to be with Brother, Panda, and the Pussywillows.

She kneels down to her bedside table where she keeps the Pussywillow's house, slides it out, and sets it before her on the floor. She knocks. No one answers, which is strange, and she feels her heart kind of collapse at the thought they, also, will no longer speak with her.

She lifts the lid on their house and peers into what had been neatly divided rooms. Walls have tilted, furniture fallen, and every single one of the Pussywillows has brown, withered threads sticking out of them, their silky, grey fur gone. Dead, she realizes, and tears are sudden. Her fault, she realizes. They're dead and it's her fault. She should have taken better care, been with them more. But no, she'd been too busy. Always too busy. And now it's too late.

And that makes her wonder if she doesn't spend time with Panda, will he die too?

She looks up to where Panda sits on her bed, says, "I won't let that happen," takes him into her arms and goes to find Brother. When she does, he's in the pen Uncle set up in the backyard, made from withy fences they use for sheep.

Brother grins up at her when she joins him, leans on the brown, woven fence.

"I've brought you someone to keep you company," she says, finding it hard to catch her breath, to say this thing without blubbering like a baby. "You have to take good care of him now. His name is Panda, and I love him very much, and so must you." Panda says nothing at all to her as she hands him over to Brother who reaches out and giggles, clutching the black and white bear tightly, thumps down to his bum and immediately sets into a chatter with her old friend. She's trying hard not to cry, but the pain in her chest is like she's being ripped open, so she just stands there for a little while, gulping, refusing to let herself give way. And when finally it's clear Panda now has a good friend, and that the two of them are talking, she turns back to the house where she collects the Pussywillows, and then buries them in the rose garden where she's promised never to play. But this isn't play. This is serious work. And she realizes she's never really played where Rose Guardian lives. It's always been about figuring out how to deal with problems. A lot of that had been about spells and promises. The spells had always gone wrong somehow, ended creating other problems. And the promises now were all broken, because sometimes things forced you to make hard decisions.

When she pats the dirt over the Pussywillows, she finally understands what it means to be responsible, about not allowing the fact you're afraid to force you into a bad decision. And knowing that, she also knows she's alone.

Summer passes, school starts, winter and biting cold, study and study and more study. Ma's always barking at her, at Uncle, and now that Gran's dead—Ma hates it when she says dead rather than passed away, but dead is dead—Ma has time for little else besides the farm and her roses. Spring comes, and she defies the call to church at Easter. Uncle supports her. Ma is furious and bangs out the door and digs a whole patch of garden, for the second time. This becomes a familiar pattern between them. She stops seeking comfort in Ma's company, and Uncle fills in, the two of them conspirators. And so, another summer, another fall.

Time and time and time. Words thrown like spears. A crack growing in her heart and then shattered the day Ma says to Brother, who's now old enough to begin to understand the real meaning behind words, "She's not really your sister. Her father left. Just like yours." And the look on Brother's face as his world shifts and shatters. A rift now between them. Somehow, she's to blame for everything.

She's watching Brother chatter to Panda out in the garden. Her window is open, and his voice drifts up to her with the scents of roses and earth. She wonders if she sounded much the same as her brother at that age. Decides not. Brother's all about rough and ready, boy-stuff, and charges through the garden as though he owns it, his laughter as raucous as jays. He brutalizes dear Panda as he goes. She realizes it's been six summers since she gave Panda into his care. And the loss of her friend still smarts. But they seem happy together, so there is solace in that, even if she wishes for conversation with her old friend. Brother now crashes toward the bed of roses where she used to find direction and advice from the Rose Guardian. The white rose is in full bloom, bright in the early morning light. Last evening, she visited again.

Are you there?

And there was only the scratch of crickets.

Will you never come to me again?

And a catch in her heart when a breeze stirred the tall stems, yellow pollen scattering like gold dust, and only a rose where there had once been a guardian.

She turns from memory and the scene out her window and looks back down to the books open on her desk, the classical sculptures she's studying for the summer course she's taking, one not allowed by Ma during the school year. Were it not for Uncle, this course would never have happened, and she's grateful for his interference. She has thrown herself into her studies, preened when Uncle has praised her for her good marks, and withered when Ma has asked why she hasn't gotten perfect. She's come to understand being second-best isn't the best, and nothing else is good enough. So, she studies.

But this morning there had been a call for her during breakfast, and a voice: "It's Dorothy."

"Oh hi," and disappointment already suffocating her.

"Mum's taking us swimming and I'm allowed to bring a friend. Can you come?"

A friend? Was she a friend? Dorothy as lonely as she. "Let me ask," she says, and turns the receiver into her chest. She looks over to where Ma's talking to Mrs. Hamilton, watches the frown that seems to be forever on her face. What was the point in even asking?

She turns the receiver back to her face, and says, "I'm not allowed."

"Oh, you're never allowed."

"I have school work to do, and Ma wants me to work on the farm this afternoon."

"Well, it is summer holidays."

"I know."

"You sure you can't come? It would be so fun."

She looks back up at Ma, watches the way her hands are punctuating every word she says. "No. Sorry. Maybe another time."

"Oh, okay. Sure."

And she had the feeling that would be the last time

she'll be asked, because it's always been no. Ma and Uncle argue about this all the time. She doesn't want to hear another argument, and so she goes to her room and studies. Study means escape. Study means she might finally be good enough.

But she's also discovered that when her studies are finished, and she can steal some time just for herself, she climbs into another world with pencil and paper, filling time with things she's seen, and some she hasn't. While long ago Rose Guardian stopped speaking to her, she speaks of what she remembers through colour and shadow, shape and form. And if Rose Guardian no longer communes, then her drawings do. Sometimes it's almost as if the trees, the rocks, the plants, and creatures she creates out of nothing whisper to her, secrets of a life which now feels very distant, like an ache left long after the wound has healed.

Summer becomes autumn, and autumn becomes winter, the colours out her window shifting from green to gold, gold to white. She's worked in the orchards with Uncle and the labourers, scything and pruning, netting and harvesting. The books across her desk open and close, information and worlds condensing in her mind. She's learned to walk through the house like shadow: lurking, insubstantial. It's best this way.

But her sketchbooks grow and bulge with life, secreted away from judgement and knowledge.

The summer hubbub below also has shifted from buzz to patter, and now to long hours of quiet. She lifts the pencil from her sketchbook, listens. There are no voices raised in anger, no disagreement that echoes and rattles up the stairs from the back parlour. She looks out her bedroom window to snow skirling, glad for the winter that closes up the guest house for a few months, glad for the privacy that comes with that. It's as though the farm sleeps, which isn't entirely true, she knows, because there's always the stock to tend, and always the hired hands coming and going.

She tilts her head again, listening. There's a footfall on the stairs, heavy. Uncle, she's sure, and turns in the chair at her desk toward the door where there's now a soft rap of knuckles, and Uncle's voice, "Are you accepting visitors?"

"Of course." And she watches the doorknob turn, the door slowly swing open, steadily, and there Uncle in his raggedy brown cardigan with the elbows out, blue flannel shirt buttoned near to his neck, and his old leather slippers beneath trousers too long and grown threadbare. He looks an old wreck, she thinks, like the hobos who come to their back stoop on Sundays when Ma has Mrs. Hamilton feed them soup and bread in exchange for a few hours work mucking pens.

Uncle has a large, flat, black briefcase-like thing in his hand. A portfolio, she realizes, narrows her eyes and looks up at him, question quick in her mouth but left unsaid.

He smiles at her, steps into the soft glow in her room, and thumps down on the edge of her bed. He sets the portfolio against the footboard.

"I thought you could use a safe place to store all these drawings you're making."

There's a flutter of pleasure in her chest. She looks down at the beautiful leather of the case, up at Uncle's bright blue eyes. She knows the exact colour of those eyes now, names it to herself, watches the way the light shines through their lenses like a candle through a glass of water.

"You've bought me a portfolio," she says unnecessarily, feeling foolish for the obvious statement.

He gestures to it. "Aren't you going to take a look?"

She slides off her chair and crosses to the footboard, sinks to her knees and runs her hand over the cool surface of the gift. "It's wonderful," and tugs at the tapes that tie it closed, watches as it unfolds, revealing hidden gifts, reams of paper, graphite pencils, and most precious of all, a small enameled travel palette and box with small tubes of watercolours. "Thank you," she says, and feels that's small gratitude for so great a gift.

"You just be sure to store all your work in that."

She looks up at him. "Keep it out of Ma's way."

He nods. "She was none too pleased."

"When is Ma ever pleased with anything I do?"

"Now, that's not entirely true."

"Seems so to me. I heard you two arguing down there earlier. Probably over this."

"This and other things."

"And you're not going to tell me."

He shook his head. "You've enough to worry about with your studies without concerning yourself about matters you can't control."

"I think I'd like that."

"What?"

"To be able to control things."

"Careful what you wish for, my flower." He stands and touches the curls on the top of her head. "I'm glad you're chuffed."

"I am. Thanks again."

And after he closes the door and leaves her to her own domain, she realizes Uncle has given her the ability to escape, that she now has discovered what it means to be *created in His image.*

<h1 style="text-align:center">Over There</h1>

In the days that followed I played backgammon with Uncle, laid out a ridiculously huge jigsaw on the dining table, and for long stretches we sat there, sorting pieces, fitting, discarding a choice, finding another. Silence drifted in the house, comfortable, eloquent.

I'd bundle him up and the two of us would set out in the clear cold, walking the property and the shore. Not for the first time he said, "I am so glad the show went well." And: "I'm proud of you, my flower."

I watched him, careful of his age, of his dicky heart, resolved to make what time we had left together good days. They would never come again. The past summer taught me that. I'd squandered so much of my life chasing after things that would never be, only to find myself in a bitter cage. And now, after the show, somehow I'd walked to a threshold. I was still afraid to step through. A cage is, after all, a sanctuary of sorts.

It was upon one such perambulate Uncle chose to go in ahead of me.

"I'll come make you tea," I said.

"No such thing. It's a fine afternoon. You enjoy your walk. I've a mind to just sit by the fire and pretend I'm reading."

I laughed and bussed his cheek.

"You have your phone?"

He patted his pocket.

"And you'll text me if you need anything?"

"You expecting your old uncle to kack off while you're communing with the cardinals?" He laughed at his pun, a wild light in his eyes I knew so well and loved. He turned away and shuffled to the house, leaning heavily on his cane. I watched to be sure he managed the steps to the porch, saw him swing open the door and close it. He lifted his hand behind the glass to wave me off, both an admonishment and thanks.

I wondered, if in a way he'd found sanctuary here on this isolated bay as had I? Had his attempt to offer me support all those years ago also been a way to unburden himself of the black hole that had been Ma's universe?

And so, Meldrum Bay. A life of relative isolation, of quiet, in a way of indulgence. The Cotter Farm was now a business of consideration, managed perfectly well by the team he'd helped to assemble, as much as Ma. The patent for the Cotter Rose was now protected under my management, and Bennett could manage all else. The legacy was complete. Only now did I understand that, accept it, recognize the shift on the political map of my life.

I made my way to the dock, brushed away snow from the bench and settled to its cold surface. The wind had died. There was a skim of ice on the cobble shore, but the bay was open, calm like my heart.

I remembered the last entry in Ma's journal: *Perhaps our greatest fears remain so because they are inescapable.*

It was only then I realized she'd never discovered

the door to her cage could be a journey to something better, that she'd allowed herself to remain the victim despite all her considerable achievements. Did that knowledge grant me the grace to forgive her? Perhaps. But I had to wonder if the act of forgiveness didn't also require the need to be forgiven. Was forgiveness perhaps a dialogue? And this dialogue with Ma would never happen, not then, not now. Which left only regret. Ghosts.

And just as I knew she would, there was Lettie beside me on the bench, watching the gloaming, that distant bank of clouds so like a far-away shore. Between us and the mirage over there, the lake became molten with light, and if you looked carefully you could make out the specs of distant ships.

My breath caught. I pulled Lettie onto my lap.

"So, Lettie Cotter," I said. "Looks like the Ambassadors from Over There are finally coming for you."

"I've waited so long."

I kissed her cheek, feeling the cold air, feeling release, and she climbed off my lap, stepped to the end of the dock and beyond.

I watched her go. It's a strange thing to witness part of yourself leaving, to know somehow you've sent your heart out into the world. It's a perilous thing this thing of love. And without it we are fractured, unable to accept the wonder of a gift so simple as a trick of light, or the formation of clouds.

About the Author

Lorina Stephensis aneditor, freelance journalist for national and regional print media, author of six books both fiction and non-fiction, a festival organizer, publicist, lectures on many topics from historical textiles and domestic technologies, to publishing and writing;teaches, and continues to work as a writer, artist, and publisher.She has had several short fiction pieces published in On Specmagazine, Postscripts to Darkness, Neo-Opsis, Deluge, Strangers Among Us,and Sword & Sorceress X.Lorina Stephens is presently working on a new novel entitled, The Rose Guardian, and another, Caliban.She lives with her husband of four plus decades, in a historic stone house in Neustadt, Ontario.

Shadow Song

By Lorina Stephens

Vengeance in the backwoods of Upper Canada. An uncle insane with retribution, a midewiwin following a vision, and the girl caught between both worlds.

Danielle Michele Fleming, 10 year old daughter of a French aristocratic mother, and the second son of English gentry, finds herself caught in the economic ruin that surrounds the failure of the Bourbon Monarchy. She finds herself aboard ship, destined for the Queen's Bush of Upper Canada and a life with the catalyst of her doom, her uncle, Edgar Fleming. Relentless in his hunt for her, her uncle has her tracked not only by bounty hunters, but in the end through another shaman of evil intent and a blood-debt to settle with Shadow Song.

Shadow Song
By Lorina Stephens

I remember the summer I met Shadow Song was so green it hurt my eyes. It was as if the world were carved from jade — something sacred and equally fragile. I, Danielle Michelle Fleming, was to become mesmerized by this world. This land, this Upper Canada, was a place where I would learn to breathe.

That had been the summer of 1832. What brought me across the ocean from England, ultimately, were dreams. The priests said these visions were devil's work. I was a child. How was I to know there were things the priests feared? How was I to know my visions were ambivalent? The irony of it is I never asked for this gift. I was content with a life revolving around a household of parents, governess and servants.

My journey began earlier than that green summer of 1832. It began with the July Revolution of 1830 in France. I will forever remember that day, young as I was, remember how my safe English universe unravelled around a slip of paper quivering in Papa's hand. Such moment can ensue from something as simple as words on paper.

I'd heard the bell ring at the front door, heard Mrs. Barton, our housekeeper, answer, the usual banter between her and the courier. As always, being curious — nosy my governess called it — I crept along the landing to watch. Papa would come to the foyer I knew. Mail was always important. It carried news of his business, news of the world, news of family. In this case it was to be news of all three. By the time I reached my favorite place, face pressed between the railings, Maman joined Papa in the foyer.

Sunlight gleamed on the white marble floor, like lace where it passed through the transom over the front door. There were lilies, white and frail, in a vase on the table against the paneling. The lilies' fragrance was pungent, like a drug to calm the nerves.

"Que est que c'est?" Maman asked, pointing to the letter in Papa's hand.

He paled. He shook his head slowly, as if the weight of what he thought were more than he could bear. He looked up from the paper and over to Maman where she stood in a halo of light. The expression on his face chilled me. A gentle man, Papa had never been wordless, never shown the slightest indication he was anything less than invincible in his steady, calm manner. Completely bewildered was how he looked. Bewilderment faded and was replaced with something I could only think of as fear. It was there in his voice when he said, "The French government has failed."

Maman, I was sure, was on the verge of shattering. She had always been delicate, like the lilies in the vase — intoxicating, enchanting, and tender to any misuse. Today she was dressed in russet silk, fashionably high-waisted with enormous gigot sleeves, her hair arranged like a dark, sleek ribbon on the crown of her head. For a moment Maman searched for words and when none sufficed she touched Papa's arm. Finally: "King Charles?"

"Has exiled himself here, England."

"And the indemnity?"

He shook his head.

"Nothing?"

Again he shook his head.

"But it had been made law. All émigrés who had their lands confiscated by that Republican nonsense were to receive an indemnity. The King guaranteed it."

He didn't even meet her look when he answered, "There is to be nothing."

Another moment of silence passed. I could hear the floor-clock down the hall ticking, ticking, ponderously ticking. Its sound thumped in my head like those ominous words, meaningless and yet full of portent. It echoed the thump of my heart. Then Maman asked, "Will Edgar foreclose on the loan?"

Edgar, the elder Fleming, my uncle. Just hearing his name gave me a shiver of apprehension. I drew into myself on the staircase. My uncle's name always connected to bitter words and hardship. I didn't know him. Uncle Edgar sailed away before I was born, taking the family fortune and his luck with him to the colonies of Upper Canada, yet somehow he always seemed present whenever bad news blew in. I had come to think of him as the maker of ill fortune, and came to know him as the engineer of my misery.

"Edgar has no security now," Papa answered. "Everything I borrowed from my brother was secured against your lands in France, and the indemnity guaranteed by the Bourbon government."

"But will your brother foreclose on the loan?"

"Yes."

Another moment. Maman asked another question. "Have they taken everything?"

"Yes."

Maman smiled, although it was plain her smile

was one of those let's-be-brave smiles. "Ça va, my Lord Fleming. Now we are both titled and indigent. You the youngest son of an English nobleman, and I the exiled aristocrat of France."

"At least we have our heads."

Maman let out a small gasp, poor attempt at a laugh, and laid her head against Papa's chest.

The demise of the Fleming mercantile house of Gloucester came swiftly, although I understood little of what occurred, only that the loss of my home, and my belongings, were because of an uncle in some land over there, the colony beyond the ocean. The first few months staff disappeared from our household: the above-stairs maid, then the scullery maid.

The day my governess was paid off Maman arrived in the classroom, arranged herself on the chair beside where I waited at my desk. She was attired in sensible grey linen, a spotless apron of white tied at her waist, a cap of white linen on her head. Such a contrast to the brilliant silks and rich, printed cottons and wools I was accustomed to seeing her in.

She was pale in the morning light, the shadows of a sleepless night around her eyes. Her mouth, usually full-lipped and rosy, this morning was pale and thin.

"Are you not well, Maman?" I asked.

"Eh, bien. De rein."

"Where is Miss Abbott?"

Maman looked away out the windows of my study to the view of the kitchen gardens. I had climbed the window seat earlier and opened the casements to let in the air which was rich with the scents of the herbs that grew there. Two weeks ago there had been two gardeners who worked for us. One of them would have been there in the garden, harvesting the cook's needs for the day. Today it was the cook herself who harvested.

"Maman?" I said when she gave no response.

"S'excuse moi, ma cherie," she said, turning her attention back to me. "We have had to let Miss Abbott go."

"Did she do something wrong?"

"No, no. Nothing wrong."

"Then why did she have to go?"

"We have to make economies, Danielle."

"So I'm not to have a governess?"

"Your papa and I feel you are quite capable of governing yourself, and I will continue with your lessons." She managed a wan smile. "You will of course honour our trust in you?"

"Of course, Maman." I wanted to hug her, to make her laugh and see her face brighten, but I knew it was important I conduct myself in an adult fashion. They depended on me to be responsible. I swallowed the lump in my throat along with my wish to have at least been allowed a leave-taking with Miss Abbott. "What shall we study today?"

That seemed to settle Maman's concern. She smoothed her apron. "I believe Miss Abbott had you working on maths and ancient history."

"Yes, Maman. I completed the assignment she gave me yesterday." And handed her my work.

And so we passed the morning without speaking again of the new arrangement. I became accustomed to studying under Maman's guidance, and over the next weeks her time with me became less, usually brief instruction in the morning as to the path my study of the day was to take, assignments given, assignments collected.

While I was lonely, I didn't mind the solitary study I undertook. In fact I quite enjoyed the digressions while reading about one thing and discovering another. After awhile Maman allowed me free access to the library with the comment all knowledge was valuable.

Cook was paid off shortly after that. Along with her went Maman's lady's maid and Papa's valet.

Shortly after that furnishings and possessions went out the door with businessmen my father invited and saw to and from our home by himself, without the aid of Mrs. Barton who had left some weeks before, chewing on tears.

Maman took to cooking and cleaning, and I found myself in her wake, scrubbing floors and chopping vegetables along with her. The grand home with its grand grounds proved too much for we three, and so the final economy was made.

Within six months I found myself shuttered into two small rooms shared with Maman, Papa, and the rats scurrying through the tenement. None of Papa's former associates came to call, which to me was amazing. Our home had always been full of people, meetings in Papa's study, business discussed over elegant dinners, ladies in rustling gowns. Considering we no longer had the floor-clock, the silver, the study or the garden, I supposed my parents didn't wish to entertain in rooms as these. The reasoning of a child can be so facile, and sometimes so utterly clear.

The positions Papa found between then and the

November of 1831 were many and varied, and never enough to keep us. He seemed distant, still as a pool of water before wind ripples its surface and obliterates its reflections. I learned what it was really like to be hungry, to have your belly churn in the dark so you couldn't sleep. We subsisted on barley, bread and cheese. I think Maman could have published a book of receipts on the uses of barley. We ate a pottage of barley with rationed bits of salted pork. Endlessly. She made a sort of savoury barley pudding augmented by whatever vegetable greens she could scrounge from the waste at the Gloucester market, and when greens weren't in season it was rotten onions and turnips she carefully pared down. I am sure she cried enough over these dishes to preclude the need for salt.

Papa tried very hard to keep our spirits bolstered when we would gather to table. Always there was some little anecdote of the day, some absurdity with which he would try to tease a smile, perhaps even a laugh from Maman and me. When anecdotes failed he'd resort to mimicry of some street-seller or market-person or character of note we knew.

It was upon one such moment of escape Maman slammed down her knife and fork, her hands fluttering to her eyes in an attempt to staunch another flow of tears. "I wish he were dead!" she cried. "That he should visit such suffering upon his own family! May there be a special place in hell for him!"

I turned to Papa, watching for his reaction. He raised his eyebrows, looked down to the table and then seemed to gather his resources. "Hell, my dear? Oh, I think even hell is too strong a punishment for my brother."

"How can you say that? He has shown nothing of human compassion whatever. Just look at what he's done to all those families of fallen soldiers! Thieved them of what little estate they had, left them penniless and he attempts to justify this by saying better invested as he would do than squandered.

"And just look at what ruin he has wrought upon his own!"

"Agreed. But neither has he done anything so heinous as to warrant eternal damnation. Forgive me, my dear, but I believe he will receive his punishment. I think the Almighty is too clever at dispensing justice to offer him mere purgatory. I do believe that instead of joining the congregation of angels and rewarded souls, he will be relegated to the menial tasks of heaven. Perhaps my brother will receive the position of Midden Master, shovelling human waste for all of eternity."

My mother removed her hands from her face and looked across the table at my father as though he had gone quite mad. And then she laughed, truly laughed. "Midden Master! Oh, I would like to see that!"

And from there they amused and comforted us all with speculation of just how Uncle's heavenly reward would unfold.

That evening Papa tucked me into bed and we continued telling the story we were creating. I found myself distracted, concerned for the welfare of my parents, and when it was my turn to add a bit more to the tale, I turned my face away, blinking away tears.

"What is it, Child?" Papa said, brushing my cheek. "Are you not well?"

I sat up and threw my arms around him, trying

hard not to give way to the sobs that were there. Papa enfolded me, rocking back and forth.

"Why does Uncle hate us so?" I asked when I felt I could speak without giving way to histrionics.

"Oh, now, that is a tangled story. I'm not sure you would understand."

"Papa! I read a great deal of what was in our library. You know I can handle maths and sciences beyond what most girls — no, children — my age and even older can comprehend. Surely I can make sense of what lies behind Uncle." I looked up at him, watched the way the fading light of day softened his angular face.

"It's complicated, Danielle."

"Please!"

He sighed, ran his hand through his hair. "I think Edgar despises me because he thinks I received the attention and love that should have been his."

"What do you mean?"

"Your grandpapa, my father, was always hard on Edgar. Edgar was the oldest. The family fortune was to be settled on him and Papa felt, and rightly so, that Edgar should be responsible. But in doing so Papa indulged me where Edgar was given no latitude. And then to add insult to my brother's injury there is the question of your Maman."

"What about Maman?"

"It was my brother who knew her first, and my brother who loved her first. She didn't know. Neither did I. Edgar had learned to hide his feelings rather well, part of being the responsible heir. And so when your Maman and I finally met, and found ourselves in love, Edgar saw our happiness as just one more proof of his ill-treatment. We quarrelled. And then Papa and he quarrelled. Papa took a stroke and died. Edgar blamed me for that as well."

"But none of that is your fault."

"I know this. But sometimes the heart doesn't allow us to see clearly, Danielle." He gave me a hug and kissed the top of my head. "Now come, Child. I have said too much. And you must sleep."

Reluctantly I separated from his embrace and lay back on the straw mattress, feeling it scrunch under my head. "I love you, Papa. I think you're a good man."

He inhaled sharply, his face set with profound emotion. "As I love you, Child. Always. Forever." He bent and kissed me again, rose and pulled the curtain across my wee corner of the room.

It was shortly after that the dreams came, dreams that were like waking moments. It was like staring through a keyhole into a situation that was, or might be. My stomach would lurch and I'd lie there in bed half aware of the rats, half aware of the scene playing out before my eyes. I wondered if it was a demon in me, threatening to violate the temple of my body as the priests often warned. Maybe it was nothing at all but hunger.

For a while the daylight hours were safest. One didn't have dreams in the sunlight. One didn't fear demons. Soon even the sanctity of the day failed. I dreamed of Papa and his stillness. I dreamed of all his reflections shattering. I wished it not to be so. My wish was in vain. Papa withered as an apple kept too long in the sun, as if something important shrank away inside him. When once he would have dandled me on his knee, he now only allowed me to sit there, his blue eyes pale like the faded colours of the curtains.

It was in this quiet, still way he died, with me on his knee. We wandered early that morning down to the Gloucester docks. Such industry there. Everywhere were longshoremen, spectres in the river-mist, unloading and loading, transporting to and from warehouses. All sound was muffled, deadened by the heavy air. The grey spires of ships could be seen in the river. Shouts rippled through the air, the toll of a bell aboard ship for the change of watch. I wrinkled my nose to the smell, something despite familiarity I could never abide: the stench of refuse and urine, tar and tobacco, sulphur and in the distance salt.

Papa overturned a used nail cask that had its top head stove in, settled onto it and pulled me onto his knee. I could feel the frailty of his frame. His wrists were raw from flea bites, the cuffs of his coat stained and ragged. I lifted his palm to my cheek. He inhaled sharply.

"Once, child," he said. "Once ...."

He didn't need to say the remainder. I knew. Once some of those ships were his, once the timber and corn and commodities of the dockyard were the currency of his life. Once, before that letter, and those that had come subsequently on its heels. Uncle, through the arm of his lawyer, pursued Papa for payment, which had been settled with the sale of our home and chattels. But existing after that proved a hazard. Papa found other positions, means of supporting us, only to have Uncle reach again to destroy yet another hope, close another door.

This morning Papa had been told the firm of Bosworth and Boone could no longer employ him as a junior clerk. Seemed one of their new investors was Edgar Fleming, and one of the conditions was to refuse employment to his recalcitrant brother, my father, whose only sin it was to believe in the sanctity of family.

"Once," he said again, and said no more.

I knew he was dead. That stillness growing in him simply pooled out over his limbs so that, finally, after all these months, he rested. I leaned to his cheek and brushed my lips against him, missing the small nuzzle he would give. I thought I might never be able to breathe again there was such a cramp inside my chest.

"S'excuse moi, Papa," was all I could say. Perhaps he might hear me wherever he had gone and forgive me for dreaming of his death. I knew God would never forgive me. It was my fault he died. Dreams, you see, did come true. Whether you wanted them to or not.

It was late in the afternoon when Maman found us and said nothing, dried eyed as I. Funeral arrangements were made, paid for with bitterness and harsh words. A pauper's grave for Papa. The loss of our two rooms for Maman and me.

I celebrated Christmas in the streets. Maman tried to find employment, but it seemed a lady, especially an aristocratic lady, was suited to no occupation, and it is amazing how quickly friends and associates forget you when you are indigent. She tried to find work using her skill with the needle. Neither milliner nor glover would consider her. She attempted to teach, but her lack of references and fall from financial grace barred all roads. Remarriage was as unattainable as our lost paradise. In the end she plied the only trade that ignored social status or lack thereof. The men who called were from our former class of people, men who salved their conscience with fripperies and coin.

I took to lurking in Gloucester's cathedral. It was dry. When the sun shone I'd dare to sit in a lake of colour cast upon the stone floor from the stained glass, and I'd turn my hands this way and that, watching the ripples of blue, red and yellow, and sometimes, when I felt alone and in need of benediction, I'd turn my face up to the lofty windows and let the blessing of colour shine full upon my face. I was sure if I sat still enough, was good enough, I would dissolve into colour and become this liquid light.

It never happened. But, as I said, it was dry. Periodically someone would throw me a coin with which I would return to the streets and haggle for bread, sometimes the luxury of cheese. The night dreams became worse so that they haunted me constantly, leaving me confused. Like Papa, Maman retreated farther and farther, shrinking, withering. Maman died coughing blood on the dawn of a brilliant day.

It had been a mistake that day to retreat to Gloucester cathedral, for my situation was discovered by a well-meaning priest, and it wouldn't do to have an orphan lurking around the grand edifice. Bad enough I begged on her steps.

All I could do was press myself against the stone wall of the cathedral, mumbling apologies. Of this, also, I had dreamed. All of it was my fault, a fact made painfully clear when I was hauled off to an orphanage.

In all fairness the orphanage was better than the streets, and at least afforded a box with straw for my bedding, although I shared the straw with lice. I didn't mind. The lice crunched satisfactorily when I pinched them from my skin, and it was a familiar task by now.

We received a thin gruel of either oat or barley once a day, and lessons on God's justice throughout. We hired out as servants and sweeps, runners and labourers, our earnings going to the orphanage to assist in our keep.

Throughout my brief stay dreams dogged my days. I was thrown out of an embroidery shop where I worked as a monkey shoving needles back up through the massive frames for the deft hands of the workers who stitched. For me the blue ground of silk dissolved into water, the threads and needles ripples stirred by paddles. The master of the shop took me for a useless idler, hinting I was touched in the head.

My keepers then placed me in a laundry where my job was to scrape soap flakes into the vats of steaming water, except the soap flakes became a white blizzard of snow through which I trudged on strange wood and sinew shoes. I nearly drowned that time. A hazard to the laundry, I was deemed. My punishment, back at the orphanage, was to be denied my rations for two days and beaten to rid me of the evil of my dreams.

Even a child learns to be stoic about these things after time. It's called survival. And I was becoming good at it.

By then Nanabush — the one the Ojibwa call the Trickster — had begun his vigil, though I realized this much later. Edgar Fleming, my uncle, was notified that his niece was in need of her next of kin, had been placed in an orphanage and could no longer be kept in light of the fact she had living kin. It is to be noted I had also become a liability to the orphanage, as I was unemployable.

On Monday, June 11, 1832, I boarded the *Baltic* out of Yarmouth, a brig of 400 tons and carrying 152 passengers, and I, for my part, with ice in my heart and dread for my future, ploughing through heavy seas toward a rendezvous. I spoke little, although I was certainly a curiosity to the others who shared the foul-smelling hold. There were mostly men, a few nervous-looking women going to an uncertain life in a wild land, and among them children, although few of us. While I shared uncertainty with them, I was sure I shared little else. None of them dreamed like me. None of them killed off their families.

As for my passage, it would seem my uncle was not a man to spend money freely; I slept in the hold with the other poor passengers as there had been no provision for a cabin. It was like living in debtor's prison, I imagined. The hold stank, a vile, gut-wrenching mix of faeces, urine, vomit and bodies. For all of us there were only 11 beds, and those made up with thin straw mattresses that quickly soiled. The rest of us slept on the rough planks below decks, which was in itself a misery that left many of us with cuts and splinters that quickly infected. Many were sick, or became so. Babies cried. Women moaned. Men quarrelled. I found a dark space and made myself small. Cold, hungry, I wasn't optimistic that my lot in life would improve greatly when finally I met Uncle Edgar. The only thing for which I could be grateful was that it seemed I was well-suited for naval life, as the pitch and roll of the ship bothered me only slightly at the outset.

What was a plague were the dreams. There was a man

who became a hawk and flew to England. He knew Papa. He knew Uncle Edgar. Sometimes the dreams showed the man with a woman. He spoke the name of Katherine. There were books that became swords, and swords that became walls. And the walls dissolved into water through which the man swam, and from which he emerged into a world dense with forest and dark with ancient spirits.

Sometimes, when my turn would come to climb onto the deck and take some air, I found it difficult to navigate, unsure if I walked through dreams or reality. At such times I would curl into the hollow of a flaked line and hang on to whatever shred of sanity remained while the passengers took their wobbly way across the decks.

We had, apparently, sighted the coastline and made contact with a mail packet out of Halifax the day Captain Earbage summoned me to his cabin. It caused quite a stir among the passengers. They hissed secrets behind their hands, thinking I was too young to understand. For a girl of ten years I was sure I knew more than they suspected.

The first mate escorted me and an older girl appointed as chaperone; he paid me no more mind than he would a mop. He opened the door onto an oaken cabin, closed it firmly behind me. My chaperone stood discreetly at my back. I stepped away from her. The captain's cabin was small but orderly, gleaming from polish no doubt he didn't sweat over. There was a repeater clock ticking loudly on a table behind his desk, mahogany and brass, carved, expensive. Standing there all I could absorb was the ticking of the clock. Tick. Tick. The way another clock had measured off the minutes, like a woman measuring fabric, cutting. So much for this. So much for that. Only so much time for each of life's courses.

Captain gestured to a silver plate of sweets on his desk, a rare commodity on land let alone aboard ship.

"No, thank you," I replied, watching his weathered face, his sharp blue eyes, the way a bald patch on his head shone. My mouth watered for want of one of those rare and almost forgotten delicacies.

"Not hungry?"

"No, Sir."

"Every girl your age is hungry for a sweet."

"I'm not every girl."

He arched a brow at that. Clearly he thought me impertinent, but I'd earned that right. Impertinent, was I? Had he had his whole life taken from him? Had he suffered from dreams that all too often bloomed into terrible reality?

"Indeed I can see that," he replied, now studying me as if I were some specimen. I became aware of my unkempt frock of faded calico, the way the collar hung askew because of a seamstress too harried to bother to correct it. My shoes pinched. I balled my hands to hide the dirt. "Sit yourself down, child."

By now my heart thudded in time with the clock. The ship groaned around me. Carefully I settled myself into the hard ladder-back chair across from him, watching him over the desk.

"Do you know why you're here, girl?"

What a thundering stupid question, I thought. My parents dead. My only living relation in the backwoods of this colony. "Yes, Sir."

He affected a smile and leaned back into his leather

chair, his fingers tented before him. "How about you tell me so I can be sure?"

"I'm being shipped to my Uncle Edgar in Upper Canada."

"Shipped?"

"Sent, Sir."

"Aye. Baggage is shipped. Young ladies are sent."

"Yes, Sir." Which, I wondered, was I?

"A letter from your uncle arrived in the mail packet." He extended the much abused envelope to me. I stared at it a moment, hesitating, remembering all the hardship that descended with the opening of a letter. When I still had not accepted the letter he gestured, withdrawing the letter slightly.

"Of course, if you are not lettered, I would be pleased to read this to you."

"I can read."

"Ah." His hand moved forward again, and this time I accepted the letter.

"I see from my passenger list that you're to disembark at Quebec."

I glanced up at him. "I thought I was to go to Montreal?"

"That may be, but the *Baltic* only goes as far as Quebec after having stopped at Prince Edward Island." He gestured to the letter. "Perhaps there is further instruction?"

I nodded and broke it open. It was from Uncle Edgar through his lawyer in York, instructing me once in Quebec to inquire aboard the *Preston*, or at the counting house of Messrs Isaac Preston & Son regarding passage from Quebec to Montreal, and then with the stage proprietors of Messrs. Norton & Co to catch the Sunday noon stage from Montreal to Prescott. Once at Prescott I was to take the steamer, the *Queenston*, to York, and from there to travel by series of stages to Orangeville. This journey was to be aided through a guide, a Monsieur Paul Rogette, whom I was to meet in Quebec.

"Is it as I thought?" Captain Earbage asked.

I nodded. "Although I barely know how to undertake all this."

"May I be of assistance?"

I glanced up at him, unsure. How to know who to trust? But he was a captain, and although that status was no guarantee of a gentleman, at some point I would have to hazard the risk. I offered him the letter, which he accepted. After a moment he looked over to me.

"I know this Rogette," he said. "He's a fair guide." He frowned as he watched me and added, "And a fair man. You'll be in good hands."

"Thank you, Sir."

He stood then and I stood also, sure my interview was over. With a wave of his hand he motioned me to be still, came around the desk and bent down before me so that we were at eye-level. "I knew your father."

I made no reply. None seemed to be required.

"Well, I suppose you could say I knew of him. I often ran goods for his company." I watched his blue eyes, the weathered seams of his face. He seemed puzzled. "Be you afraid, girl?"

Oh that was so close, so clever. I shook my head in denial.

"You know, there isn't a sailor aboard my ship who isn't afraid from time to time."

I tried to look as brave as possible, stared him right in the eye and answered, "I'm not afraid."

He touched my cheek with his fingertips. Why was he doing this? What did he want? He stood and now I was truly afraid for he was a tall man and his height only added to the authority I knew he wielded. Anything he wanted aboard this ship would be his. He was the law here.

"How'd you feel about sharing the captain's quarters?"

I stiffened, my heart lurching. "No thank you, Sir."

He cocked his head. For a moment I thought him angry and then watched his features soften so that it was more sorrow. "God in heaven what's become of you, girl? You're only a child."

What was I to reply to that?

He turned away from me and then wheeled back around. "Look, I meant nothing other than offering you a safe and warm place to sleep, a separate cot and a screen for privacy." He nodded to my chaperone. "And of course she accompanies you. I'd do the same for my own daughter."

"You have a daughter, Sir?" I asked.

"Aye. About your age."

"If you were so concerned about me why didn't you do something before?"

"Because I can be a fool at times. Do you accept?"

I nodded. His offer seemed safe enough, and almost anything would be better than shivering below deck for the next few days. It was. For the first time in a long while I was relatively warm, I felt safe, and my future was something that didn't preoccupy my every thought. Just to hear the captain snore was a comfort.

It was also a sorrow for there was another man snoring I remembered and mourned silently in the night.

I was allowed to sleep and stroll the decks as I wished, ever shadowed by the girl appointed to be my companion. She was afraid of me, rarely spoke. I never even learned her name. Conversation with her proved futile. I was given the luxury of warm water in order to take a sponge bath, for which I was grateful. I spent my waking hours either huddling in blankets in the captain's quarters, or above-decks watching the industry of the sailors. Below-decks I'd indulge in a much-missed past-time of reading. Captain had a modest but excellent collection of works. I found myself drawn to Milton's *Paradise Lost*, and although the vocabulary was difficult, I soon found the tale compelling. Above decks I learned the names and properties of all the sails, spars, and rigging when I'd eavesdrop on the midshipmen's lessons.

Quebec came, as surely as the next hour and the next. Dawn was dreary, damp when we sailed into the roads, and yet despite the gloom of the day the forest rose magnificently above this grey settlement town. As to the city, all I saw was as dull as the slate skies — building upon building of pine board and stone, like skeletons rising from the mud. Everywhere the rain fell in a curtain so thick you could barely see. I shivered in my thin coat.

This couldn't be Quebec. An established settlement had to be better than this, but I knew my incredulity for falsehood even before the captain stood beside me. Rain dripped from the black brim of his cap, sheeting off his oilcloth.

The boom of cannon fire rolled across the harbour, puffs of smoke like ghosts.

"Drop anchor," the captain shouted, and in answer orders echoed across the decks. "Return the salute."

I could hear two of the four nine-inch cannon below decks squealing back on their trucks, felt the impact of sound in my chest when they fired. Shouts fell from the tops as men fisted the canvas into submission. An exclamation went up from one of the other passengers on deck. The first lieutenant drew abreast of Captain Earbage, saluting with British Naval efficiency, evidence of former employment.

"Sir."

"Mr. Aldritch."

"The quarantine flag is up, Sir."

"So I see."

"As do our passengers by now."

I glanced over to where the exclamation had come from the passengers on deck, watched their fear, their despair.

"Aye," Captain Earbage answered. "Much good that will do. Still, we'll have to wait for the city's doctor to arrive and do his inspection. It had been my understanding when we picked up mail the cholera had passed."

"Perhaps it's a precaution, Sir."

"Perhaps." He looked back out across the harbour to the city and the island between. "It's likely we'll have to disembark them at Grosse Isle, sail back downstream. It seems to have been made a quarantine station. Be so good as to have our ship's Surgeon meet me in my quarters. And then our Navigator." At that he turned and left. I remained at the rail, wondering what was to happen now with the threat of cholera or some other plague upon us.

In the end what happened was the city's doctor had us sail back downstream as Captain Earbage had suspected, and disembarked at Grosse Isle, which was a world of suffering if ever there were one. So many Irish who had fled the famine found their graves here, or as I learned while we were interred there, buried at sea. We were summarily inspected and marched back aboard a cleaned and fumigated *Baltic*, and held there while eight of our number were admitted to what they blithely termed the hospital.

Privy as I was to Captain Earbage's dealings because of my accommodations, I overhead an outraged report from the ship's chandler regarding provisioning the passengers.

"And to add insult to injury," the chandler said, "the commandant has dutifully informed me he can accommodate us with straw when he next receives a shipment!"

"So I am expected to bear the cost and responsibility of our passengers entirely myself?" Captain asked.

"It would appear to be the case, Sir."

"Outrageous!"

"Indeed, Sir."

"And I'll wager my next profit there will be straw and provisions aplenty, of inferior quality and superior prices if I were to inquire after purchase."

"Very likely, Sir."

"Well, I cannot leave them to further suffering, can I?"

"No, Sir."

I could hear Captain thump his desk. "Then be about it, man. And bring me the bill."

"Ah, Sir — I was informed any purchases would have to paid in cash."

"Cash!" I could hear him sputter. "Then see the purser. But be sure every farthing is accounted!"

"Yes, Sir."

I heard the cabin door close, and then Captain mutter, "Blackguards, the lot of them. Damn their eyes!"

So it was over the next fortnight we were fed and made a little more comfortable at the grace of Captain Earbage, and finally given a clean bill of health and able to continue on. For the passengers that meant being able to disembark at Quebec proper and there make our way to whatever holdings, or work, we had arranged. For me it meant making my way toward the man who had written my suffering.

The morning I was to leave a sailor dumped my one small valise near me where I waited at the rail. The girl appointed as my chaperone had already left without so much as a farewell. I stared at the valise, wondering how my life had been reduced to this small, tentative parcel. I used to have three dresses for every day, petticoats and underslips, stays and stockings, drawers and chemises, and shoes so varied there were a pair for every need and occasion of my life. Now there were only the clothes upon my back and the one good frock in that sad, battered valise. Some priests said it was because of my family's greed that we'd fallen from financial grace. Some said it was my dreams. Whatever the reason I was convinced I was damned by God. Perhaps I was one of his fallen angels, like those of Milton's epic poem.

Resolutely I walked to the valise and clutched the unlikely handle into my hand.

"I'll accompany you," I heard Captain Earbage say.

I jumped at that, unaware he stood near me. "You don't need to take me." I raised my gaze to him, forcing myself to look at him steadily. "It's not that I'm ungrateful, just that I already owe you more than I am able to repay." That sounded adult, responsible. It was important I sounded responsible. I was sure my well-being was my own burden.

"Lady Fleming, you owe me nothing."

Lady Fleming — a blow to the order of my thoughts, that. The title set me off balance. It had not occurred to me I was titled, should have been privy to all of England's opportunity. I smiled although it felt like a disguise. "Then if you would please tell me where to find my guide, I'll take my leave."

"It would give me pleasure to escort you."

A gentleman, this captain. I'd seen enough of men to know one. Maman, I was sure, would approve. I nodded my acceptance and allowed the sailors to truss me into the bosun's chair, held my breath as they swung me out over the side and down into the boat. Captain followed down the ladder and settled beside me, nodding an order to the men. Without thought I slipped my hand into his. He closed his fingers tightly around mine, and I felt safe if even only for a little while.

Once onto the streets of Quebec it became clear walking meant a sloppy journey whether on cobbled streets or those not yet paved. A carriage awaited us. I climbed in, settled across from the Captain and set to observing this world through the windows. At an intersection just beyond our route a wagon had become mired to the axles. Everywhere there were soldiers, odd spots of bright red against all that grey. There were men in slops, women lifting their skirts to an unthinkable height against the sea of mud and filth. Trees loomed beyond the streets, a forest so tall and seemingly endless it was almost a threat. Never had I seen such trees. To me the threat was lost. Beyond this settlement, so recently crippled by cholera, was a wild freedom that whispered freedom from all the guilt with which Church, priests and events burdened me.

My attention came back to our journey when the carriage came to a halt, and Captain Earbage led me out before the Nelson Hotel, ushered me in and ordered himself a room, a bath and food. Furnishings, décor, all were sparse.

"I'm expecting a Monsieur Paul Rogette to call," he told the desk clerk.

"I'll send him right up," the clerk replied, making a note.

We climbed the stairs to the second floor and walked down a bare board floor to one of a series of doors and entered our room. It was larger than those to which I'd become accustomed, but certainly not as spacious as those in my lost home. There was a tester-bed placed between two windows, covered in gaily-coloured counterpanes and pillows. Shutters were folded back from the window. A bed-stand with a rush-light stood to the right of the bed, a dressing table with a mirror and a plain wooden screen against another wall and a writing desk and chair against the third. Two battered ladder-back chairs were arranged beside the fireplace.

There was a knock upon the door. The captain bid whomever it was to enter. An older woman — the innkeeper's wife I assumed — with two lads and another girl bustled in, she with a tea cart filled with covered dishes, the lads with a copper tub.

"Maggie here will attend upon you," the woman said.

We dined before a fire that was laid with all haste, while the boys came to and fro with buckets steaming with water. A cot was arranged for me at the foot of the bed.

"And the bath is for you," Captain Earbage said.

A bath! What a delicious thought. I was aware I was filthy, likely stank. "Thank you," was all I could say and that inadequate enough. Dabbing at my mouth with the linen, I excused myself and stripped out of my clothes behind the screen and eased myself into the lavender scented water, first to my waist, then to my chin, and then immersed myself completely to wash out the infestation of my body. Maggie gingerly plucked up my clothes and ordered one of the boys to have them laundered immediately. I scrubbed and I scrubbed until my skin and scalp tingled and then, sure I was at last clean, slid back down to my chin and closed my eyes to lap at this luxury. I would not think. I would only feel. In that sensual state I must have fallen asleep for I became aware of a change of sensations.

Yellow lamplight now painted the room. I watched reflections from the fire dancing off the rose-stencilled walls. I lay in the large bed, nestled among those soft counterpanes and clean linen sheets, a veritable mountain of pillows under my head.

Voices rose and fell from before the fire, one louder than the other.

"The child's asleep, damn you," Captain Earbage said to a dark man in the other chair. "Lower your voice."

"But the governess — "

"There isn't one."

The man in the other chair was only partially visible to me, but his profile was sharp and clear. His hair was dark, tied at the nape with a leather thong, rather out of fashion. He was large, as though built for carrying terrible weight, his face swarthy where it wasn't covered by a bush of a beard. His clothes were all of deerskin, a fringed shirt and breeches, long boots upon his feet. Hanging off the back of his chair was a fur cap with the tail of some animal dangling near his arm.

At the moment the man shovelled the remains of our luncheon into his mouth.

"So, there is no governess," said the man with a noticeable French accent. I assumed he was my guide, this Paul Rogette.

The captain shook his head in reply to Rogette's statement.

"I doubt Monsieur Merde de Fleming will find his pockets deep enough to hire one," Rogette said. "They're rare enough out here."

"To what am I sending this girl?"

Rogette shot the captain a look. "An uncle."

"Aye, an uncle, but what sort of man?"

Rogette shrugged. "A man."

"For God's sake — is he decent?"

"No." Earbage arched a brow that prompted Rogette to add, "He's the one who bankrupted the girl's father. His own brother." He nodded in my direction and I shuttered my lids so as not to be discovered eavesdropping. "The poupee's papa," Rogette finished.

"Sporting of him."

"And the maman?" Rogette asked. "Do you know what happened to her?"

"I've learned the mother and child were turned out to the streets after Fleming died. For a Christmas present her maman died. Retribution, some have called it."

"Mon Dieu!"

"Even some of the passengers said the child is cursed." He glanced over to me. "What could be cursed about such a child?"

"I make no judgment on the church."

"Lest they judge you, eh?" Earbage replied, looking back at Rogette.

"It is wisest not to interfere, especially not out here."

"So. We send her to the only living relative."

"Oui. Le seulement."

"And he's in — "

"Hornings Mills. It's a new settlement in the Queen's Bush started by this Horning from St. Catharines. He's too old by all accounts to be undertaking such an enterprise, but he and this Lewis are going to try to make a go of it. There nothing else around them. Nearest settlement is days away. Fools, if you ask me."

Earbage shook his head. "Out to the Queen's Bush." As if it was some kind of death sentence.

Paul nodded. "By foot. Fleming allowed for no ox, no horse, no wagon, no canoe in which to transport the child once past Orangeville. Not that there's much past Orangeville but a blazed trail, and then not much of one."

"She's not able."

"That, mon ami, I can see too plainly." He braced his hands against his thighs. "So, Monsieur Merde de Fleming will have to wait — won't he? And you can be sure I will be recompensed for the expenses of this journey." He grinned, all teeth. "I'm not a slaver, and I'm not a murderer. If it takes us longer, and with a little more cost than Fleming would like, well, so be it. We'll have fine weather for many weeks to come — one thing for which I'm thankful."

Earbage smiled, lifted a mug as did Rogette, and drank. Rogette rose all in one motion, paused at the foot of my bed and then swept from the room. When left the captain stood with his back to the door, watching me. I wondered if he knew I was awake for he studied me a long while before saying, "So, my little woman. You're off for the backwoods."

Shadow   Song
By Lorina Stephens

Available in trade paperback, ebook and audio
From your favourite online retailer worldwide
And www.fiveriverspublishing.com